For the Love of Abbey

By Paul James Jeff

Published by:

BAICO
Publishing Consultants Inc.
102-C McEwen Ave.
Ottawa, Ontario K2B 5K7
Tel: (613) 829-5141
www.baico.ca
E-mail: baico@bellnet.ca

Printed by Documents Majemta Inc.

© Paul James Jeff

ISBN 978-1-897449-20-2

Cover designed by
David Craig

Title designed by
Travis Craig

Edited by
Paul M.J. Legault

For Orders Contact
pauljamesjeff@sympatico.ca

For the Love of Abbey

Chapter 1

She was born on the 17th of July 1961. This was the second daughter for Sam and Maggie Walker. Their other daughter Heather was four years old.

Maggie had a hard time with this birth. The doctors put it down to stress during the pregnancy. She almost lost the baby twice and on two occasions, she had to be hospitalized with very high blood pressure. Her husband Sam knew it was over their concerns for Heather – their first born.

When Heather was born, she was a healthy baby girl, weighing in at 8lb 2oz. Just after her third birthday, she started having problems. Tests were done and x-rays were taken, but nothing major showed up. Heather would cry constantly for hours for no apparent reason. She would be sick, would not eat her food, and she was in and out of the hospital. They did tests on her heart, liver and kidneys, but still could find no reason for her problems. Then she would be okay again for a few months. Just when they thought they were through the worst, the symptoms would reappear. When Maggie became pregnant again, the worry of Heather would rear its ugly head again and again. Trips to the hospital with her young daughter became unbearable.

Heather would stay in the children's ward for days on end, still no sign of what was causing her problems. Maggie spent endless hours at her daughter's bed side, until she herself started showing signs of exhaustion. This started to worry Sam, who phoned Maggie's sister, Jennie, to see if she could come and stay for a while.

Jennie lived on St. John in the Virgin Islands. She arrived two days later and was a great comfort to her sister. She helped with Heather, and she made Maggie take a lot of rest. When the doctor sent Maggie into the hospital, her blood pressure was dangerously high. Two days later, Heather was back in the children's ward with the same symptoms recurring. This was a very troublesome time for the whole family.

Maggie's mother, Susan also spent a great deal of time at the hospital. First with Heather, and then with Maggie who had also been admitted. She was there to help where she could. Her being there was also good for Jennie, who found that looking after Heather was harder than she had thought possible. Jennie herself could not have children. It had been a huge disappointment to both her and her husband Richard, but after a while, they reluctantly accepted it and were able to move on.

Maggie became very depressed worrying about Heather. The doctors decided with the family that they would perform a caesarean to avoid any possible complications with the birth due to her high blood pressure.

The baby was born at 8:45 in the morning – a beautiful baby girl. The whole family was there at the hospital, even Richard had flown in from St. John.

Sam was delighted, but worried at the same time, as Heather was in the other wing of the hospital. They all assured Maggie she was fine. They did not let on at that time that Heather had actually gotten worse.

Jennie was in the hospital room alone with Maggie, when to her surprise her sister asked her, "If you had been able to have children, and you'd had a daughter, what would you have named her?"

"Abbey," she replied instantly.

"Then Jennie, if Sam agrees, would you mind if we name our child Abbey Susan?"

This immediately bought tears to Jennie's eyes. She was overwhelmed.

"Abbey ... really? You would do that ... for me? And Susan ... after Mother ... that would be the sweetest thing anyone could do. Thank you, Maggie," said Jennie.

She wanted to squeeze Maggie with all her might. Instead, she hugged her sister carefully, because she had stitches and was very sore.

Jennie picked up Abbey and cuddled her, holding her very gently. She looked at her and whispered softly, "I'm your Aunt Jennie, Abbey, and I will always be here when needed." From that day on, they would have a special bond that no one would ever break.

After Maggie and little Abbey went home from the hospital, Jennie stayed on. Her husband Richard flew back home. Problems had arisen on the island, and being Chief of Police, he had no choice but to leave immediately.

Sam was at the hospital with his mother-in-law, Susan. They stayed by Heather's bedside. She improved again over the next few days and was allowed home. Maggie was so pleased to see her – she now had two girls to cuddle.

Jennie went home two weeks later. At that time, Heather had improved, and all looked good. Sam and Maggie would take the girls out for walks in the sunshine, Abbey in the carriage and Heather in her stroller. This was a happy time for the proud parents.

Sam knew that when they grew up, he would have three women to contend with, and he would be outnumbered every time, but just the thought of them being together as a family was enough.

They showed off the girls to the whole neighbourhood. Sam was making sure everyone could see the two most beautiful girls in the world and he was the father. This was a happy time in the Walker household, and Maggie's health continued to get better, which was a blessing in Sam's mind. He wanted his wife back now more than ever.

Their happiness was not to last. In late November, Heather became ill yet again and more intensive tests were carried out. Jennie had flown back to help look after Abbey. Sam and Maggie were at the hospital day after day. This time, Heather did not improve.

When the test results were completed, Heather's doctor called them in. He sat them down and explained that after extensive tests, they had found a tumour on Heather's brain. He needed permission to do a biopsy which would then determine the next steps to be taken. Both of them sat there stunned.

Sam asked, "What do you mean a tumour? Did this not show up before?"

The doctor's answer was short and to the point. "Sometimes these types of tumours don't show up until they have enlarged. We need to do the biopsy to determine whether it's benign or malignant," he said.

The doctor did the procedure the next day, but Heather's health was not improving at all. They sat that evening at home talking trying to make sense of the whole situation. Susan, Maggie's mother, tried in vain to comfort her daughter who had become very distraught. Again, her blood pressure was high. Sam and Jennie put her to bed and gave her a sleeping pill, which knocked her out and at least she got some well needed rest.

Jennie spent all day, every day, with Abbey. She had come to adore this little baby. "You're gorgeous." She would say. She loved bathing her with those big brown eyes and jet black hair. Though she played with Abbey for hours, in the back of her mind, Jennie was concerned for Heather and Maggie.

Sam and Maggie were called back to the hospital – the test results were now ready for review.

They were in Doctor Bennett's office with two other doctors. In spite of his best decorating efforts, the room was uninviting.

Dr. Bennett leaned forward as he spoke. "May I introduce Dr. Gitano and Dr. Lake? Dr. Gitano is a leading Neurosurgeon and Dr. Lake is his assistant." He turned his head toward Dr. Gitano, who took over the conversation and began to explain their findings.

"I'm sorry to inform you that the growth on Heather's brain is malignant, it is cancerous, and we need to operate immediately if we are to save her."

Maggie nearly fell to the floor. If Sam had not caught her arm, she could have hurt herself. She passed out. Dr. Lake managed to bring her around. She was shaking, but still managed to ask, "Will my daughter be okay?"

Dr. Gitano quickly answered Maggie's question.

"If we do not operate immediately, your daughter will only survive for a few months. The growth is very virulent. If we operate now, I still can only give your daughter a fifty-fifty chance."

Sam was now realizing the seriousness of the situation. He quietly asked Dr. Gitano, "If you operate, why can you only give my little girl an even chance?"

Dr. Lake jumped in and addressed Sam's question, "Mr. Walker, until we actually go into Heather's brain, we can't tell how much of the tumour we can remove. It's not an exact science, but we may be able to save her life, and we feel this is the only avenue open to us."

Sam asked if he and his wife could have a few moments to discuss their request.

Sam held on to Maggie, and asked her what she thought they should do.

"I don't know," she replied. "I'm too confused. I don't want to lose my little girl."

"Then we have to go ahead," Sam implored. "We have to give her a chance to survive."

They informed Dr. Gitano to go ahead and prepare Heather for the operation. When he and his assistant left the office, Maggie insisted on an answer from Dr. Bennett.

"How good is the surgeon?"

She could not remember his name. Her fainting had left blanks in her memory, and she was still a bit confused.

He assured her, "If anyone can perform miracles, it is Dr. Gitano. He is one of the leading doctors in his field."

Sam felt a little more at ease with this answer. Maggie however, was not so sure.

Dr. Gitano and his team carried out the operation. Heather was in surgery for ten gruelling hours, and Sam and Maggie were there the entire time – waiting, pacing, sitting, and pacing some more. The only time they left the waiting room was to visit the washroom or get coffee. They had both been up for thirty-six hours, and now the whole dilemma was causing so much anxiety for Maggie, that Sam himself was under real pressure. Sam had to show his wife that he was strong and help get her through the day, but it was very hard on him too.

When they eventually emerged from the operating room, they looked drained. Both doctors came to the room where Sam and Maggie had been waiting.

"How is she?" Maggie blurted out. Sam held her.

Dr. Gitano had a sad look on his face. When he answered, he had a little stutter in his voice.

"We removed a lot of the tumour, but not all of it. We now have to wait and see how Heather responds. She will be heavily sedated for a few days. All we can do is pray she gets stronger so we can take another look. You may see her shortly." After he finished speaking, he left the room.

Maggie started sobbing and eventually became hysterical. Sam had to call a nurse for help. Dr. Bennett had to give Maggie a mild sedative to help calm her.

Sam called Jennie at his home and told her all he knew for now and how Maggie had broken down. He then called his mother-in-law Susan, who immediately went to help. Sam helped Susan get Maggie into her car so she could take her home to rest. He stayed at Heather's bedside all night, even when nurses and doctors came in to do checks, he did not budge.

Sam was so worried, that he did not sleep again. He was near exhaustion in the morning when Susan arrived to take over the watch. She sent him home to sleep, which he did for ten hours straight. When he awoke, Jennie informed him that Maggie had gone back to the hospital. It was early in the evening. He showered and shaved, had a small light meal, held Abbey for all of ten minutes, and went back to the hospital.

Maggie stroked Heather's hand and talked to her, even though her daughter most probably could not hear what she said. As Sam walked in, Maggie started to cry again. He held her tight, and said, "We must have faith."

Maggie was at the hospital day after day. Sam had to go back to work and came in when he could. Even though their daughter was no longer under sedation, she had not stirred for weeks. Dr. Bennett came to see them. He held their hands. Sam asked what was going on and he informed both of them that Heather was still in a coma, and all they could do was pray and wait.

Maggie was on the verge of a break down. It was Christmas Eve and still no response from Heather. They visited together with Susan, and went home to try and salvage what they could of Christmas. This was Abbey's first Christmas. Even her Aunt Jennie was feeling the strain. She called her husband Richard to wish him a Merry Christmas. This was their first apart since they had been married, and though she had consolation in Abbey, she missed her man.

When the phone rang on Christmas morning, Maggie answered. It was the hospital asking them to come in immediately. She felt all funny and her mother had to help her sit.

"What is it?" Sam asked.

"It's the doctor. He wants us there ... now," she replied.

Sam drove as quickly as he dared to the hospital. Susan sat in the back of the car with Maggie. She was having a panic attack, and kept telling Sam to drive faster. He didn't answer her. He did not want to make matters worse.

They went straight to Heather's bedside. Her breathing was laboured even with the oxygen.

Dr. Bennett came in and took Sam aside. Maggie was stroking Heather's arm and holding her hand. Then the doctor explained the situation.

"She's slipping away Sam. We have tried everything. Your daughter is not responding."

Sam went over to the side of the bed. Maggie was in tears. She looked at Sam.

"Tell me what he said," she demanded.

She was becoming hysterical again. He tried to hold her, but she was too distraught.

"Tell me what the doctor was saying," she repeated. Sam had tears in his eyes.

"We're losing her Maggie," he sobbed. "We're losing her."

Susan came over and held Maggie's head and tried to comfort her.

Sam walked to the other side and took his daughter's hand. He felt the life go out of Heather - she stopped breathing - her machines were flat line.

Sam and Maggie's daughter died at 10.32 on Christmas morning. The hospital staff had tried to revive her, without success. Heather was gone. Their daughter never regained consciousness.

They sat by her bedside for a long time. Maggie was still talking to her, but she had calmed. It was as if Heather was talking back. They all went home. Sam knew he had the horrible task of making funeral arrangements. Jennie put Maggie to bed. She took Abbey in to see her, but there was no response, she just laid there looking at the ceiling.

Susan, Jennie and Sam sat in the lounge, little Abbey was on the floor. Sam looked at his daughter.

"She's grown," he commented. His face softened and his eyes saddened. "I never realized she'd grown so much. We have been too busy at ..." he stopped. He could not say how he felt. He just bent down and picked up Abbey, held her tight and cried.

The funeral was a solemn affair, not a dry eye in the church. Maggie held on to Sam's arm. Jennie held little Abbey, her husband Richard by her side. Susan stayed behind Maggie to give extra support to Sam, just in case. Maggie was near the breaking point.

Life at the Walker home would never be the same. Heather was cremated and Maggie insisted that in the spring, she would spread the ashes on her rose garden, so that she knew she would always be close. Jennie had asked Sam if they would all come to St. John for some sunshine and get away from New Jersey and the cold for a while.

Sam called his boss, Joseph Brady. Of course he understood that Sam needed time to come to terms with the loss of his daughter, and assured him he would have his work covered.

"Take as long as you need Sam," he said. "You come back when you're ready. You have my condolences."

While they sorted out all the last details, picked up Heather's ashes from the Funeral Director, Richard would go on ahead to get his home ready for them. He called his cleaning lady from Sam's, explained what had happened and asked her to get the other rooms ready.

Jennie stayed to help Sam with Abbey and Maggie. Susan would stay behind to answer any phone calls and greet visitors. She would visit her daughter later.

They flew out of Newark the following day. Her doctor had prescribed Maggie antidepressants and they were helping to keep her calm. She even cradled Abbey in her arms, and Sam noticed that when she held Abbey, she actually smiled.

For the first time in months he felt a little relief. Sam prayed that this holiday would help his wife come to terms with the loss of their child, but deep down he knew it would not be that easy. He had to stay calm and collected because he knew it was also hard for him.

Chapter 2

They arrived in St. John. It was a glorious day, the sun was shining and the temperature was around seventy-six degrees. Richard met them at the dock. They had taken the ferry from Charlotte Amalie on St. Thomas. They loaded the minivan and drove up the road to their cottage.

Jennie had realized that her sister was close to having a nervous breakdown and that a holiday away from New Jersey would hopefully help dull her pain. Luckily for Maggie, having her family close to her would help immensely.

Sam was normally a very strong individual, but he was also feeling the strain. He knew it would be hard to come to terms with losing his daughter, and at times during the vacation, he would go off alone just to collect his thoughts.

He knew he would have to be strong in front of Maggie and be there when she needed him.

The cold winter weather in New Jersey, and running back and forth to the hospital every day had taken its toll on everyone. Sunshine, warm weather and relaxation can be a tonic for just about anyone.

They went swimming every day. The weather was wonderful and they got to spend a lot more time with Abbey. It was a tonic they all needed.

They took a trip to St. Thomas and did a lot of shopping – which in its own way –was very therapeutic. Jennie and her husband Richard's home was called Cinnamon Cottage and was located on Cruz Bay, within walking distance of the main part of St. John.

It was a beautiful cottage with lattice windows and black shutters. The exterior walls were rendered and painted white, with two stone chimneys jutting from the roof. It had a kidney-shaped pool in the back garden with patio doors from both the lounge and kitchen overlooking the garden and pool. A picket fence separated the garden from the beach. Inside was a large style farmhouse kitchen with a huge oak table that could seat ten, two very modern bathrooms with showers, and a huge L-shaped lounge with granite floors to help keep the home cool. All the bedrooms were a good size. It was a beautiful home. *'It's our slice of paradise,'* Jennie would tell them.

Richard had inherited the cottage on the death of his grandfather who had moved to St. John in the late 40's. He bought the cottage and named it, Cinnamon Cottage.

Richard's grandfather told him he had renamed the cottage because his wife, Richard's grandma, was always in the kitchen cooking and made the best cinnamon rolls in the world.

Richard could not disagree, having tasted those many, many times. His grandma passed away suddenly in 1954. She had a major stroke from which she never recovered.

His grandma was buried at the little local church they had attended every week for seven years. She always said it was one of the nicest places she had ever seen, with its tall trees and beautiful grounds, and had made it quite clear to her husband that if anything ever happened to her she wanted to be buried there, so that every day she could hear the ocean.

Her wish was carried out. Richard knew his grandma's sudden death was very hard on his grandfather and certainly was not surprised when he announced his retirement six months later.

He had decided to take up painting and could now spend time traveling and painting scenes of all the wonderful shorelines and bays that St. John had to offer.

As it turned out he was quite good, but refused to sell any of his work though he did give some of his pictures away to friends and family.

He passed away in 1958. He went to bed and never woke up. The cause, according to the doctor, was heart failure, and Richard being his only living relative was left his entire estate. That same year, Richard had been successful with his appointment as the new Chief of Police for St. John. His grandfather would have been very proud.

Abbey and her parents visited St. John every year. Even when she attended university, Abbey made sure she could vacation with her Aunt Jennie and Uncle Richard and became even closer to them.

She loved the cottage with its kidney-shaped pool, even though it was just a few steps from the beach through the little picket fence, she still loved to swim in the pool as sometimes the beach could become crowded.

Aunt Jennie had to spend a lot of time at the gift shop she had bought in the village, many years before. She loved her store, and she made it a point to sell only the high end gifts that many tourists and quite a lot of locals liked to buy.

Jennie's store was called Serendipity, and had grown in reputation over the years. It had become very successful, which eventually allowed her to employ full time staff to run the store, while she would just be involved in the buying and pricing of the stock.

Jennie had worked very hard over the years, and felt she had achieved more than she could have hoped for. Now was the time to relax more and enjoy life. The store offered her that freedom she felt was deserved. Richard and Jennie were never fortunate enough to have had children of their own, it just was not meant to be, but they were really happy together. They had a good life here on St. John and both Jennie and her husband

loved being visited by friends and family – especially Abbey.

Since they inherited the cottage, Richard and Jennie had done many upgrades. They added another bathroom, and made the kitchen much larger with all stainless steel appliances and granite counter tops, causing Richard to joke with his wife, "Why do you want a bigger kitchen? You never use it."

His wife smiled and snapped back without missing a beat. "Maybe not," she said, "but doesn't it look good?"

Their main lounge had been redone in antique brick with Mahogany doors, trim, and a huge beamed cathedral ceiling. Even with all the changes they had made, it still had a nice homey feeling.

As Abbey grew older, her father found it harder to go on vacation as much as he would have liked. His company had now expanded and he had to spend even more time at work. He had been appointed General Manager. The salary was really good, but of course a lot more was expected of him.

Maggie would always go. She loved spending time on the island with her sister, Abbey, Richard, and Joanne. They would make trips to St. Croix and British Tortola, but most of the time she was quite content to stay on St. John, or take the ferry to St. Thomas for their main shopping.

One evening Maggie was invited out with Joanne Morris, her sister's next-door neighbour. Joanne had also lived on St. John for a very long time. She was an author and had over the years penned several romantic novels – three of them had made The New York Times top ten bestseller list.

Maggie and Joanne had clicked immediately years before and their friendship would last a lifetime. Whenever Maggie visited St. John, she always spent time with her. She always felt relaxed around Joanne, and her husband Sam had always encouraged their friendship. He believed it had helped his wife immensely.

Maggie had read a lot of Joanne's books, even before they became friends and they would spend hours discussing any new book she was writing or life in general. Maggie felt so at ease with her, she could even talk about Heather's death, which was something she still found hard with her family.

St. John is the smallest of the Virgin Islands with St. Croix being the largest in land mass, and the main island St. Thomas in the middle. Richard had come to work in the police force on the island after transferring from New York. He had been a policeman since he was twenty-one and never thought of doing any other occupation.

He met Jennie at the Christmas party in 1954. She had traveled from Rockaway to stay with an old school friend for a few days before Christmas. Her friend had fixed her up with a blind date, that blind date turned out to be Richard.

They married nine months later and moved to St. Thomas and bought an apartment overlooking the harbour in Charlotte Amalie, even though Richard's post was on St. John. He took the ferry to work. When his grandfather passed away, they moved to the island. Jennie adored St. John, with its beautiful beaches and a few National Parks, and she loved the cottage. She had stayed a few times, when invited, but when she moved in, she made changes immediately.

As she told her husband, "Let's hope we will stay here forever."

After Abbey was born, it became a home away from home for Maggie and Sam. This was truly paradise in Jennie's eyes.

They had an idyllic life. The only set back was when they found out they could not have children. That hurt Jennie deeply, but her loving husband helped her get over that heartbreak and they became even closer. She bought the business on the island and never looked back.

Joanne had become very wealthy over the years. She had never married. She was sixty-three and could easily pass for fifty. She had been dating the same *man-friend,* as she liked to call him, for twenty years.

"I will never get married." She had confided in Maggie. "Andrew is a sweet man and I adore him, but I like my independence too much to change and luckily for me he feels exactly the same way."

Andrew was an artist, and had his own art gallery in Charlotte Amalie, situated on the dockside in St. Thomas. He made a good living, but more importantly, he was happy with everything in his life. He traveled the islands painting landscapes and beaches and the yachts that would adorn most of the harbours.

Andrew had a studio cottage on the other side of St. John where he used to sometimes spend weeks finishing his work - which in a way, was why their relationship worked. They always tried to spend at least one night together each week, either at his place or hers and they also phoned each other once a day to say hello.

Joanne and Maggie would also visit the local inns and restaurants, not just for the food, but Joanne liked to talk to the locals. She used to say to Maggie, "I get some material for my novels from them." And over the years, she too had become quite a celebrity.

In 1985, Sam managed to book two weeks winter vacation. His company had become quite successful and he had more staff to delegate the work to and could get a much needed break.

The winter was a bad one this year and the cold temperatures were really affecting him, so Sam was more than happy to take a break.

Abbey had finished all her training and was applying for a teaching position in Rockaway, but she flew to St. Thomas with them. As they left the plane in St. Thomas, they could instantly feel the warmth.

"It was a tonic," Sam commented.

They then took the ferry to St. John. Jennie and Richard were there at the dock, waving like lunatics – hugs and kisses flowed.

They loaded the luggage and drove the mile to the cottage. Abbey was in the pool within fifteen minutes of arriving, everyone else sat on the patio that had just been finished. They had added a Tikki bar, a garden swing and an arbour with vines covering the roof that gave great shade from the hot sun. Richard had brought out a bottle of champagne and glasses.

"What's going on?" Abbey asked. "And where's mine?" she laughed.

Her Aunt Jennie smiled.

"Please join us. We have some news to share."

"It sounds very mysterious." Maggie commented to her sister.

"Not really." Richard replied. "I have decided to take early retirement, and as of next month, I am a man of leisure. We wanted to wait until you joined us to let you know. I suppose we could have phoned, but we both thought this would be nicer."

"Congratulations Richard." Sam shook his hand. "You deserve it. Do they have a replacement in mind?"

"Yes," Richard replied, "my deputy has been appointed and they could not have picked a more qualified person."

Abbey kissed her uncle on the cheek, and asked if they would be leaving St. John.

"We will never leave here," Richard replied. "This is our home and there is nowhere else we would rather live. We were even thinking of changing the name of the house to Paradise Cottage, but my grandparents are just down the road and I know they would not approve."

Maggie had tears in her eyes.

"I am so happy for you both. I hope that one day, when Sam decides to call it a day from his job we will be able to sell up and move here and not have to put up with the cold winters anymore."

They were hugging each other, when a voice from nowhere said, "And when were you going to let me in on the secret?"

It was Joanne, holding a large bottle of champagne.

"I heard you from my garden." Her face was beaming, she walked over and gave both of them a big kiss.

"I am so happy for both of you," she said. For some unknown reason, she had a tear in her eye.

"I think we should all get tipsy," were her very next words, and that afternoon, they all did.

That night, they went to the local inn and had a noisy dinner. They were laughing and joking and by the end of a very intoxicating night everyone in the village had heard the news, and Richard had never had his hand shaken by so many people in his life. He never realized how so many of the *Islanders* held him in high regard. It really was an eye opener.

The next morning the cottage was very quiet. Everyone had a hangover and the black coffee and Tylenol flowed freely. Next door, Joanne, who could certainly hold her liquor, was in her garden singing happily. She had never suffered from a hangover and was certainly bright and breezy this morning.

She had called her *man-friend*, Andrew and told him the news. He suggested that it would be a fine idea to take them to the best restaurant on the island so that he could congratulate Richard and Jennie himself.

Joanne said she would make the arrangements for Saturday evening. They had a wonderful time that night. The wine flowed and the dinner was fantastic. They all had the lobster special, except Sam, who was a red meat fanatic. He had a New York Strip Loin with a peppercorn sauce, which he commented afterwards, was the best he had ever had.

Andrew congratulated them and handed Richard, and Jennie, a very special package.

"It's your retirement present. I hope you like it."

When they opened the parcel, inside was a painting of Cinnamon Cottage. Andrew had painted it a few years ago and finished it quickly to present to them.

You could have knocked Richard over with a feather.

"It's wonderful," he said, and thanked Andrew for his kindness. The evening had finished on a happy note.

Though Abbey was miles away, she was thinking of her childhood and of this man that she could not get out of her mind.

Although Abbey had grown up as an only child, she had a happy childhood. Her loving parents, her aunt, uncle and her grandmother had all made certain that Abbey was secure in every way possible. Once a year without fail, she would travel to St. John. Her mother always went with her, though sometimes Sam, her father could not. On these occasions, Susan, her grandmother would go with her daughter.

She would spend at least two weeks in the summer with her grandmother, they would go off walking through the woods, and it was a time that Abbey looked forward to most. Her grandmother was the one, over the years, that taught Abbey how to cook. She had often commented that when she was married this would be important.

One day while they were making brownies, Abbey who was then ten years old asked her grandmother what her sister was like. She had often daydreamed about her and how she would have liked to play dress up and other things that girls do. Although she never knew her sister, she would have liked too.

Abbey explained to her grandmother that she had once asked her mother, but she had avoided answering because it upset her to talk about it.

Her grandmother sat her down and told her about Heather. She was a lovely girl, a lot like Abbey. They were similar in many ways, but unfortunately, she was always sick, so it was very hard on her mother, and as her sister had passed away at such an early age, it was hard to say what she would have been like.

"It is good to think about her like you do. I am sure you would have played together a lot," she explained to Abbey.

Abbey was not sure she understood, but thanked her grandmother and never brought the subject up again.

After kindergarten, Abbey went to private schools. Maggie, her mother, wanted the best education that they could afford, and Abbey was given every opportunity. For some unknown reason though, she did not make friends very easily. Her best friends were her Aunt Jennie, Uncle Richard and her grandmother.

She was also close to her parents, but more so to her father than her mother. Sam would always take whatever time he could to spend with his daughter. He would tell her stories of how he was just a boy during World War II and watched his father leave to go off to Europe to fight the Germans. That was the last he saw of him, but he had fond memories of the times they spent together.

Then he told her about her grandmother that she had only seen in photographs, and what a wonderful person she was, and how she looked after him. Although he knew how much she missed his dad, she never tired of talking about him. He explained that when he was eighteen, she took sick with pneumonia and never recovered.

He joined the Navy and went to sea for four years and visited many places. Once, when he had returned home on leave, he met Abbey's mother Maggie and after a whirlwind romance they got married. He was discharged from the Navy and joined Brady Industries and had been there since.

After marrying Abbey's mother, he moved to Rockaway in 1956. Her mother was born here and he fell in love with the town. They had decided to raise a family here, and as far as he was concerned he never wanted to live anywhere else.

Abbey loved to hear his stories. She used to imagine all the places he had been and all the people he had met. It made her quite content.

After leaving *finishing school* and attending teachers training college – again, the only friends she made seemed to be fair-weather friends who would come and go. She did get involved with one young man, Peter and eventually their relationship went further and they did end up having sex.

Abbey was not comfortable with him and quickly discovered he only thought about himself. His idea of sex was *get in, get out, and get off* – so she never really enjoyed it. When she found out from some of the young women there that Peter was bragging about his latest conquest, Abbey dumped him immediately. After that, she stayed away from men for a long time.

She did enjoy her time at the college and had always wanted to be a teacher, graduating with honours at that time was the happiest day of her life.

Although Abbey had temporarily sworn off men, there was one in particular who gave her cause to reconsider. Her first meeting with this young man happened just before she had graduated, when the car she had just purchased, broke down on her way home. She had just pulled over on the shoulder and put her hazard lights on, when out of nowhere this man pulled up and asked what the problem was. After Abbey explained it to him, he pulled the hood and within two minutes the car was running like it should. Abbey had noticed his smile and rugged looks, and she was impressed by his nice manner and willingness to help. In fact, Abbey was attracted to him immediately, but then he was gone and she did not even have time to ask his name.

That night while lying in her bed, she thought of that nice young man who had helped her and wondered if he was local, and was there a chance she would meet him again. All these wonderful thoughts went through her head. Abbey, over the next few months, would think of him many times.

Then, when it happened and they did see each other again, and he disappeared for the second time – she knew he was someone she would like to get to know properly. Every time she left home or saw a Honda Civic, she would wonder if that was him. Abbey did not know if he was married or going steady, but she thought about him more and more and at least now she knew his name. She did not realize at that time, she was falling in love with a complete stranger.

The following morning, Abbey went for a swim in the bay. After the previous evening, the cottage was noisy, and she needed some peace and quiet to think. After her dip, she sat on the sand wrapped in her towel so she would not burn in the hot sun. She was deep in thought and was miles away, when suddenly she heard a voice call out to her. It was her Aunt Jennie.

"Penny for your thoughts." She sat down beside Abbey. "You looked like you were on a different planet."

"I'm sorry," Abbey replied. "Yes, I was just thinking of someone."

"Oh, do give me all the sordid details," her aunt said jokingly.

"No. It's not like that," Abbey said. "I had a strange dream last night."

"Must have been the wine," her aunt teased.

"Maybe," Abbey agreed, "but it was very life like."

"You can tell me." She winked at her niece and smiled.

Abbey stared long and hard at the sand for a few moments, and then told her aunt the story of her car failure, and of the man who stopped and helped her.

"He was very kind and considerate. Just jumped out of his car and had mine working in minutes," Abbey said, and chuckled.

"He was also quite handsome in a rugged sort of way, and his smile was something you only see from a movie star. I actually went weak at the knees. I know that sounds childish and stupid - but it's true."

"Then I ran into him a couple of weeks later," she said. "Well, actually I had run into the pharmacy on Main Street. I had left my car idling because it was an extremely cold day. The pharmacy as usual, was really busy, so I had to wait in line longer than I anticipated. One of the customers in at the head of the line kept changing her mind and everyone was getting impatient. You had to be there to hear some of the comments being made. It was really bad. Eventually, I paid for the things I had wanted and went rushing out. I opened the door without thinking and knocked this man over. I did not know at that point it was him as he was face down in the snow. I was really scared. I thought at the time that I had hurt this poor man. He rolled over and looked up at me and I had the shock of my life when I saw his face - it was him again. I started stuttering like a fool. I asked him if he was hurt, he just laid there looking at me and said jokingly, *'Yes. If you don't like me, tell me. Just don't beat me up in public like this. It could get embarrassing.'*

"There was that wonderful smile again. I honestly can't remember laughing so much in all my life. He picked himself up, and asked why we always met under strange circumstances. Then just when I thought he was going to talk to me, he said, *'I'm sorry. I have to go. I am already late for an appointment.'*

"He handed me his business card." *'This is in case I sue you for assault,'* he said. "Then he flashed that smile again. I watched him disappear into the crowd. I must admit, I was very disappointed."

Aunt Jennie kissed her on the cheek and asked, "Have you seen him since?"

Abbey replied, "Yes, if you can believe this. Last night in my dream, it was like he was in the room smiling at me. In some ways it scared me."

Jennie hugged her niece and held her tightly.

After a few minutes, her aunt asked if she would like to see him again and Abbey replied, "Yes. I would too very much. It's funny Aunt Jennie. We live in a small town, and yet apart from those two occasions, I have never seen him around and believe me … I have been looking. It's like he has disappeared."

Jennie thought for a moment and then said to Abbey, "You have his card. If it was me, I would call him."

"And what would I say?" Abbey asked.

"Just ask him if he is okay, and that you were wondering if he had healed from the bruising you gave him." This time they laughed together.

"You know," her aunt said, "maybe running into him the way you do is fate. I have a feeling you will meet again."

Abbey really did love her aunt, and hugged her more.

"By the way," her aunt said, "what's his name?"

"Jake," Abbey replied. "Jake Lockhart."

Chapter 3

B ack in Rockaway, Jake had been invited to dinner at his best friend's house. When Jake had first moved to New Jersey, his mother found him his first permanent school, Valley View Elementary in Denville. He was at last not moving from school to school.

Jake soon made friends. Daniel was in his class in grade seven and had Jake's sense of humour. They instantly bonded. Elizabeth and Nancy were also in the same class and were Daniel's pals. They became like a foursome and went everywhere together.

Jake found it strange to have girls as friends. This had never happened before, but he soon got used to the idea.

The movie theatre, the bowling alley, even shopping at the mall on Saturday's – over the years they would do most things that kids enjoy.

Even at that time, Jake could tell that Elizabeth was special to Daniel. They held hands under the table and over the years became inseparable. Nancy and Jake would just tag along, but their friendship remained very strong.

As the years went by, Nancy became more and more dependant on Jake's friendship - even after they graduated high school.

Daniel had always wanted to work with cars and at eighteen could do most repairs, so he went to Automotive College in Queens, New York. For two years this meant he stayed in New York during the week as he was taking very demanding courses. He obtained his ASE certificate, and his Degree in Automotive Management, and went on to be a first class mechanic. Eventually he would be able, with help, to open his own garage.

Elizabeth did not go to college. Instead, she worked in her parent's bakery in Rockaway. She loved baking and cooking and her dream was to marry Daniel. This came true, not long after Daniel had finished at Automotive College. They had been childhood sweethearts. He had always been in love with Elizabeth and after settling at work in Ivan's Garage in Denville, eighteen months later, on Elizabeth's twenty-fourth birthday in 1983, they were married at the Parsippany Presbyterian church, which was only twenty minutes, from the home they had bought in Rockaway.

It was a beautiful July day and around one hundred family members and guests attended the wedding.

The only guest who did not look happy was Nancy, even though Jake had accompanied her. She was jealous that her friends were marrying each other, and not the other way around. She wanted to tell Jake how she felt, but could not bring herself to tell him her secret after all these years.

Elizabeth looked absolutely stunning in her white silk gown, with a train that went on forever. The bridesmaids wore pastel blue dresses in the same style. Her mother had made all of them. Daniel was really nervous, but Jake was there to make sure he was okay and give support.

Parsippany Presbyterian was built in 1828. It was a beautiful stone church on the edge of the town, a super place for wedding pictures. The reception was held at the Hilton Garden Inn in Rockaway.

Jake was the *best man*, and gave the speech of his life. He informed the guests that growing up with these two was the best thing that could have happened to anyone. Their friendship meant more to him than words could express, even though they were now Mr. & Mrs. Smith. He assured everyone that that was their real name, not one made up for the Honeymoon Suite at the hotel. At that moment, the room erupted in laughter. Jake kissed them both, and then toasted the happy couple wishing them much happiness in the years to come and to one day make him a godparent.

"I love them both," he finished, "and hope we stay friends forever no matter where life takes me."

Nancy Ross was in some ways different from the other three. She loved Jake, though she had kept the secret to herself. Elizabeth had a feeling that when Nancy looked at Jake, it was with love, and not friendship. She once asked her if this was true, but Nancy flatly denied it and made it quite clear she did not appreciate the accusation. Elizabeth then assured her that as a friend, she was just asking. Nancy emphasized the point by reminding her it was none of her business anyway.

Elizabeth had always thought that Nancy had a dark side and never mentioned it again, but their friendship from that day onward was never quite the same.

She recalled not long after her marriage that she invited Nancy for dinner. Jake was away in New York for a seminar. Elizabeth was quite shocked when she declined the invitation, it was her tone when she said the word *no*, yet when she invited Jake and Nancy to a barbecue the following week she jumped at the idea and was really charming. Elizabeth got the feeling there was definitely something strange about her friend, but could not put her finger on it.

When she spoke to Daniel about the way Nancy sometime seemed to have mood swings, he said, "She will never change. Remember at school, sometimes she could really be horrid to some of the other kids. If she liked you, then it was okay. If she did not, then get out of her way. It's best not to pry. Some things are best left alone."

Daniel had purposely avoided telling his wife that he knew Nancy was in love with Jake. He had watched her on many occasions. It was the way she looked at him and always wanted to sit by him, because that is the way he was with Elizabeth, so it did not take a brain surgeon to work that out.

Daniel thought of Jake more as a brother than a friend, but even though he knew about Nancy and her feelings toward him, he could never tell his best friend. He did not want to be the one to drive wedges into their friendship.

Nancy had left for University. She was a very intelligent woman and was studying for her Degree in Medicine. She had said all along that one day she would become a doctor.

Of course, Jake kept in touch with Nancy, and on a few occasions traveled to Connecticut to spend the weekend. They would go to parties, which seemed the thing to do. Jake was not a heavy drinker, but now and again he would have one too many.

It was while he was there one weekend that it happened. They went to the usual round of parties, had far too much to drink and went back to Nancy's apartment. She could afford to live off campus. Jake used to sleep on the sofa bed in the lounge - Nancy had her own bedroom. He was dozing, nearly asleep, when Nancy slipped in beside him totally naked and started running her hands all over him. He tried, but not that hard, to stop her. They started kissing and as their desire grew they ended up having sex. It had been lust than anything else – a spur of the moment thing, until Nancy blurted out, "I have always loved you Jake – always."

After they were finished, Nancy went to sleep. Jake just laid there, he was stunned. *'What the hell have I done?'* he said to himself. *'This should never have happened.'* He was full of remorse, but knew he was as much to blame. He decided to talk with Nancy, in the morning.

Jake was making coffee, when Nancy stirred. He had been up a long time thinking what he could do and say. It was eating at him – driving him crazy.

Her first words were like a knife to his heart. "Good morning darling," she purred.

Jake stood frozen to the spot. *'Oh God,'* he said to himself, *'What have I done?'*

He poured them both a cup of coffee, and then he beckoned Nancy to join him in the kitchen.

She came over and tried to kiss him. Jake gently pushed her away.

"Please don't," he said.

"Jake, you must have known that I was in love with you," she said. "And I always had a feeling you loved me and last night you proved it."

"Nancy, we have to talk about last night."

"Last night was wonderful," she said.

Jake started to tremble. Sure, he had sex with girls before, but this was different. He plucked up the courage. Looked straight at Nancy, and said, "Last night was wrong. It was a mistake, and should never have happened. I know I'm to blame, but this can never happen again. You're my friend Nancy and always have been. I love you, but I'm not in love with you. I'm sorry."

Nancy was absolutely stunned.

"You bastard!" she shrieked. "I have loved you all these years and you treat me like a *whore!* You screw me and then don't want to know. *You utter bastard!"*

Jake had never felt so low, so dirty.

"Nancy, it was wrong. It should never have happened. I am truly sorry."

"You don't mean it Jake! We can work this out! *I love you!* We can. We must work this out!"

"I can't Nancy," he replied. "Last night was a huge mistake. It should never have happened. I am truly sorry. I think I should leave."

"Yes ... go ahead!" she ranted. "You had your way, and now you want to run away. *You bastard!"*

Jake closed the door on the way out.

Nancy was still screaming obscenities.

He knew this would haunt him – maybe for the rest of his life. They had been really close friends for so long. Jake stopped by his car. He threw up all over the side of the road.

At dinner, Elizabeth commented to Jake, "You seem miles away. Is there something wrong?"

Jake hesitated for a moment then told them what had happened in Connecticut the week before. Both Daniel and Elizabeth went quiet. Daniel was the first to speak.

"It's funny you know, but Elizabeth has had the feeling for a long time, that Nancy wanted you to be more than a friend."

Daniel was being careful of what he said. "It was just a mistake buddy. Don't beat your self up over this. She'll get over it. Nancy is a very strong minded girl."

Jake replied, "I hope so ... but if you could have seen her ... she was a different person. I don't mean she was just upset. It's like she changed into a *demon*. She was spitting venom. In some ways – she scared me."

Then Daniel told his friend about some of the things she used to get up to in school, which Jake did not have a clue about.

"She has always had a strange side. My advice as a friend – yes, it was wrong, but put it behind you."

Elizabeth's dinner of Duck a l'Orange with Duchess Potatoes and assortment of vegetables was absolutely divine.

"I'm stuffed," Jake said. "You are the best cook in the world Elizabeth. There's no doubt about it. Thank you for inviting me."

Elizabeth replied, "You will always be welcome in our home, no matter what, always."

Jake smiled. "Thank you kind lady."

After dinner, Daniel took Jake out to the patio so he could feed his addiction of one cigar a day. He offered Jake the box, and much to his surprise, he took one. Jake had never smoked, but it was a crutch he felt that evening would help.

Elizabeth joined them on the patio.

"Well, go on," she told her husband, "tell him."

"Okay. Okay," Daniel said. "Jake old buddy. You are going to be a godfather."

Jake smiled and hugged the pair of them. "Congratulations to both of you and thank you for cheering me up."

He enjoyed his cigar that evening, but Nancy was still on his mind. *'If I hadn't been so stupid, maybe we could still be friends,'* he thought.

Back in Connecticut, Nancy was on a downward spiral, drinking every night sleeping with anyone, and was now into drugs. Her life was in the toilet. It was affecting her studies. She was missing seminar after seminar, not going to class, had numerous warnings for her conduct and was slipping deeper and deeper into depression. At this precise moment in her life, she hated Jake. She would phone him at his home and leave atrocious messages. Swearing and calling him every name under the sun. *'You have ruined my life!'* she kept repeating, over and over. Though later, she would not remember most of this, because most of the time when she did this, she was high on whatever she could get her hands on.

Her intense hatred had taken over her life.

Abbey, having finished Teachers college, had now secured a position at Copeland Middle School teaching math to sixth graders. She loved the school and being so close to home could not have been more idyllic.

Living only minutes from the school afforded her the opportunity to walk there most days. She really liked working with kids of that age group and secretly hoped this would become a permanent position.

Abbey had only been there a few months when they broke for summer holidays.

She was hoping to go visit her aunt and maybe spend the summer in St. John, but that was not to be – fate would take a hand.

She had become friends with Mrs. Granger, one of the older female teachers at the school, who had given Abbey some good advice on how to handle the behaviour difficulties. Even at that age, some of the kids could wreak havoc, and Abbey being a novice appreciated her help.

On the last day of term, which fell on a Friday, Mrs. Granger had invited Abbey for supper.

"Please come?" she urged her young friend. "It would be so nice to have a different face at the table, and my husband Leo is dying to meet you. He's retired now and we don't have people over that much anymore. Leo is a delightful cook."

Abbey agreed to be there for seven as requested and thanked Mrs. Granger.

"That's okay for school," she replied. "Please call me Nora. Here's my address and phone number. You can bring your boyfriend as well. It would be nice to meet him."

Abbey explained to Nora that at the moment she was alone.

On the Saturday evening, Abbey pulled up to Nora's cottage, which sat on Lake Hopatcong. It was only a twenty minute drive from Rockaway.

'Oh my,' she thought to herself, *'it reminds me in many ways of Aunt Jennie's in St. John. This is really quaint.'*

Nora greeted her at the door.

"I'm sorry I'm a few minutes late. I had to stop in town," she said, handing Nora a huge indoor plant, and a bottle of wine.

"You didn't need to do that," Nora said grinning, "but that's very thoughtful, come in Dear, and meet Leo."

He was in the kitchen leaning over the stove. He was a tall man, very distinguished looking with long white hair.

"You must be Abbey," he said with a big smile. "I have heard so much about you from Nora. I'm Leo." They shook hands.

"Can I get you a glass of wine young lady?" He was still smiling.

"Thank you."

"White or red?"

"White please," Abbey replied.

Just then the doorbell rang.

"That must be Martha," Nora said. "She's our next door neighbour. We thought it would be nice to invite her. She is a real sweetie. I hope you don't mind. She said she was bringing a date. How mysterious. I have never known Martha to even have a boyfriend. She is a widow, and has always been content to stay that way."

Martha came straight to the kitchen and gave Leo a big kiss. "Here's my date," she said.

Abbey's eyes widened – it was Jake.

"I'd like to introduce my new colleague from work," Nora said. "Martha, Jake –this is Abbey."

"Pleased to meet you," replied Martha.

For a moment, Jake stood motionless. He could not believe that the beautiful young lady that he had thought of so often was standing right in front of him. Then he broke the silence, "Hello again Abbey. How are you?" He took her hand. "And yes, before you ask, as you can see, I did recover." They both laughed.

"You both know each other?" Nora asked.

"Yes we do, in a strange way," Abbey replied, "but it's a long story."

Jake could not take his eyes off Abbey. His mind was racing. *'So here she was again, the beautiful girl that I bump into now and again. There she was with her jet-black hair, those big brown eyes, and that little dimple in the middle of her chin that made his heart race.'*

The story of how they met on two different occasions was told over dinner. Abbey had elected Jake to tell it. Everyone found it amusing, though Martha, who was very protective of her son, did not say a word.

Though she did notice, the way Jake was looking at Abbey. There was a sparkle in his eye, and being a mother she knew Jake liked her very much.

Then Martha remembered after listening to her son explain how they met. *'So this is the girl that he spoke about. Jake's ramblings, and going on and on about a girl that he had bumped into. I can see why he is taken with her she is very beautiful. Just be careful son,'* she thought to herself. *'Please tread lightly. I do not want to see you get hurt.'* But she also noticed the way Abbey looked at Jake. *'It's like she was dancing on his every word.'* Martha smiled.

After dinner, they all sat in the lounge talking. Jake wondered if Abbey would like to take a walk in the garden and get some air. It was late June, the evening was very warm. They strolled down to the lake.

"It's lovely here," Abbey commented.

"Yes, it is."

"I grew up next door, so I have always loved the lake."

Jake found it hard to find the words, but eventually he blurted them out. "Abbey, may I take you out for dinner one evening?"

She replied instantly, "That would be really nice … when?" Abbey smiled at him.

Jake knew there and then, this was the woman he had been waiting for.

Martha had always been very protective of Jake. Even when he had moved to his apartment, she called him most days. He was only twelve when his father died, and he was all she had in the world. Seeing Jake look at Abbey the way he did, made her a little jealous, though she had always hoped that one day he would marry, and give her the joy of grandchildren.

Jake was born on January 31, 1958. He was an easy child and gave great comfort to Martha with her husband always on the road, though he would come home at night when he could.

They had moved to New Jersey not long after her husband died. She had settled by the lake and loved this part of the country, not even minding the cold winters. She loved to see the lake freeze over in winter and then thaw again in the spring.

Jake had settled here, had made friends for the first time in his life. Even though she missed her husband, who was a wonderful partner, they had moved from state to state with his work. They had never owned a home, always rented. Now at last she had roots. She had often told herself that Gary, her husband would have loved it here, what a shame he never got to see this beautiful spot.

Gary, her husband, was an engineer on state highways, spending no more than two years in one place. They had lived in Florida, Alaska, New York, North Dakota and Virginia. Gary went where he was needed. Their savings had grown over the years, and with his life insurance, Martha was very comfortable for money, but she missed him. Not a day went by that she did not talk to him still.

Gary was killed in an accident at work. A speeding driver had gone through the intersection too fast and could not brake in time. Gary was killed instantly. The car had thrown him twenty feet in the air eye witnesses had testified at the Coroner's inquest.

The driver of the speeding car was charged with vehicular homicide, but that would not bring her Gary back.

She did hear some time later, that the driver received a light prison sentence but she did not care about that. She just would not, could not, ever forgive him for destroying her happiness. Her only consolation now was Jake. She was sad that her husband never got to spend more time with his son.

Jake also missed his father. After his death, he would still stand by the door

waiting for him to come home, then he would remember, and it would make him feel very sad.

He was resilient, and after time, started to come to terms with the reality of losing his father.

His mother helped him through it. She would sit and talk for hours. Telling him about what a good man he was, how much he loved Jake, and that he was always sorry that by the time he arrived home in the evening, Jake would be in bed. *'He always came to your bedroom to tuck you in. Remember Jake, on weekends, we would if possible, go the park and your dad would play ball with you for hours. He really enjoyed the time that he could spend with us. Promise me that you will never forget.'* Jake promised.

And his life improved when he started school in Denville. He now had friends, and homework and a lot more to occupy his thoughts. He would never forget the promise he made to his mother, and every few months they would visit his father's grave in Wilkes-Barre in Pennsylvania and leave flowers.

Jake was growing up now. He helped his mother as much as possible around the house and weeded the garden. His friends would come over and all four of them would swim in the lake, or take out the rowboat and fish. The girls caught more fish than Jake or Daniel. They had some happy summers at his home.

Although Daniel was born in Rockaway, until Jake arrived at his school, he had just two friends – both of them girls – Elizabeth and Nancy. He had no male friends. He found them tiresome, but hit it off with Jake immediately. Martha would call them, *'the infamous four'*.

Jake had always been interested in the stock market, and on leaving high school he attended the Centenary College in Hackettstown which was about thirty minutes from home. His mother bought him his first car, a little red Honda Civic. This enabled Jake to travel there and back every day. He earned his Business and Accounting Degree.

He was so happy that summer, he sent his resume to every financial institution in New Jersey scored lots of interviews and was offered a position with a small investment firm in Rockaway. Being close to home, he jumped at the chance.

He would be taught to sell investments to clients, insurance, be able to deal in the stock market. Jake was a natural, and after only two years had a number of his own clients and his portfolio was building every month. Even his mother bought stocks and shares.

Jake was really happy his hard work was paying off, and he loved the adrenalin rush when he picked good stocks for his clients.

'He is a natural', his Manager had commented to the Director, *'he will be a fine asset to this company'*.

Jake still lived with his mother, but had put an offer in to buy a small condo in town, not far from Daniel and Elizabeth. He had told his mother who was very apprehensive, but understood that it was time to live his life, his way.

He was driving home one evening when he noticed a car with its lights flashing on the side of the road. He pulled over to see if he could help, and then he saw her. For the first time in his life, Jake was lost for words. She stepped out of the car and was standing in front of him, the most beautiful girl he had ever laid eyes on.

She had dark flowing hair, huge brown eyes, and the sexiest little dimple in the chin.

'Wow!' he thought. *'She is gorgeous, but what the hell would anyone like that see in someone like me?* Though he dealt with the public every day, when it came to women, Jake was always a little on the shy side. But he did jump out of the car. He fixed hers within minutes. It was only a loose connection. She smiled and thanked him, and he drove off. But he would never forget that beautiful girl he met on the side of the road. He passed the same spot every day, but alas he did not see her again. He wished now that he had known her name, but he had not asked for it.

Chapter 4

Abbey awoke on the following morning. She had really enjoyed last evening. The nice dinner at Nora's, and especially meeting Jake again. She felt all warm inside. Abbey could not remember feeling this way before. She was to visit her grandmother later in the day, but all her thoughts were about Jake. *'I hope he calls today.'*

In the meantime, Jake had been up for hours pacing the floor. *'Should I call her today, or wait a few days?'* He could not make up his mind, he just kept pacing and pacing. He was in turmoil. He had wanted to call her at six this morning when he woke up. He just could not get her out of his mind.

Jake picked up the phone, started to dial, put it down again. *'You're acting like a schoolboy,'* he said to himself. He picked the phone up again. This time he dialled –Abbey answered.

"Hi," said Jake. "Remember me?"

"You would be hard to forget," Abbey replied.

His heart was in his mouth. "Would Wednesday be okay for dinner?" he managed to ask.

"Yes," Abbey replied, "that would be fine."

"I'll pick you up around seven."

"I look forward to it."

"I had a nice time last night, and I'm glad we have at last met under better conditions," he said and laughed.

"Yes," she agreed, "it was a lovely evening."

Abbey sat there. She was thrilled that Jake had called. Now her only problem was to call Aunt Jennie and delay going to St. John. She had made arrangements for travel on Tuesday, but she had been waiting for this Wednesday for a long time. She was on the phone for over half an hour with her aunt, related the story of meeting Jake again, and the dinner and Jake calling, she rambled. Her aunt congratulated her, but also showed some concern.

"Just be careful Abbey, I would not like it if you were hurt."

Jake arrived at Daniel and Elizabeth's in time for the Sunday barbecue. He could not wait to tell them about his dinner the night before, and meeting Abbey again. He went on and on, *'I'm seeing her Wednesday'*, and *'how sweet she was'*, the *'pacing'*, the *'phone call'*.

"We get it," Daniel replied. "You're love-struck, totally lost. Come back down to earth."

Jake apologized. "I'm sorry, it's just…"

"Yes," Elizabeth said. "We know. Daniel and I have always felt like that Jake. It's called love. Don't ruin it."

She kissed him on the cheek. "Now eat your ribs please."

Abbey was driving to her grandmas. She was passing the spot on the highway where she had broken down. She pulled over and sat there for a few minutes. She had butterflies.

'This is ridiculous.' she thought to herself. *'I'm a grown woman. I have been out with other boys, and men. What is it about Jake?'*

She drove on.

At last, she arrived at her destination. Her grandma was pleased to see her and appeared to be quite excited, almost giddy.

"How was the dinner last night?" she asked, barely giving her granddaughter time to settle in.

"Absolutely fantastic," Abbey replied. "Guess what? I met Jake again. He was at the dinner party."

Her grandmother looked at her in surprise.

"Is this the same young man you told me about before?"

"Yes," Abbey said. Her face suddenly felt hot. "The same."

"Oh ... do tell," her Grandma said with a playfully wicked grin on her face.

Abbey then related the events, and her evening, and the phone call from Jake, and her conversation with Aunt Jennie.

"Yes," her grandma said. "I spoke with Jennie myself not long before you arrived. She told me you have delayed going to the island. I know you Abbey. You have good insight, so I don't need to worry."

Abbey's parents were away that weekend, so she would have to wait to tell them all her news.

When Jake arrived home, he called his mother. He thanked her for the invitation to Nora's, and told her how elated he was at meeting Abbey again. He informed his mother, "If it had not been for you, this might never have happened." He was still walking on air.

His mother replied, "She is a charming young lady, and Jake it was nice to hear you laugh again."

Wednesday came. Abbey was flustered. She had tried about ten different dresses, blouses and pants, she had no choice but to ask her mothers help. After what seemed a lifetime, she was ready. She wore a two-piece summer suit, with a delicate print and a small wrap as it could still get chilly in the late evening.

"You look really nice," her mother said in approval.

At exactly seven, Jake arrived and rang the bell. Abbey answered the door, he stood agog.

"Wow," was the first word he uttered, "you look beautiful."

"Jake, I would like you to meet my mother."

Mrs. Walker came to the door and shook his hand.

"It's a pleasure to meet you," she said. "I hope you both have a lovely evening."

The evening was still warm.

"Abbey, I hope you like Italian food."

"Yes," Abbey replied, "I love Italian."

Jake drove to Regigalia's Restaurant in Cedar Knolls.

"It's a delightful restaurant, very romantic, with a great ambiance."

Jake had been here many times before. He did not know it at the time, but so had Abbey. They both had Calamari with hot sweet sauce to start, and then Abbey had Vitally Rossini, veal scaloppini, prosciutto, sun dried tomatoes, mozzarella cheese, in a light Dijon sauce. It was her favourite. Jake tried something new. Gamberi Fradiablo Jumbo shrimp, in a spicy tomato sauce served over tomato infused risotto. They both had a nice glass of Chardonnay, not too dry, not too sweet. They talked endlessly and by the end of the meal, Jake felt he had known her all his life. He could not take his eyes off Abbey.

She had told him about losing her sister, St. John, Aunt Jennie, just about everything there was to tell. She had never been this relaxed around a man in her life.

Jake also opened up about his life, his friends, the loss of his father, and that he was to be a godparent, which had made him very proud. Basically, the only detail he omitted was his problem in Connecticut. He was still ashamed of himself over his behaviour there with Nancy.

On the drive back to Abbey's, again they were passing that place on the highway where they first met. Jake pulled in and stopped his car. He had bought the new Volkswagen only a few months before. He got out and stood there. Abbey also opened her door and stood staring. Jake looked straight into her eyes, he had had only one glass of wine, but he felt really intoxicated. He had to say it.

"Abbey – this spot will always be very special – may I kiss you?"

Before he uttered another word, she had flung her arms around his neck, they kissed long and passionately. When Abbey stopped for air, she looked at Jake.

"This is my place also."

They kissed again and again, and then he said, "I had better take you home before it gets out of hand."

He hugged her tightly, and then drove her home, in silence. Jake glanced at the beautiful woman beside him. He wanted this moment to last forever, but they had arrived at her home. The return drive seemed much shorter. Jake pulled up outside her home, turned, put his hand on her cheek, and whispered, "I have to see you again. I need to see you again."

She leaned over and kissed him. "I need to see you again."

They both laughed. He watched her walk to her door. His chest was pounding. As she opened the door, she turned and waved.

Jake sat there for a minute then drove home the long way, Friday could not come quick enough.

Abbey lay in her bed, and thought to herself, *'I know Jake is the one. I know.'* She was experiencing feelings that were completely alien to her.

Rockaway and Denville were like twin towns in Morris County. They sit beside one another, both different, but alike in many ways, only thirty-five miles from New York, and the same distance to Newark. They are commuter heaven, abounded by beautiful lakes and an easy drive to the Delaware water gap, one of the nicest areas of New Jersey.

Over the years, Jake came to love living in such nice surroundings. Even after being offered work in New York and Newark, he wanted to stay where he had grown from a boy to a man. His favourite was Indian Lake, though his mother had bought the house on Lake Hopatcong because she could not afford the price of a house on Indian Lake, it was at that time out of her reach.

Though Jake liked living on the lake at Hopatcong, his dream was to one day own a waterfront property in Denville so he could live in town. Since Indian Lake was only a few minutes walk from the centre, which was where he would buy land and if all went well in his life, spend the rest of his days.

Jake knew that would be many years down the road and a lot of hard work. He used to think to himself, *'There's nothing wrong in dreaming.'*

As a boy, Daniel and Jake would visit the lake with the girls whenever they were able, and as Nancy had a friend who lived there, they would go water skiing as much as possible.

There were also many other places to visit very close to the town. Jake hoped he would never have to leave again. He had spent his early childhood going from place to place, and did not want to live anywhere else.

That summer, Jake and Abbey went everywhere – they were inseparable. On numerous occasions they caught the train from Denville to New York. They spent their days shopping, and sightseeing, and they had a picnic in Central Park. They visited museum after museum, and had a day on Ellis Island, then came the Statue of Liberty and Wall Street. They had virtually covered the city. They were having a wonderful time, coming home late in the evening where they would curl up on the train together.

Abbey did not want this summer to end. She hoped it would go on forever. She had never been happier. She was also hoping that her relationship with Jake would move to the next level. Abbey wanted him badly, she had never wanted anyone like this before, and she was getting urges that were hard to explain. When Jake kissed her, she felt she was floating on air.

Jake was at the same time, thinking on the same lines. He knew he was in love and wanted to touch her and caress her, and make love with her, but he did not want to appear pushy – so he waited.

She never did get to St. John that beautiful hot summer of '85 – Aunt Jennie understood. They talked on the phone every week and her aunt was now very encouraged by her relationship with Jake. Abbey was happy, and that's all she cared about. Her niece was important to her, and she knew they were in love.

Jennie had also spoken a few times with her sister Maggie, who was not so enthusiastic. She had certain reservations about Jake, and just thought her daughter could do better with her choice. Jennie though, would have none of this, and on one occasion told her sister, she was living on a different world to the rest of us.

This did not please Maggie. She so wanted to pair Abbey with Simon, who was Sam's boss, at the pharmaceutical company. She adored Simon, but could not convince her daughter to go out with him.

It was eating away at her and she would not give up. She was certain that Abbey's relationship with Jake would fizzle out. What she did not know – was that it was getting stronger.

Abbey was talking to Jake on the phone.

"This is the last weekend of my summer holidays. Have you made any plans?"

"You've forgotten already. We're invited to Daniel's for a *shrimp on the barbie* tomorrow evening," he joked.

"Yes, I remember that. I mean you and me. Can we go somewhere, just the two of us?"

"Are you okay Abbey?" Jake asked concerned.

"I want to be with you. I'm being selfish. I just want to be alone with you," she replied.

"Of course honey," he said, but he was not convinced. "Are you sure there's nothing wrong?"

Earlier that day, Abbey and her mother had an argument over Jake. She had never seen her mother like this before, and it scared her.

"What have you got against him?" Abbey shouted.

"I just don't think he is good enough for you. There are better catches out there. You have not even looked."

"I don't need to look," Abbey replied, but her mother went on.

"It will end in heartbreak. Mark my words!" Her mother stormed out of the room, leaving Abbey in tears.

That evening Abbey drove over to Jake's place. She didn't call him, she just turned up, and as he opened the door, he could sense something was wrong. She flung her arms around him. He just stood there and hugged her, he could hear the sobs. He kissed her.

"Sit down," he said. "Tell me all about it."

She relayed the conversation she'd had with her mother to Jake. He did not say anything for quite some time. He was angry, but did not want Abbey to know that. Then Jake held her again.

"I love you Abbey. I love you with all my heart. I would never hurt you in a million years."

Her grip tightened on Jake. "I love you too, and will forever."

That evening was the first time they made love. It just came naturally. They kissed and they started undressing each other. Both of them were clumsy. Jake carried her to the bedroom. He laid her on the bed and slowly kissed her body. In return, Abbey caressed him – it was wonderful. Her breath quickened as she pressed her hips against his. With each passing second, their desire intensified until they could wait no longer. Abbey trembled as she slid her hand down between them and guided Jake home. They made love. It did not last as long as they wanted, but they knew it would only get better when they learned how to satisfy each other. All that did not matter, as they lay there, holding each other, afraid to let go.

Abbey stayed the night, holding Jake as if her life depended on it.

She had never been happier. When they made love again in the morning, they this time came together. He entered her and their lovemaking was slow, but deliberate. They climaxed together. Jake wanted this time to last forever, he could not stop kissing her, but he had to go to work. He made coffee and sat on the bed. He kissed her nose.

"I must take a shower and get going. I'm sorry."

Jake was ready to leave. He walked over to the bed. Abbey stared at him.

"I'm really happy."

"So am I," Jake replied, and kissed her passionately. He gave her huge hug as if he was leaving forever.

After he had departed, Abbey called her aunt, she knew Jake wouldn't mind. She told her Aunt Jennie about the argument with her mother and confessed to staying the night at Jake's.

"You really love him Abbey?" was her aunt's next question.

"Yes," she sighed. "I can't explain, but I want to be with him all the time."

Her aunt understood, but she did not say a word.

When she did speak, it shook Abbey a little.

"Go home. Make peace with your mother. If you can't do that, then leave. You're a big girl now, and you have your own life. Call me soon."

Back at home, her mother was frantic, more worried than anything else. Abbey had never done this before. *'We've had words before, but she had always come home, or phoned to say she was staying somewhere.'* This was new to Maggie, and she did not like it.

She heard the car pull into the driveway. She ran to the door.

"Are you okay Abbey?" She had tears in her eyes. "I'm sorry." She hugged her daughter. "I'm so very sorry," she repeated. "I should never have said those bad things about Jake. Please forgive me. I was stupid. I love you Abbey and your future is important to me. I promise to get along with Jake. I know now how much you love him."

Abbey held her mother tightly. "Thank you Mum," was all she said.

She sat with her mother and over coffee and she explained what had happened to her over the past few months. She wanted her mother to know everything.

"I met Jake last year. He was kind enough to help me when my car broke down. Then I bumped into him again. I can't explain how I felt, because I had never felt that way before, and then when he turned up at Nora's – I knew he was the one. I wish I could elaborate more, but this is the truth. I did not know I would or could fall for anyone so fast and so hard, but I have. I can't imagine life without him Mum. I just want you to understand how I feel about Jake, because it's so hard for me to comprehend. I know he is everything to me, and I hope he is for the rest of my life, because I could not be happier."

Maggie sat there somewhat stunned by her daughter's explanation.

"I will try my best to accept him. I promise," she told Abbey.

When Abbey answered, she was quite stern. "I hope so Mum, because nothing will ever change my mind. I know I have not known him for very long, but it feels to me that I have known him forever, and what I feel inside – I can't explain."

Jake, was very busy with clients that day, but he never stopped thinking about last night. He had girlfriends before, he'd had sex with some of them, but this was new to him. This was different. This was everything. *'Abbey,'* he said to himself, *'what have you done to me? It's like you've weaved a spell and trapped me, and I'm so glad you did.'*

Abbey called him at noon. He was just about to go out and get a sandwich.

She told Jake what had happened when she arrived home, and that she now felt a lot better. He asked if she had any regrets about what happened between them the night before.

"No Jake," she replied, without hesitation, "after staying with you last night, I wish it had happened sooner. I'll see you at six." She hung up.

Abbey thought about what Jake had said. *'Regrets ... how could I have regrets? I love the man. My only regret is the time wasted when we could have been together.'*

That afternoon, Maggie called her sister in St. John.

"Hi Mags," she replied. "What is it?"

She proceeded to tell Jennie the events surrounding Abbey not coming home, and their argument. Jennie did not let on that she had already spoken with Abbey. She thought it might hurt her sister's feelings. She told Jennie that she was sorry, and she was sure she would *'never'* do that again, but Jennie knew her sister too well, and knew that would not be the case. She just agreed with Maggie and left it there. There was no point in having an argument. They went on to other topics – how Richard was enjoying his retirement, the weather - they chatted for over half an hour.

When Jennie had finished talking to her sister, she went to work in the garden. Richard was in the pool cooling off. He had replaced the picket fence. Some of it had rotted, so he renewed all of it and painted it white. Now he could relax for the rest of the day.

Jennie dived in the pool and swam up to him, and gave him a big wet kiss.

"The fence looks nice," she commented.

"Thank you kind lady," he said, with a contented smile on his face. "How is everything back in New Jersey?"

Jennie hesitated before she answered. "Not brilliant. Maggie and Abbey were at loggerheads over her boyfriend, and I really get the feeling that trouble is brewing."

"What's this poor guy done?" asked Richard.

"Absolutely nothing," Jennie assured him. "His only crime is he loves Abbey and Maggie does not approve. She has it in her head that he is not good enough, which is absolutely ridiculous. I have spoken many times with Abbey, and she has assured me he is hard working, thoughtful, kind, romantic, and funny. Sam likes him – no problem there. It's just Maggie. Why can't she be happy for her daughter? If Abbey was ours, I would have no problem."

"She's a smart girl." Richard commented. "And her boyfriend Jake is a lucky man … just like me."

Jennie splashed water on him.

"Behave – you. I'm just concerned about her. I love Abbey very much, and I do not want to see her hurt. Not by Jake, but Maggie. My sister can be a pain sometimes."

Jake rang the doorbell at precisely six. Maggie opened the door.

"Come in," she smiled. "Abbey will just be a minute, she couldn't find her jeans. How was work?" she inquired.

"Very busy," Jake answered, as Abbey appeared.

"You look nice," Jake commented. She took his hand.

"Have a nice time," Sam said cheerfully, as he walked through from the kitchen. He kissed Abbey on the cheek.

"Nice to see you again Jake.   Are you keeping well?"

"Yes, thank you sir," replied Jake, and they shook hands. Maggie was still smiling, but never said a word. As they drove away, she was watching out of the window.

"What is it?" Sam said.

"Oh, nothing," Maggie replied. "Nothing."

Elizabeth greeted them as they arrived, gave Jake a friendly kiss on the cheek, and hugged Abbey.

"Nice to see you again. Come on through the back. Daniel's already started. We're having shrimp and steak tonight." Jake laughed.

"What is it?" his friend asked.

"Oh nothing," Jake answered. "How are you Dan? I like your apron." He laughed again.

Daniel always did the barbecue. He was not allowed in Elizabeth's kitchen.

"He makes a mess, so he is banned. He's a menace in that room," she said, trying to be taken seriously. They all laughed.

Other couples had been invited, which filled the tiny garden. The beer and wine flowed and there was lots of food. Jake, out of the corner of his eye, saw Abbey talking to a couple that he had never seen before. She beckoned him over.

"Jake, I would like you to meet Simon and Laura. Simon is dad's boss."

"Hi, pleased to meet you both. How do you know Daniel?" Jake asked.

"Oh, he's my mechanic," Simon replied. "And a damn good one. I would not let anyone else look after my cars."

"Cars?" Jake asked.

"Yes, I have three," Simon chuckled. "I love cars."

Jake smiled, but he did not know why he took an instant dislike to this guy. Maybe it was the way he looked at Abbey. No matter where she went or who she talked to, his eyes followed, and he was with a very pretty girl himself. Jake pondered.

They left the party, which was still in full swing around nine-thirty. Abbey explained she had a headache. They said their goodbyes, and as they got in the car, Jake asked, "Are you okay?"

"I'm fine," Abbey replied. "I lied. I'm sorry. I just wanted to be alone with you," She kissed him and said, "Let's go to your place."

"But what about your mum?"

"Oh, that's okay," Abbey replied. "It's been sorted. Why do you think I bought an overnight bag?"

They made love for most of the night. Their lovemaking was more intense than Jake thought was ever possible. They just could not seem to get enough of each other.

Abbey awoke at around eleven-thirty. She felt safe and warm. Jake still had his arm around her. He was sound asleep. She slipped quietly out of bed and put on a pot of coffee. Jake stirred. He could hear Abbey singing in the shower. He poured himself two cups of coffee and knocked on the shower door. When she opened it, he handed her the coffee, smiled and said, "Not the best woman's voice I've ever heard, but you are the most beautiful." He kissed her.

She dragged him into the shower. His shorts were soaked.

"Look what you have done," he said.

"Take them off," Abbey demanded.

Jake happily complied and they kissed passionately and fondled each other until they could not take anymore. He kissed her breasts, slowly, methodically, as she moaned with satisfaction. She kissed his neck, pulling him closer. They came together, and joined as one while they made love. Jake shuddered as he climaxed with such sheer intensity that he felt like he would pass out. He jokingly said to Abbey, "If you carry on like this, I will be dead before I'm thirty."

She giggled, and quickly replied, "Well, at least we will have a couple of years of insanity." They laughed together.

Later that day, they drove to Lake Hopatcong to visit Jake's mother. She was pleased to see them both. She realized now, that Abbey was a part Jake's life, and was happy that he was settled.

Abbey went for a swim in the lake. Jake sat in the garden with his mother. He was quite taken aback when she said, "So when are you going to ask her to marry you?"

"Mum," he replied, "it's a bit soon for that, but rest assured I would like nothing better. I love her Mum."

"Yes, I can see that," she said. "It's such a pity your father's not here to see her. He would definitely approve. She's lovely son."

"Yes," he said in complete agreement, "she certainly is."

His mother cooked them a delightful dinner, simple but nice. Jake loved goulash, with potatoes and green beans, followed by apple pie and cream. Abbey had the pie with ice cream. Jake was not a big ice cream lover, but he loved whipped cream. He had lots on his pie.

"Your dad used to like to eat pie exactly the same as you," his mother reflected, "with lots and lots of cream." Jake smiled. It was something he remembered.

He watched his mother with Abbey. It was like they had known each other for years. They talked and laughed and after dinner she helped Martha stack the dishwasher while Jake took a stroll in the garden. He was happy that they liked each other. It was, it seemed to Jake, another hurdle out of the way.

They drove home stuffed. Jake commented to Abbey, "I was absolutely famished, and I'd forgotten we had not *eaten all day.*"

"That was super," she replied. "Your mother is a very nice lady. I like her a lot. She made me feel very welcome."

"She adores you," Jake said. "She thinks you would make a wonderful wife."

"And what do you think?" She looked at him intensely, as if trying to read his thoughts.

"What do I think?" Jake chuckled. "Who am I to argue with my mother?" Abbey smiled.

He drove her home. He knew she had to get all her things ready for the restart of school on Monday.

He stopped in the driveway. The house was in darkness.

"No one home?" Jake asked.

"No," Abbey replied. "They are at a dinner party. Simon's dad's boss, he has them a few times a year, invites staff members and their wives."

"Ever been?" Jake inquired.

"I've been two or three times." She smiled at him. "But not since last year."

He kissed her, and held her very tightly.

"What is it Jake?" she asked. She seemed to sense that something was not quite right.

"Oh nothing. Just going to miss you tomorrow." He kissed her again and said goodnight.

As he drove home, he wondered if there had ever been anything between Abbey and Simon. He could not understand what was making him feel like this. He was not the jealous type. He told himself, *'Don't be such an idiot, so what if there was, she's with you now.'*

He arrived home. There was a message on his answering machine. He tapped the button, it was Abbey. "Hi Jake, it's me. I love you." It was short but sweet. *'Thank you,'* he said to himself.

He settled down to watch a movie on TV, but started dozing, so he went to bed. He felt totally exhausted. He smiled when he realized why he was worn out – Abbey.

Chapter 5

On Sunday morning, Jake turned over as he awoke. She was not there. He was still dozy, and then he remembered he had taken her home. *'Jesus. What's wrong with me?'* He did not understand ever feeling this way. *'If this is what love does, it's scary.'* He put on some music, made coffee, and started pacing. Just then, his doorbell rang. *'Abbey?'* No, it was Monica from across the hall.

"Hi Jake."

"Oh, good morning Monica," he replied. He was hoping it had been someone else.

"What's up?" she asked.

"Nothing," he answered.

"It's good to see you. How's Abbey?"

"She's good. Thanks for asking." He was a bit short with her. "What can I do for you Monica?"

"Oh, nothing. I just wanted to say hi."

He felt guilty now. She was a sweet kid.

"I'm sorry," Jake replied apologetically. "I didn't sleep well and I'm not fully awake."

"That's okay," Monica said. "I'll see you later." He closed the door. He did not hear Monica whisper, "Grumpy."

Jake showered, and walked to the corner store to get a newspaper. He liked to read his paper on a Sunday. It was a beautiful day, so he sat in the park and read for about an hour, he then strolled home.

The phone was ringing as he entered his apartment. He smiled, "Abbey?" but the voice on the line, he had never heard before.

"Is that Jake Lockhart?"

"Yes," he answered.

"I'm sorry to disturb you on a Sunday. We have met once in Connecticut, at a party. My name is Brian Groves. I found your number in Nancy's address book. I thought I should let you know she's in hospital."

Jake shook. "What do you mean, she's in hospital?" He wasn't thinking straight. "Who's in hospital?"

"Nancy," the voice replied.

He then proceeded to tell Jake that Nancy had overdosed on heroin at a party the previous Friday. Then he told him that she was in the *Yale New Haven Hospital* on Temple Street.

"The reason I called you Jake, is that I knew you were once friends. We can't help her. We have tried. Maybe you can."

Jake thanked him for calling.

The guilt came flooding back with a vengeance. *'Oh my God!'* he said to himself. *'What should I do?'*

Jake called Abbey. Her father answered. "Hi, how are you Jake?"

"I'm fine thank you, sir."

"Please don't call me sir. It's Sam. I would like you to call me Sam."

"Thank you sir … I'm sorry … Sam. Is Abbey around?"

"Abbey, it's Jake!" he heard him bellow.

"Hi baby," Abbey said lovingly. "I miss you."

"I miss you too," Jake replied. "Listen Abbey, I have to go to Connecticut first thing in the morning, so I won't be home for a few days."

"What's wrong?" she asked. She could now tell by his voice if something was up.

"It's my friend Nancy. The one you've never met. She's in hospital and needs help. I have to go. I'll call you as soon as I can. I must go, I have other people to call. I love you." He hung up.

He called his company Director at home and explained what had happened. "Sorry sir," Jake said, "but she needs me. She's an old friend. I have to take a few days."

He understood. "Jake, take whatever time you need. We will make sure all your work is covered."

"Thank you," Jake said sincerely.

He stood there in a daze. *'What have I done? Is this my fault?'* Jake was trying to come to terms with the phone call. This was something he did not need right now, not with the way his life was improving every day. He felt like saying, *"To hell with her!"* but he could not. She was a friend that needed help. He then realized, *'No matter what happened, she is still your friend.'* He gathered his thoughts together and knew he had to do this.

Then he drove to Daniel and Elizabeth's. He did not want to tell them over the phone. Lucky for him, they were at home. Most Sunday's they normally go to Elizabeth's parents. He then again explained the phone call from Connecticut, and the problem with Nancy. They understood that she needed help, but could not understand Jake's rush to go to her.

"I have to go," Jake said.

Elizabeth asked Jake to call her. "I can come up if you need me," she implored. "I'm not working now at the bakery. I don't think my baby likes the smell. I've had a lot of sickness. Call me Jake."

He said he would. He drove home to pack, knowing the reason he had to go, was guilt.

Abbey called him that evening. "Are you okay Jake? You were upset. I didn't know what to say to you this afternoon."

"I'm fine now that you've called," he replied.

"Have a safe journey and call me if I can help," she said.

"Thank you Abbey. I will call you anyway. I will see you soon. I promise."

That Monday morning, the traffic was horrendous. It seemed to take forever to get to the hospital. At the inquiry desk, he was having a hard time to find her room.

"Sorry," they said, "but only relatives can visit at this time."

Jake lied, "But I'm her brother, I have to see her."

Nancy looked like death. He could not believe his eyes. She was a shadow of herself. She had lost weight, her eyes were sunken, and her face was gaunt.

"Hello Nancy," Jake said. She looked at him and started to cry.

He held her close and stroked her hair. "I'll help you through this," he promised. "Let's get you better." She sobbed harder now. Jake's shirt was soaked, but he did not mind.

He stayed with Nancy for three days. They talked for hours, about everything. He arranged for her to go into Rehab, at a private clinic just outside New Haven. He thought it would be better for her. She did not want her parents called, but Jake took no notice of her pleas.

She needs their help as well. They thanked Jake for calling and assured him they would be there later that day. They kept their promise, and they arrived at the clinic at four-thirty. They thanked Jake again. He asked them to wait a few minutes so that he could talk to Nancy. He told her he would be back on the weekend, and that she must stay and get her health back. He made her swear on the bible – she did.

He explained to Nancy that the only people that knew back home were her parents, Daniel and Elizabeth, and no one else, and that they would visit with him at the weekend. He also mentioned that Elizabeth was pregnant and that they were looking forward to the birth. Nancy cried again. Jake noticed her eyes, they were brighter. Their colour was coming back and that was a good sign. He did not tell her yet, about Abbey.

Jake had called Abbey a dozen times in those three days. He just needed to hear her voice. It was the only time the sadness left him. He felt he was to blame over Nancy's demise, but could tell no one, not even Daniel and Elizabeth. Sure, they would understand, but they were blameless. They had no idea really of how much he thought about what happened over the months, but he also knew that one day, he would have to tell Abbey. He wanted nothing to jeopardize their relationship, and if she found out from anybody else, he was not sure how she would react.

Jake had good drive home, and was making coffee when Abbey came in. They just threw themselves against each other. He must have kissed her a thousand times that evening, and when they made love, it just seemed to get better and better. He held her so tightly afterwards that she looked at him concerned.

"Hey," she said, "you'll crush me if you're not careful." He eased his grip.

"I'm sorry," he replied. "I just missed you so much Abbey." He kissed her again.

Jake thought his lungs would *explode,* but he pressed on, his legs moving as fast as he could push them. He turned the corner. There in the distance was his apartment building. He tried to push harder, the sun was shining. It was a great day for a run.

Stopping outside his building to catch his breath, he looked down at his watch. *'Wow!'* he said to himself. *'I've broken thirty minutes. About time you loser. Yes! Yes! At last!'*

A voice from behind him asked, "Who the heck are you talking to Jake?"

Monica, his neighbour, stood there. She was waiting for her school bus.

"Just myself!" Jake exclaimed.

"That's a sure sign of madness," she chuckled.

Jake laughed. "Cheeky devil," he said pretending to be hurt.

"It's okay Jake," she shot back, "I promise not to tell." He smiled.

They had always had a special relationship from day one. He was moving some boxes into his apartment, when this voice asked if he needed help. It was Monica. *'Sure,'* said Jake, and it started there. *'How old are you?'* Jake asked. *'Nearly fifteen,'* she replied, and that started their big brother, little sister relationship.

Monica lived with her parents, Jonathon and Mary Gitano. They occupied the apartment opposite. They had immigrated to the States in the early sixties, and had come originally from Nigeria. They had spent six years in England and then moved to the States.

Mary qualified as a nurse in England, but the lure to the States was strong. A better life, more money, and Jonathon's brother who was a surgeon had moved to New Jersey five years earlier, and assured them this was the place to be. So, they immigrated and had never looked back.

Mary, with her brother-in-law's help, secured a position at St. Clare's Hospital in Denville, and her husband found a job at the local building supplies store.

They had managed to save some money before they arrived and rented a small apartment in Rockaway. In time, they managed to buy their first home, and when Mary gave birth to Monica they were content. Mary had always wanted a daughter – her wish came true.

Jake and Monica's parents spent hours together at the poolside at the back of the apartment complex. They had all become very friendly. They had confided in Jake that one day, maybe Monica, if possible, and a lot of luck, would have the chance to be a doctor or lawyer. They just wanted their daughter to have a good life.

"I'm sure she will," Jake said. "Monica is very intelligent, and by what you have told me, and what I have learned, she is the top pupil in her school with fantastic averages."

Jake had often spoken to his friends about Monica. Daniel and Elizabeth were very supportive of his big brother type relationship with this young girl. Nancy was not quite as enthusiastic as the others were, and warned Jake *to tread lightly.* He thought she was just being protective – she was not.

Nancy was jealous. She felt Jake was spending far too much time with Monica, and she took an instant dislike to the girl even though she had never met her. Jake was totally unaware of Nancy's feelings. He had never looked at Nancy other than as a good friend.

He didn't have a clue that she was in love with him, and Nancy was not about to tell him, not yet.

Nancy would wait, and when the time was right, she would make sure that she got what she wanted. She always got what she wanted. Even as a child, she basically had everything. Her parents were filthy rich and wanted Nancy to go to private school, but Nancy being Nancy, would have none of that. She went where she wanted and she would choose her life, not her parents. Whether or not it's because they were always traveling for business, and Nancy was left with a nanny most of her childhood, or they felt guilty on leaving her so much – only Nancy knew the answer.

A few months back, on Monica's sixteenth birthday, she had been allowed to have a party and invite some friends. That morning, she did of course ask Jake if he would pop in. Jake apologized, but he had a late client that evening, so he would not be home until very late. He wished her a happy birthday and gave her his present.

"Can I open it now?" she pleaded.

"Of course," Jake replied.

She opened the card. It read, *'To a special friend.'* She gave Jake a *thank you* kiss on the cheek. Inside the card was a gift certificate for the local record store.

"You are a big softy Jake. I'm lucky I have a big brother like you." They both laughed.

At Monica's party, two of her so-called friends smuggled in alcohol. Marty and Steve were the class clowns. Her father noticed they were getting intoxicated and asked them to leave. They did, but did not go far.

After the deadline of ten-thirty, everyone had gone home. Monica's parents were tired. It had been a long day. She thanked her mother for a wonderful time and apologized for the behaviour of the other two. "It's not your fault." Her mother kissed her goodnight.

Monica decided to clear some of the empty pop cans and paper. She took all the garbage down to the recycling bins which were situated in the underground garage.

She opened the door of the bin room, and there stood her two classmates that had been asked to leave. By this time, they were pretty drunk. They grabbed Monica and started trying to touch and kiss her. On struggling, she fell to the floor.

The two boys thought this was funny, but Monica was upset. They went to grab her again, just as Jake opened the door.

"What the hell?" Jake pushed one of the assailants, who fell over and hit his head. The other just backed off.

"I'm sorry," he said. "I'm sorry."

Jake was livid. "I've a good mind to…"

"No!" Monica pleaded. "Please don't Jake. Just get them out of here."

She was very cross. The other boy got up, a bloody nose, but no real damage.

"Jake, please take them home."

"You should call the police."

"No, because you know, and I know, I will be blamed just as much. It always seems to end that way. No Jake, just get them out of my sight."

He drove them both home, and instilled in them how lucky they were. Both of them said sorry.

"It's not me you have to be sorry to. Never let me find out you have bothered Monica again."

That is a secret Jake and Monica share. She never told a soul and she made Jake swear never to repeat what happened that night. He never has, not even to his friends.

He had decided that he would always look out for her. He always inquired how she was doing, and would spend time talking to her when he could.

Even when he started dating Abbey, Monica was not pushed aside, and when Abbey took an interest in her, Jake was happy. She would help her with her homework if it were needed, and always found time to talk to her about boy and girl things. If Jake asked what girl things were, he was told that it was private, and he used to laugh.

One evening, Jake invited everyone over for dinner – Jonathon, Mary, Monica and Abbey. Mary did not realize that he could cook and got a very nice surprise. They had spring salad with mandarins and almonds, followed by roast duck, which was Jake's favourite. Then on to dessert, Elizabeth had made him a chocolate hazelnut meringue. They all enjoyed the meal. In conversation over dinner, it came to light that Jonathon's brother was a neurosurgeon, and through the conversation it was evident that he was the same surgeon that had operated on Abbey's sister. He was retired now, but had spoken to his brother about the sadness he felt on not being able to save her.

Abbey of course, said that she had never known her sister, but had been told by her father that everything possible had been done. He had a lot of admiration for the doctor and his team who tried to save Heather. She excused herself from the table.

Jake thought it best to change the topic, so he asked Monica how she was doing in school, and about any new friends she had made. It was just idle chit chat from there until everyone went home.

Before Abbey left, she kissed Jake tenderly and thanked him for being so considerate. She knew that he had realized that the conversation was a little upsetting. She thanked him again and Jake walked Abbey to her car. She kissed him goodnight, and as always, he watched her drive away.

Chapter 6

He knew he needed a shower badly. He put on a pot of coffee. *'Thank God I have the day off.'* He never took time off during the week, but had decided to have a long weekend. Jake finished his shower, put on his favourite CD and poured himself a big steaming cup of coffee. He sat and listened to *"Dr. Hook."* They were singing, *"Sharing The Night Together"* - just then, the phone rang. It was Abbey.

"Hi gorgeous. Do you miss me?" Jake asked.

"You know I do," replied Abbey. "Listen Jake, you know I have to go out with Mum and Dad this evening. It's this Gala thingy, I have no choice. Dad's company is up for an award."

"I take it Simon will be there?" inquired Jake.

"Of course," Abbey replied. "It is his company. And Jake, before you ask ... Yes, we will be on the same table. I do believe I detect a hint of jealousy."

"I'm sorry."

"I love you Jake Lockhart, but I must go. There's a class waiting for me. Call me in the morning. Oh ... Jake, I nearly forgot. Is the party at Daniel's still on for tomorrow night?"

"Yes," he said. "I'll call you."

Jake finished his coffee and turned off the music. He sat pondering for quite a while. He had been seeing Abbey for just over a year. He knew she was the one, he had never felt this way about any other women. He was totally and completely in love, and did not want anything or anyone to ruin their relationship in any way. He felt he was the luckiest man on earth and knew Abbey loved him too – so why the jealousy? *'You're stupid he told himself.'*

When Abbey awoke that morning, she could hear her mother calling.

"Abbey, Abbey! Are you awake?"

"Yes Mum. I'm going to take a shower. I'll be down shortly."

Abbey dressed and appeared ready for work. She had a coffee and two slices of toast, which was her morning ritual. Her mother came in the kitchen.

"You wanted me?" Abbey asked.

"Yes Dear. Please don't forget about this evening. It's very important."

"I won't Mum," she replied. "Don't worry."

"I can't help worrying," her mother said. "Your father is very proud that all the work they have put in on this new drug … it's starting to escalate. What, with the positive results so far on testing, this could be a massive seller in the marketplace. The company could very well make a lot of money."

"Mum, I will be home in plenty of time." Abbey smiled at her. "I've already spoken with dad. I know how he feels and it will be a pleasure to be there. The only question I have," Abbey probed, "is why Jake can't escort me?"

"He is not a member of the family," her mother came back at her harshly.

"Yes Mum, but he is my boyfriend, and you know how I feel about him."

"Yes," her mother replied, "but you are on the same table as Simon. He invited you, so please make the effort to be nice to him. You know he likes you. I don't understand why you did not go out with him before? He has asked you a few times."

"He asked me as a friend – that's all. And yes mother, Simon is a super guy, but he's not Jake. Why can't you understand that I love him, and when I'm with him I couldn't be happier?"

Her mother's tone was quite upsetting. Abbey did not understand why she got like this.

"I just think you could do better!" her mother said sharply.

Abbey quickly replied, "Mum, you will have to get used to Jake. Why is it dad likes him and you do not? It's really worrying." Abbey had a tear in her eye. "What have you got against him? He's a sweet, caring man. He is the best thing that's ever happened to me. So Mum … get used to it!" Abbey opened the door and left.

As she walked down the driveway, she had to wipe away tears. Her mother had upset her again.

Abbey tried to analyze why her mother would not accept Jake. She did not understand. He had always been the gentleman, had not tried to put his hands everywhere like some previous dates, and had always treated her like a princess. She knew from their time together, that he was very special.

Of all the boyfriends that she had dated, and there were not that many, Jake was the one she wanted to be with and even in this early stage of their relationship she hoped it would be forever.

Her mother watched, and as Abbey walked out of sight, she then picked up the telephone.

Her husband Sam answered. "What is it? Has something happened? You never phone me at work."

"No," Maggie replied, "it's just that I have been talking to Abbey." She then repeated the long conversation she had had with their daughter.

Her husband did not answer her immediately, and when the reply came, Maggie was stunned.

"Maggie, stop trying to run Abbey's life! She knows what she wants, and I have no intention off trying to change her mind. Jake is a good man. He loves Abbey very much. Why can you not see that she is happy? And if he and Abbey should get married, I could not wish for a better son-in-law. Come on Honey ... Be happy for them. Come to terms with it. Please don't blow it out of proportion."

"Look what happened to us, with your *mother*, who made it quite clear to me that I was not good enough for you ... but we're still together after all these years."

"Sure, we have had our moments, good times, and sad times, but we stayed the course. We got through everything Maggie. You are, and always will be my life. I know it sounds corny, but it's the truth."

"Listen, I have to go. I have an important meeting before the gala this evening. Simon has some issues to discuss."

"I love you honey. See you later. Bye."

Maggie stood holding the phone for quite some time after Sam had said goodbye. *'I know he is right,'* she thought to herself. *'So why do I feel this way?'*

Later that day, Maggie was taking a bath, getting ready for the special evening when the phone rang. It was Sam.

"Hi honey," he said. "Can we talk? Do I hear water?"

"Yes, I'm in the tub."

Sam continued, "There is something I think you should know. You were upset earlier and I knew I was needed at the meeting. There is something I should have told you before. It could wait, but knowing your feelings about Abbey and Jake, I would rather it be now. Do you remember that summer you went to St. John to see your sister Jennie for a week? You needed a break, and I stayed at home. Abbey asked if we could go visit her grandma, and I thought it would be a good idea. While Abbey was in the kitchen making a pot of tea, your mother confided in me. Though at first she was really against our marriage – which of course was no secret to either of us – she actually for the first time opened up and really started talking to me and what she said *totally stunned me.*"

'Sam, you have always been good to Maggie, especially through that tragic time with Heather. My daughter told me if it had not been

for Jennie and Richard's help, she would have gone insane – but most of all Sam – you were her 'rock'. She needed you more than ever, and in my eyes, you came through. You were there for Maggie and little Abbey and I have completely changed my mind. You showed me what a good husband and father you really had become. Now I'm eating humble pie, and I deserve to. I just hope you can forgive me for being such a bitch to you Sam. I should have told you years ago.'

"She actually hugged me. When Abbey came in from the kitchen, the words she spoke caused both your mother and me to look at each other. *Remember now*, she was only fourteen years old."

'It's about time you two became friends.' Then she kissed her grandma and I heard her whisper, *'Thank you. I love you both.'*

"Maggie, those few words from your mother mean a hell of a lot to me. What I am trying to say honey is, be happy for Abbey. She is all we have now."

"I'm sorry," she said. "It's just that I worry so much. This is her first serious relationship, and she has put her heart and soul into it. I wish she would take a step back and not rush into things. I'm not saying Jake is a bad person. It's just we don't know him, and I'm sure Abbey has only told us the good things. But I promise to try and get to know him a lot more, and then hopefully set my mind at rest."

"Thank you Maggie," Sam replied. "I'll be home shortly. Oh, I forgot to tell you. Simon wants me to collect the award this evening. I feel very honoured. I could not wish to work for a nicer guy."

When Maggie hung up the phone, her thoughts went straight to Abbey. If only she would realize, that Simon was so right for her.

She finished bathing, and poured herself a glass of Glenlivet. This she did most days. *One a day is good for blood pressure* was her excuse. One would turn into two or three.

Maggie had never gotten over the loss of her daughter Heather. She hid it well, but over the years it had started to eat away at her, and she turned to alcohol. The only person in the world she had talked to about this problem was Joanne, but she was sworn to secrecy, though even she had implored Maggie to get professional help on many occasions.

She just could not bring herself to tell Sam or Jennie, even knowing they would help. Her husband was the kindest man in the world. She knew this, but still refused to discuss it. And Jennie, her sister, was a no nonsense person and would have her in front of a psychiatrist immediately.

Maggie poured herself another scotch just as the doorbell rang. She drank it fast. It was the florist's delivery man. He had a large bouquet for Abbey, two dozen roses, with a small card which she was tempted to open as Abbey walked in the door.

"Hi Mum." She gave her a kiss on the cheek. "Who are those for?"

"For you."

Abbey opened the card, it read, *'Have a nice time. I love you. Jake.'* She opened the bouquet. They were beautiful, her favourite, yellow roses, with fern and baby's breath. *'Oh Jake,'* she said to herself. *'Thank you.'*

"I will take a shower." Abbey informed her mother. "Then I will be ready on time."

She took the flowers to the kitchen. After putting them in a vase, she took them to her room. She called Jake immediately.

"You're spoiling me."

"I will always spoil you, because I love you and you are worth it," he replied. "Listen Abbey, I have to run. I'm sorry. I have a new client waiting. I'll see you tomorrow … and darling … have fun." He hung up.

Chapter 7

The evening was busy. The Mayor of Rockaway greeted them at the door, alongside him stood the Governor of New Jersey. They had champagne cocktails. Everyone was dressed in dinner suits and evening gowns. Simon greeted the family and informed Maggie and Abbey that they looked absolutely divine.

He kissed them both on the cheek. Maggie wore a black silk gown and Abbey's was rose colored. He escorted both ladies to their table. He stood for a while talking to Sam – work was the topic. Then they sat, Simon next to Abbey. He then went though the motions. *How are you? How is school? Did she enjoy teaching?* She liked talking with Simon. He was intelligent and considerate. He let Abbey talk. She knew that, at times, it was impossible to get a word in with some people. The dinner was served, it was okay, hotel type food, mass produced, but edible. Soup, followed by salad, then a sorbet, the main course was Chicken Kiev with Parisian potatoes, baby carrots and broccoli. The dessert was Crème Brûlée or fruit salad.

Then it was time for the awards. The Governor of New Jersey was the announcer. One after one, different companies collected their plaques. Then the Mayor called the nominees for Business Excellence. Four companies in New Jersey were nominated in this category. There was hush in the banquet room, *'And the winner for 1985 is Brady Industries, for their innovation toward fighting Alzheimer's disease.'*

Abbey's father stood, and walked to the stage. The whole room stood and applauded. She could tell by the smile on his face that he was a very proud man this evening. He had worked really hard on this project, now came the reward.

Sam accepted the prestigious honour. *'Thank you Mr. Governor.'* Then he gave his speech. Very graciously, he thanked all the members of his staff.

"Without you," he said, "this would not have been possible. I want to thank you again for pulling together as a team. We still have a long way to go, but if we carry on the effort, we will achieve our aim of helping people with this terrible disease. I would also like to say a few words about our Managing Director, *Simon Brady*. He is an inspiration to all of us. He is thoughtful to employees, and has, as long as I have known him, never been afraid to roll up his sleeves. He is his father's son. Mr. Joseph Brady was exactly the same and this award is as much for them, as it is for all of us. I thank all of you for your support."

As this was the last award for the evening, the Mayor once again took the stage. "Ladies and gentlemen, I would like to thank you all for coming. Now the fun begins. So please, take your partners for the first dance."

Maggie and Sam were the first on the floor, followed by other couples.

"May I have this dance Abbey?" Simon asked. Abbey stood, and soon the pair was flowing through a waltz.

Simon also danced with Maggie and a couple of other guests, but most of the evening was spent dancing with Abbey.

She was so graceful. The dancing lessons that she had taken years earlier certainly paid off this evening. Abbey really enjoyed herself. Simon was the perfect gentleman she told her mother, who inwardly was delighted. She had watched the pair dance. She knew Abbey loved to dance, and the devious side of her was hoping for better things to come. Maggie smiled.

Simon asked Abbey if there was anyone special in her life, so she opened up and told him about Jake. How he made her feel, what a kind and thoughtful guy he was and how she felt about him.

"Sounds like love to me," Simon said smiling.

"Definitely," Abbey replied. She was in love with Jake.

She then turned the tables on Simon.

"I've known you for some time, but I don't really. You have never said much about yourself."

"Oh, my story's boring," Simon replied. "There are a lot better things to talk about."

"Okay," Abbey said, "what about that lovely girl, Diana. The one you were at Daniel's barbecue with. Where is she this evening?"

"She's just a good friend," said Simon.

What he didn't tell Abbey was that he had asked Diana to marry him, but she did not want to be tied down. She wanted to enjoy life, and did not want to end up as a bored housewife with three kids running around.

Abbey changed the subject.

"This award tonight, for your company. Why did you not go up and collect it?"

Simon smiled. His reply surprised her a little.

"Abbey, your father worked really hard on this drug, and I felt he put in endless research and testing. He is my General Manager, but he was in the lab all the time. He *deserved* to get the accolade." Simon excused himself and got up to speak with some of the other guests. Abbey realized Simon was a very private person.

All the while, her mother had been watching out of the corner of her eye. She was so pleased with herself, not knowing that they had in part, been talking about Jake. She felt another couple of pushes and she could get the two of them together.

The following morning, Abbey called Jake. "I was wondering if you would like to take me to breakfast?"

He agreed and they met at the small café alongside Indian Lake in Denville. It was a quaint, old-fashioned building. They had eggs and bacon with lots of coffee, they sat watching the boats come and go from the small docking area.

"How was your evening?" Jake asked.

"It was enjoyable," replied Abbey. "Dad was so proud on receiving the award for his company."

"That's great," Jake said. He wanted to ask more, but decided to leave it alone. He had to control his jealousy. He did not want to be stupid and end up putting barriers between them.

"Listen Abbey, I have to go to Connecticut this afternoon with Daniel and Elizabeth to check on Nancy. I will be back tomorrow afternoon. Would you like to have dinner? I can pick you up at six."

Abbey got up the nerve to ask him. "Why can't I come with you?" she pleaded.

Jake was stunned and had to reply quickly, "It would be no fun for you. We will be at the clinic most of the time. I don't want you to meet Nancy yet. She's not ready for strangers."

Abbey was determined. "That's okay. I don't mind looking around New Haven while you're busy. At least we can spend the evening together."

Jake was in turmoil. He felt if Nancy in any way found out about Abbey, things could get out of control.

"No," Jake said. "I think it's best we go up alone."

Abbey sat there for a moment. She could feel the tears welling in her eyes, and inside, she was confused and a little angry.

"I have to go Jake. I have things to do. I'm sorry, but I won't be able to make dinner tomorrow evening, there's something going on at home."

She left abruptly, not even giving him a kiss. It was too late, but Jake knew he had thrown a wrench in the works. He sat there for a while and contemplated. *'Maybe I should call Abbey, apologize and ask her to join us. Why did he feel so scared?'*

Abbey was the best thing that had happened in his life. He wanted to be with her all the time. He had to come to grips with himself and get this problem with Nancy sorted once and for all so he could move on. He told himself that, *when the time was right, he would tell Abbey everything.*

He picked up Daniel and Elizabeth at noon and drove to New Haven. He was not in a talkative mood. They had both noticed this immediately.

"What's wrong Jake?" Elizabeth asked him very gently.

"Oh nothing," he replied. Then more silence.

Daniel looked at Elizabeth and raised his eyebrows. Then all of a sudden, Jake blurted out that he and Abbey had words that morning and he felt uncomfortable. He explained to them what was said.

Daniel jumped in. "Listen buddy, you should have let her come. Don't shut her out, or you will lose her, and that's the last thing you want."

Jake went quiet again. After a moment, he responded, "Yes, I should have. Sometimes I'm too dumb for my own good."

When they arrived in New Haven, they booked into a small motel. It was neat and clean, and as they were only staying one night, there was no point in staying anywhere fancy.

They drove to the clinic on the outskirts of town. Nancy was overjoyed at seeing them. Elizabeth hugged her for a long time, both of them teary-eyed. Daniel gave her a kiss on the cheek. Jake just stroked her hair.

"You look a lot better," he commented.

She smiled at him. "Thank you," she replied and held his hand. It felt like a death grip to Jake.

They talked for hours, but for most of the time, Jake's mind was elsewhere. All he could think about was Abbey.

"If all goes well…" Nancy informed them, "I can leave in two weeks. The only problem is – I don't want to go home right away. I need time."

Elizabeth suggested that she should come and stay with them for as long as she needed.

"I'm not working now."

"You're so lucky," Nancy commented. "You have the baby to look forward to."

The men were asked to leave the room so they could talk girly stuff. Jake and Daniel walked to the small café on the ground floor.

Daniel broke the silence. "If she looks good now, I would have hated to see her when you first did."

"Yes." Jake nodded. "It was a shock. I've never seen anyone right after an overdose before, and I would not like to see it again."

While they drank their coffee, Jake's thoughts went back to Abbey. *'I'm so sorry,'* he said to himself. Then he left Daniel alone and went for a walk. He told his friend he needed some air. Daniel had already guessed what the problem was, but said nothing. He just felt for his buddy.

Jake walked around the grounds. *'Maybe he was just feeling sorry for himself.'* He found a phone booth and tried calling Abbey, but there was no reply.

'Where are you Abbey? Please pick up the phone.'

At home, Abbey was still upset. She knew the phone ringing was Jake, but she refused to answer it. She lay on her bed and cried. *'Why shut me out Jake? If you really loved me, you would not do this.'* Thank goodness her parents were out. She knew her mother would have a field day if she told her what had happened.

Jake hung up. He was very concerned. He tried again, still no answer. This bad feeling was getting the better of him. He walked some more, rehearsing over and over in his mind, what he would say to Abbey when he got home.

He would never do this to her again. If their relationship was to go further, then he had to be honest with himself and confide in the girl he loved. She will be his main concern from now on.

Now that the other two had left the room, Nancy confided in Elizabeth. Nancy had asked if she knew what had happened between her and Jake. She replied, "Yes." Elizabeth did not want to lie to her. When Jake left, she went on.

"I was livid. I hated him at that time. I started drinking too much and using heroin. I was a mess Elizabeth. I don't know what happened. I just flipped. I blamed Jake for everything. I called him at home, but he never answered and I just slipped deeper and deeper into depression. Then I lost the baby I was carrying. It was Jake's baby. I had not had a relationship with anyone else for a long time. The only person I had sex with was Jake, and then he pushed me aside and told me he did not love me and that it was a huge mistake. I hated him for a long time, but that's over with now."

Elizabeth had to sit down before she fell over. The story totally shocked her.

"What do you mean, you lost the baby? I don't quite understand. You had an abortion?"

"No," Nancy replied. "With the drinking and everything else, I just lost the baby. I was only three months at that time. That's why I was calling Jake, but I couldn't bring myself to tell him. I don't know why, I just couldn't. He doesn't know Elizabeth. Please don't tell him."

Elizabeth felt dizzy. She was glad that they had now moved on to other subjects. Nancy wanted to know when the baby was due, and commented on how Daniel would be a proud father. Then Nancy asked outright who Jake was seeing. Elizabeth felt she had been put on the spot, and did not know if she should tell her.

"It's okay," Nancy assured her. "I'm over him. I just want to know that he is all right."

Elizabeth hesitated, but answered her.

"Yes, he is seeing someone. He is going out with Abbey Walker. Do you know her?"

"I know of her," Nancy said. "Doesn't her father work for Brady industries? I think my father once told me he had business with that company, and that her father was General Manager or something like that."

Nancy was fishing, and had Elizabeth cornered.

"Yes," she managed. Elizabeth struggled to find the right words. "I do believe you are right. It's just that, maybe *Jake* should be the one to tell you."

"That's okay," Nancy reassured her, "I just want him to be happy."

The men came back and said their goodbyes, and told Nancy that they would come by for a while on Sunday morning. Just as they were leaving, Nancy asked Jake if she could have a minute.

"Are you okay Jake?"

"I'm fine Nancy. Now you get some rest." He kissed her on the forehead. "We will see you in the morning."

Not long after Jake had left the room, Nancy started screaming and swearing. She threw the vase of flowers that he had bought her at the wall, and anything else that she could get her hands on. The staff sedated Nancy and cleaned up the mess.

It was early evening. Jake drove them to a small Chinese restaurant he had visited before. They discussed Nancy, and Jake was pleased to see the improvement in her. Elizabeth did not mention her conversation. She thought it best to leave well enough alone. Daniel said how pleased he was to see her again.

"It's been a long time."

They went back to the motel. Jake wished them goodnight and went to his room, and without thinking called Abbey. Her mother answered.

"Hi Mrs. Walker. Can I speak to Abbey?"

"I'm sorry Jake. She has gone out on a dinner date. Did she not tell you?" She smiled, knowing that she had just thrust a knife into him. "My husband's boss, Simon invited her out for the evening."

"Oh, that's nice," Jake said. "I'll call her tomorrow." He wished her a goodnight and hung up.

Maggie felt really good, and poured herself a Glenlivet. *'I need to celebrate,'* she said to herself.

"Who was on the phone?" Sam asked, as he came through from his little office at the back of the house.

"No one," Maggie replied. "Wrong number."

Jake left his room. As he passed Daniel and Elizabeth's door, he could hear them laughing. He walked and walked, analyzing events as he did. *'Abbey, Abbey,'* he said to himself. *'What have I done?'*

Sam was concerned that his wife was drinking a lot more than she used to.

"Another scotch?"

"Just the one," Maggie replied. "I need it to help me sleep."

Sam knew she was lying, and although he thought it best to leave it alone for now, he would definitely be keeping an eye on his wife.

It was only by chance that Abbey had gone out to dinner. She had spent best part of the afternoon sobbing. When Simon popped in around six-thirty to drop off some documents for her father, he could see her red eyes.

"What's wrong?"

"Oh, I just had words with Jake. It was my fault."

"I'm a good listener," he replied. "I'm going to take you out to dinner and then you can tell me all about it, and I won't take no for an answer. Get yourself cleaned up, wipe those tears from your eyes, and let's see if I can help."

Abbey did not eat very much, but she did open up to Simon. She told him her anxiety over the issue of Jake not letting her go to Connecticut. She felt he was a different person when it came to anything to do with Nancy.

"Listen Abbey, let me tell you what I know. I took control of the company when my father took early retirement and I've had a lot of dealings over the years with Nancy's father. What I can gather from his conversations, is that they have been friends forever, since they were quite young, and Jake has always looked out for her. I honestly think that if she's in hospital, Jake did the right thing. I'm sure this is just a storm in a teacup."

Abbey felt better already. She managed a smile and said, "Thank you Simon. You really are a good listener."

On the way home, Simon actually started to talk to Abbey about his life. He was born in New York, in the very affluent Westchester County and had a relatively lonely childhood. His parents worked all the time, so he attended boarding school all his life until he went to University and obtained his Business Degree. He told her how he had a crush on his Nanny. He explained how he joined the company, that his father had groomed him to take over, and on his 26th birthday, it happened when his father took early retirement. And that he did not lose his virginity until he was twenty-two, with the housemaid. His father found them together. Simon thought he would flip, but told him the next day to his surprise, *'As long as you don't want to marry the girl - then enjoy yourself.'* Abbey learned more about Simon in that fifteen minute ride, than she thought was possible. He was in some ways, just like Jake, thoughtful and considerate.

Though at that precise time, he was being quite the opposite and Abbey did not understand why, after talking with Simon, she was willing to give Jake the benefit of the doubt.

Simon dropped her in the driveway.

"Listen Abbey, if you need a shoulder anytime, you know who to call and don't worry, I'm sure you will sort it out when Jake gets back. Goodnight and good luck."

"Thank you again Simon. You have been the perfect gentleman." She kissed him on the cheek.

Maggie had not gone to bed. She was watching out of the window. *'Yes, yes, yes,'* she said under her breath. *'It's working.'* As Abbey came in, she asked, "Did you have a nice evening?"

"It was fine Mum," she replied. "Did anyone call?"

"No." Her mother – lied.

Abbey was more than a little disappointed.

"I'm going to bed." She told her mother. When she got to her room, she lay on the bed. *'I'm sorry Jake,'* she said to herself. *'Maybe it's me and not you that is to blame. I know you called earlier, but I was angry with you. I'm sorry. I should have answered and we might have sorted everything out.'* She fell asleep, fully clothed.

Jake had walked for hours. When he realized how far he had come, he hailed a cab. It was a long ride back to the motel. It was four in the morning. He climbed into bed and had a fretful sleep, tossing and turning, seeing Abbey with someone else. He woke with a start. It was Daniel knocking on the door.

"Come on sleepy head!" he yelled, "Time to get up!"

They drove to the clinic and visited with Nancy. Jake's mind was elsewhere, but he tried not to let it show.

"You seem chirpy this morning," Jake said, making conversation.

"Yes," Nancy replied. "I got a good night's sleep." She did not let on that the sleep was induced. "Did you all have a nice evening?" she asked.

Daniel answered her. "We had a nice Chinese dinner, then went back to the motel and slept like a log."

Nancy was looking at Jake. He looked tired and stressed.

"How about you Jake?" she asked.

"Oh yes, fine. I slept okay." He did not like lying to her, but he did not want to talk about it.

"We had better be getting home," Elizabeth chipped in. "I have to visit my mother later this afternoon. She has some presents for the baby." She realized what she had said, but Nancy smiled.

"When I'm ready to leave here," she said to them, "I will call you. Is it possible for someone to come and get me?"

Jake answered. "Of course. I will come."

Elizabeth and Daniel said their goodbyes and left the room. Jake stayed behind for a few minutes and spoke alone with Nancy. He explained that as far as he was concerned, he would always like her to be a friend.

She hugged him and promised they would be. He kissed her on the cheek and reminded her to call him when she was ready, then he left. Nancy lay in her bed and pondered on what Jake had said. Then, she said to herself, *'So you want us to be friends forever. You're a fool Jake Lockhart if you think that's the end of this, because it's just the beginning. Enjoy yourself ... while you can.'*

On the drive home, Jake was again very quiet. He hardly said a word. The two of them just talked to each other and knew it was best to leave him be.

Jake dropped them at home. He kissed Elizabeth on the cheek and helped Daniel with the overnight bags. His friend turned to him and said, "Jake, if you need to talk, we will always be there. Take comfort in your friends. Now go away and sort out this problem with Abbey before you drive me nuts." Daniel smiled.

Jake hugged him, which he did not do very often, and replied, "Thanks buddy."

He slept all night, but he still awoke tired. He got up and made his coffee, it was nine thirty. He had slept for twelve hours, but felt like he had been kicked by a horse, his joints were stiff. He went for a run, and although he had bettered his fastest time – he did not care. All he could think about was why he had been so stupid. *'If I had told Abbey the truth, I would not be going through this. I never thought real love was like this. I had a couple of flings when I was at college, but nothing serious. I even thought I was in love once, but when she dumped me for someone else, it was forgotten in a matter of days and I ended up dating another girl. But this – wow – this is different. What have you done to me Abbey? It's like I'm under a spell.'*

Jake showered and shaved. He looked at the time, it was five past eleven. He kept thinking, *'should I call her, or wait to see if she calls me?'* His doorbell rang, *Monica?* He opened the door. It was Abbey. He went weak at the knees, did not know what to say. He just looked at her. Abbey broke the ice.

"How was your trip?" she asked.

"It was tiring," Jake replied. "Do you want to come in?"

She flung her arms around his neck and kissed him tenderly. Jake held her as he had never held her before.

"I'm sorry Abbey."

"So am I." She kissed him again. "I missed you."

They kissed and kissed. Jake just held on for dear life.

"Oh, Abbey," he whispered.

They eagerly undressed each other and made love on the rug.

"Let's not do that to each other again," she pleaded. "I don't think I can take it."

"I promise," Jake replied and held her even tighter. She did not mind that he was holding her so tightly. They laid there in silence for quite some time.

Abbey asked him if Nancy was better.

"She's getting there. She is going to stay with Daniel and Elizabeth when she leaves the clinic."

"Do you want to talk about it?" she asked. "Or would you rather I mind my own business?"

"No." Jake answered. "I think its time you knew the whole story. I should have told you before. I want this relationship to go further so we should not have secrets from each other."

She kissed him again. "I love you Jake. I really love you and I can tell you now I have no secrets, and I would not keep anything from you ever. I realized when you were gone how much pain I was feeling by not answering your phone calls. I never want to go through that again."

He pulled her closer and whispered, "What I am about to tell you is not easy. I did something that I am not proud of. I made a mistake, and in some ways it changed my life. Then I met you and *wham,* I did not know what hit me."

Abbey laughed. "Jake, tell me what's on your mind, then we can enjoy ourselves properly."

Jake told Abbey the whole story. He did not leave out any details. He just needed for her to know everything. When he had finished, he explained that he still felt guilty even now, and that Nancy being in hospital was mainly his fault. She kissed him.

"Thank you Jake. I love you so much. It does not matter what happened between you and Nancy. That was before we met and why you felt you had to keep it to yourself, I don't know. Sometimes things happen between friends that shouldn't, and if it doesn't work out, then it's time to move on."

Jake looked at Abbey. "It's just that I did not know what you would think."

"I think I'm glad," she replied. "Because I know now we can move on and put this far behind us. I want to be with you Jake, and hiccups like this should not stand in our way."

"Now…" she said, "let's shower and get something to eat. I'm starving."

He took her to Charlie Brown's in Denville and they ate ribs as if they were going out of fashion.

Jake was just about to ask her how her evening went, when she blurted out through ribs that Simon had come by and taken her for dinner.

"I felt so embarrassed." She went on. "I couldn't eat anything, but Jake, he listened to me and how I felt about you. He assured me it would turn out all right and it has. In a way I'm glad he came by. It's not as if I can talk to Mum."

Jake did not say anything about calling last evening and decided it did not matter now he was here with his Abbey.

He leaned across the table and kissed her nose, it was the only part of her face without rib sauce on it.

That afternoon they took a walk alongside Indian Lake. It was a lovely September afternoon. They walked arm in arm and now and again he would stop to give her a kiss.

Jake stopped by the boat ramp. He turned to Abbey. "Are you happy?"

"I'm very happy," she replied.

"Happy enough to marry me?"

Abbey stood speechless. "Jake. What are you saying?"

"I know it should be over a candle lit dinner, at a romantic spot…" He did not utter another word. She kissed him.

"Yes Jake. I would love to marry you."

Jake had never felt so elated in his whole life. He just held her.

"I love you Abbey, and I always will … that is a promise."

"Oh Jake," she replied, "I love you too."

"Shall we drive over and tell my best man, or do we tell your parents first?"

"No," Abbey said. "I would like to call my Aunt Jennie first. As for my mother —we have to tread lightly – I'll need my father there as support. He likes you Jake and he will stand up for us – I know he will."

Abbey called her aunt from Jake's apartment and gave her the news. She could hear the tears of joy over the phone.

"Let me speak to Jake?" she asked Abbey. "Hi," Jennie said. "I've never met you Jake, but from what Abbey tells me, you sound made for each other. Congratulations! You have made her happy Jake. Thank you, and please come and see us. It would be a pleasure to meet you before the wedding. Now let me speak again with Abbey."

They talked for over half an hour. Jennie was so happy she could not wait to tell her husband.

When Abbey had finished talking, Jake told her that her aunt sounded like a really nice person.

"She is a darling," Abbey confirmed.

They kissed, and then they made love to celebrate. They were so connected at that moment that nothing could stand in their way.

They were entwined for a long time. Jake was gentle with her and she climaxed, and she kissed him at the same time. Jake could not believe the feeling when he reached his peak and finally released. *'This was so different with Abbey, it's as if she never wanted to let go.'*

They were both hot and sweaty. They took a shower together and then sat and discussed what sort of wedding Abbey would like. She explained to Jake that it would take a lot of time to plan a wedding. The only thing they agreed on was that it would take place the following June. Abbey had always dreamed of having a June wedding - ever since she was young. She had only been to two weddings in her life. One was a distant cousin, the other, was a fair-weather friend in teachers college whom she had not seen since. She moved away to Florida and had never heard from her.

Chapter 8

"Since your parents are not at home, can we drive over to my mother's and tell her the news?" Jake asked Abbey.

He was so exited. She had never seen him this way.

"Of course," she replied and kissed him for the hundredth time. When they pulled in the driveway, there was no sign that anyone was home.

Jake rang the bell. No answer.

"That's funny," he said to Abbey. "I was supposed to drop over to see her today anyway. When I called her earlier in the week, she said she would be home."

The door was locked. They walked around to the patio. The screen was shut, but the door was fully open. Jake called out – still no reply.

He opened the screen door to enter and could see his mother lying on the floor. They rushed over.

"Oh my God – Mum! What's happened?"

He checked her pulse. He could not find one and he was panicking. She was not moving. Abbey rechecked her pulse. She found it, but it was very faint. Jake quickly dialled 911.

"Ambulance! We need an ambulance!" He was flustered. "Please … we need an ambulance!"

He gave the operator the address and was assured it would not be long. Abbey had gotten a cushion off the sofa and had laid it under her head.

There was still no sign of movement from his mother.

They heard the ambulance. Abbey ran to the door to let the paramedics in. They immediately checked for signs of life.

"She's alive," the first one said. They put the oxygen mask on her and gently put her on the stretcher. The second paramedic said to Jake, "It looks like she's had a stroke."

"Oh God!" Jake gasped.

Abbey drove. Jake was too distraught. She knew how close he was to his mother. She stayed behind the ambulance all the way to the hospital, driving faster than she had ever done before.

They waited in emergency holding hands. Abbey could feel the tension emanating from Jake. She stroked his face, which she knew he loved. She tried to reassure him that everything would turn out fine, but Abbey was not sure herself. She saw a small smile.

"Thanks honey," he said. "I don't know what I would have done without you by my side?" He rested his head on her shoulder. Jake did not want her to see the tears.

When the doctor finally came to them, it was late evening. He took them to a private waiting room where he gave Jake and Abbey the grim news.

"Your mother has had a stroke. It is very serious. She is completely paralysed. We have put her in Intensive care. You may go up and see her, but please don't stay too long. She needs a lot of rest and we have more tests to do."

Jake asked him if she was going to be all right. His reply was not what he wanted to hear.

"We don't know Sir. We have to wait and see the results of the tests."

Abbey held him tight as they went up in the elevator. His mother just laid there. No movement, no sound. Jake could not hold back the tears, and by this time, Abbey was also crying. Jake held his mothers hand and spoke softly to her.

"Get better Mum. I came today to see you and give you the good news. Abbey has agreed to marry me. I wanted you to be the first to know. Please get better. I love you."

Jake drove Abbey back to his apartment so that she could retrieve her car. He promised to call her if there was any news. Jake held her.

She gently kissed him and said goodnight, she wanted to stay, but she took for granted he would want to be alone.

Abbey cried all the way home. She just did not know how to help the man she loved – she felt guilty.

Jake watched Abbey drive away in the distance. He went straight to his apartment and called the hospital. He was told there was no change, and the nurse asked if he would kindly call back in the morning.

He paced the floor. He felt helpless. *'I don't want to lose her – not now – not when everything was going right.'* He could not hold back the tears. *'I still need you Mum.'*

He did not sleep that night, endless cups of coffee kept him awake. He phoned the office and left a brief message for the Manager, explaining that he may not be in tomorrow.

Jake was at the hospital at seven – still no change. He was told by the resident doctor that there was no brain activity at the moment. His mother lay there lifeless on the life support machine. He felt sick and totally drained.

Abbey called Jake as soon as she woke. There was no answer. She knew that he must be at the hospital. She called Nora.

"Oh my God! I didn't know … and we live right next door. When did this happen?"

After Abbey told Nora the whole story and explained the situation, Nora remembered she had been out visiting, which was why she did not know that Martha had been rushed to the hospital. Abbey asked her what she should do. *'Go to school, or take a sick day to be with Jake?'* Nora did not hesitate in her response, *'Abbey, Jake is more important than any job. I will explain to the Principal. It will be okay. Go the hospital and give him what support you can.'* She thanked Nora and hung up.

Abbey sat in the kitchen trying to get her thoughts together when her father came in.

"What's up little one?" he said. He liked to call Abbey that, it was his own nickname for her. She explained in detail about Jake's mother. Her father immediately agreed with Nora.

"Go … be with him. He may not know it, but he will need you there. When something like this happens, you need all the support you can get. Go to him Abbey. Try and give him some comfort."

Abbey arrived at the hospital and found Jake sitting by his mother's bed, tubes everywhere. It did not look good.

"Hi Jake," she called out. When he turned, she was shocked by his appearance. He looked terrible. His face was drawn, his eyes were half closed. She walked over and held him.

"Oh Jake, I'm so sorry."

Jake, though not really with it, held on to Abbey.

"She's brain dead," he said. "The doctor told me she's brain dead. How could this happen? Why her?"

He was distraught. Abbey felt useless. She knew there was no way of helping him, but she wanted to be with him. She knew he had no living relatives that they could call. All of his grandparents had been killed in the Second World War and his mother was all he had. She suddenly felt sick and went to the washroom.

When Abbey returned, Jake was sitting in the corridor the doctors were in with his mother. His head in his hands, she sat beside him, he spoke to her very softly, "Thank you for being here Abbey."

She stroked his face, and asked, "Have they said anything to you?"

"No."

The doctors were with his mother for what seemed an eternity. When they finally emerged, the nurse asked them to go into the private waiting room. The doctor would be there shortly. They waited again. He came into the room and stood. Abbey could tell by the look on his face that this was not going to be good news. She held Jake's hand tightly.

"Mr. Lockhart. It's not good. There is no activity at all. Technically, your mother cannot survive without the life support. What I am trying to say is … she will never regain consciousness. She needs a miracle. I'm so very sorry."

"What are we supposed to do?" Jake pleaded.

"We can leave her on the machine for now," the doctor replied, "and see if in the next few days something stimulates her, but in my professional opinion, I can't see it happening. The stroke your mother suffered was massive. But she is in no pain. That is the only consolation. You can sit with her and talk to her, but as I expressed, I would be very surprised if there were any change."

"Thank you Doctor," Abbey said, and got Jake up. "Come on. Let's get some coffee and something to eat," she insisted. "You have to be strong Jake. You need food. Then I'm taking you home for a shower before we come back."

Jake did not resist. He was too tired to argue, he felt numb.

After they had eaten, Jake fell asleep for a few hours, when he awoke Abbey was on the telephone. She had called his friends to give them an update. They assured Abbey they would visit later. She called her mother to see if her dad had told her. He had, and she was very sympathetic.

"I'm sorry Abbey. I know you liked his mother a lot. If there is anything I can do." Maggie was genuinely sorry.

"Thanks Mum," Abbey replied. She made Jake take a shower and clean himself up. Then they went back to the hospital.

Jake and Abbey were sitting by his mother's bedside when his friends appeared. Elizabeth hugged Jake and very quietly told him, "We are here for you."

He thanked her. Daniel put his hand on his friend's shoulder. "I'm sorry buddy." He did not know what else to say.

"Has there been any improvement?" Elizabeth asked.

"No," Jake replied. "None at all. I don't think she is going to get better. I cannot see how she can."

He was a lot calmer now. Abbey could see it in his eyes. He was starting to accept that his mother would not get through this. Elizabeth and Daniel went in to see Martha. They had known her since Jake moved here and she had always been kind, never a cross word, even when they went swimming and got her floor all wet. They were kids, and she accepted that they would not always be considerate about small things like walking in dripping with water.

Elizabeth held her hand. She spoke softly, "Jake needs you Martha. I hope you can hear me. He loves you and you must pull through for him." But there was no response. Elizabeth had tears in her eyes and Daniel put his arm around her.

Jake was the first to get up. He hesitated. "Let's go," he said softly. "I need some air."

They walked out into the hospital gardens. He held Abbey's hand then he looked at his friends.

"I will have to decide in the next few days what to do. Let her stay on the machine and just fade, or to have it turned off and let her die in peace."

Daniel responded first, "Jake whatever you decide will most probably be the hardest decision of your life. She is your mum, and we all know how much you love her."

The air felt chilly to Jake. Maybe it was just tiredness, or the thought of what he had to do. He shivered. Abbey sensed this immediately. It was as if she were inside him.

"Let's get some coffee and warm up," she suggested. Nobody argued.

After coffee and farewells to his friends, Abbey took Jake home. It was getting late and he needed rest – if that was possible. She stayed with him for a while then he suggested she go home and get some rest. He kissed her very gently.

"I don't know what I would have done without your support Abbey. Thank you so very much." He kissed her again and walked her to her car.

"Call me Jake," she said, and stroked his face.

Jake went inside. He sat in the dark for a while then he went to bed. He had decided what he must do tomorrow and he knew deep down inside that this would change his life forever.

Elizabeth was the first to call, "Hi Jake. How are you? I know that's a dumb question, but…"

"That's okay," Jake interrupted. "I'm all right. Honestly I am. I will be going to the hospital shortly to talk with the doctors to get their advice, but yes … I'm okay. Thank you for calling me." He felt very confused.

As he hung up the phone, it immediately rang again. It was Abbey.

"Morning baby," she said. "How do you feel?"

"I'm trying to come to terms with it," Jake admitted. "I need to go and sort everything out."

"Call me," Abbey pleaded. "Please call me. I'm going to work, but call anytime. They will understand."

"I will," Jake promised.

He walked to the hospital. His car was still in the parking lot. With all that had happened, he had forgotten to take it home, but it did not matter, he needed fresh air and time to think.

Jake went to the doctors first and asked them outright. "Can my mother get better?"

Their response was an overwhelming, "*No.* As you know, there is no brain wave activity. She could remain in this state for a long time, but she will never recover and her other organs will slowly deteriorate."

Jake knew the answer, but he had to ask. "Do you think it's best to turn off the life support?"

They concurred. This was most probably the best thing to do, but it was his decision and his alone.

"All we can do is offer our advice," they told him.

Jake decided to call Abbey, eventually she came to the phone.

"What is it darling?" she asked. "Do you need me there?"

"More than ever."

"Give me thirty minutes. I'm on my way."

He walked to the Intensive Care, bent over his mother and kissed her forehead.

"I'm sorry Mum. I have to do this. I wish there was another way, but I am having the machine turned off. I wish you could hear me. I wish you could talk to me. I really am going to miss you. I love you Mum. I always have. You were my strength. You helped me through so much." The tears flowed down his face.

"You will always be in my thoughts. I'm going to let you go to Dad. I hope you are happy in that place." He kissed her again and called the doctors. They turned everything off.

Jake's mother was gone within seconds. She was fifty-seven years old. He held her hand.

"Bye Mum," were his last words.

He was still standing by her bedside when Abbey came rushing in. One look was enough.

"Oh Jake … I'm so sorry." She ran to him and held him as tightly as she could.

"I had no choice Abbey. I could not let her waste away. She would never have forgiven me."

"I know. I know." She stroked his face then went over to the bed.

"Goodbye Martha. It was really nice to have known you. Really nice, and I promise to look after your son. I give you my word." She took Martha's cold hand. "I promise."

It was raining that Friday morning at the small Methodist Church in Lake Hopatcong. Jake's mother had been part of the congregation for as long as he could remember. There was a lot more people than Jake expected. Just him as family, but a lot of friends his mother had made over the years had come to pay their respects. Abbey stood alongside Jake with Daniel Elizabeth and Abbey's parents. The funeral service was short, but it was carried out with dignity. It was what his mother had wanted. She was to be cremated and her ashes were to be spread on her husband's grave.

Jake invited everyone back to his mother's house, which was now his house, for tea, coffee and sandwiches which Nora and Leo had taken upon themselves to prepare.

"It's the least I can do," she told Jake. "Your mother was a good friend."

He thanked everyone for coming out. The only speech he gave was at the house, and again, it was short.

"My mother would have loved to have been here with all her friends. Thank you all again for coming."

As the guests started to diminish, Jake looked up, and to his surprise there in the doorway stood Nancy. Jake walked over and gave her a hug.

"What are you doing here? I thought you were not due to leave the clinic until next week."

"I heard about your mother," she replied. "She was kind to us as kids. *Jake* ... I had to come."

He smiled. "It's good to see you."

Jake had no choice but to introduce Abbey to her. He was pleasantly surprised when Nancy hugged her and said, "It's really nice to meet you at last."

'How did she know about Abbey?' The thought was soon gone as he said goodbye to the other guests. He took the time to offer Nora and Leo a special *thank you* for all their kindness.

After everyone had left, there were just the five of them, Jake Abbey Daniel Elizabeth and Nancy. Daniel poured them all a proper drink to celebrate Martha's life, and basically to break the ice. Nancy did not take a drink. Instead, she asked Daniel for some juice or a soft drink, which pleased Jake.

They sat and reminisced about the times they spent at the house in summers past. They raved about the fun food that Jake's mum would bring them out, cupcakes of all sorts, and Daniel commented, "Martha made the best apple pie ever, sorry Elizabeth, but she did." Elizabeth faked a frown before saying, "I agree." Abbey was quiet. She felt like a little bit of an outsider. She had never known these times, but she wished she had.

They had talked for hours laughing and joking. Who would have thought this would happen on the same day as the funeral, but it was a good tonic for Jake. They did not realize how quickly the time had passed.

Daniel exclaimed, "I'm famished! I need food."

They all laughed again, but agreed with him.

"I don't have any food in the house," Jake added. "We will have to go to a restaurant."

Elizabeth looked at Jake. "Okay, as long as nothing spicy, or I will be up all night." They walked to the local pub on the lake and ate.

When Daniel and Elizabeth were ready to leave, they insisted that Nancy come with them, she did not argue. She said goodnight to Abbey and kissed Jake on the cheek and left with the other two. After they had gone, Jake turned to Abbey and apologized.

"For what?" she said.

"For leaving you out of the loop when we were talking about old times."

"Jake, no apology is needed. It was a joy to see you laugh." She stroked his face and he kissed her.

"What would I have done without you Abbey?" He kissed her again. "I love you more than I can explain." He held her tight.

They sat and talked together. It was peaceful and nice. Jake asked Abbey if after they were married – she liked hearing that – if she would like to live in this house, as it was his. He would sell his apartment or rent it out.

"I'd love to live here," she said without hesitation. "What better place could be found? And I can't think of a nicer house to bring up children some day." Jake smiled at her.

"Where are you staying tonight Jake?" she asked him.

"At my apartment."

"Can I stay with you?" She looked at him.

"Yes please. I'd like that." They locked the house up and drove to his place.

Their lovemaking was tender and beautiful that night. Abbey was so happy to be lying alongside him again. It had been a hard week for both of them. They slept cuddled into each other like spoons.

When Jake awoke, he sat bolt upright.

"My God!" he shouted.

Abbey had already stirred. "What is it Jake?"

"I've just realized," he said. "We have been so busy this week with the funeral and arrangements that I forgot to buy you an engagement ring."

"I can wait."

"No," Jake insisted. "Why don't we go into New York today, get away for a few hours? I'll take you to every jeweller's in Manhattan, let you have some fun today." He gave her a big kiss and made some coffee.

Abbey realized that Jake needed a break from the thoughts of his mother and the funeral so did not argue. She simply said, "What a wonderful idea."

Abbey dashed home to shower and change her outfit. Jake did the same, but popped over to Daniel's to check on things there. Nancy greeted him with a kiss on the cheek, and commented how nice she thought Abbey was. Jake thanked her and asked how she was. She said she was feeling fine and had decided not to go back to the clinic for the last week. She was going to stay where she was for a while, she was sure she would be okay now.

Elizabeth was in the kitchen baking.

"Hi Jake," she said. "I know yesterday was very sad for you, but we did try to brighten up such a sad day, by the time we left I did notice you smiling more. Are you okay?"

"I feel a lot better," Jake replied then he whispered in her ear. "I'm taking Abbey to New York today. We're going ring shopping. He put his finger across his lips.

Elizabeth understood and hugged him, and very quietly said, "Out of sadness, comes happiness."

"Where's Danny boy?"

"He's working today. We're trying to get enough money together so he can maybe have his own garage." She smiled. "At least he's not under my feet."

Jake said his goodbyes and drove over to Abbey's. Sam greeted him. "Come in my boy."

He led Jake to the lounge. Maggie was there with Abbey.

"I hear you are going into the city Jake, to buy my daughter a ring. Well – have fun," she said and abruptly left the room.

Jake had still not worked out the reason why Maggie was so cold toward him. Even yesterday at the funeral, though she was polite, she had been very curt.

They caught the train from Denville to Hoboken, then on the subway into the city. They must have hit ten shops before lunch, but Abbey continued looking, she had not found that special ring yet.

Then they came across Cartier's on Fifth Avenue.

"We can't go in here Jake. It's too expensive."

Jake opened the door. The service they received was astounding. Abbey felt like a queen and before long, she found the perfect ring.

"Oh Jake … it's beautiful."

"So are you," he replied, and quietly took the assistant aside. She told him the price.

Jake said immediately, "That's the ring she loves. That's the ring she will have."

It was expensive, but not too bad. Abbey was over the moon.

"Thank you darling." She kissed him.

Jake's humour came into play. "That kiss made it all worthwhile."

They ventured on to Macy's and a few more stores. They had a delightful evening meal in a small bistro on the other side of Fifth Avenue, and a bottle of champagne to celebrate their engagement. They toasted each other and Jake said to Abbey, "Thank you for loving me." He kissed her on the nose and everybody in the restaurant clapped, but they didn't care they just had eyes for each other.

They walked arm in arm to the subway with Abbey admiring her ring the entire way. Jake warned her to be careful, "This is New York City at night, you never know if someone's lurking."

It was around eleven when they arrived back at Jake's. The only message on the answering machine was from the Funeral Director asking if Jake could please come in first thing on Monday.

He turned to Abbey. "I need to go to Pennsylvania on Monday so that I can carry out my mother's wishes."

Abbey looked at him. The sadness had returned.

"Can I come with you?" she asked. "I'm not at school on Monday. We have two days off. They are having trouble with the heating system and need to do some repairs to the boiler."

"That would be nice."

They went to bed, cuddled and slept. It was a good sleep. When Jake woke up on Sunday morning, he felt a lot better. He left Abbey sleeping and went for his run. When he returned, she had coffee made. He showered and they drove over to Indian Lake for breakfast. As they ate, Abbey said to Jake, "Do you realize it's been a week since you proposed?"

Jake looked at her and smiled.

"Abbey Susan Lockhart …it sounds good to me," he replied.

She stroked his face. "I can't wait to be your wife. June can't come quickly enough."

They drove to Daniel's house because Abbey wanted to show Elizabeth her ring. Jake was more than a little apprehensive, he knew Nancy would be there, but to his surprise she congratulated them kissed Abbey and gave him a huge hug. She could not have been nicer. Daniel bought out a bottle of champagne.

"I've been keeping this one just for this occasion."

They toasted Abbey and Jake, and laughed and smiled. Nancy excused herself and went out to the garden for a cigarette. Elizabeth turned to Jake.

"I'm so glad she has taken this well," she said.

They did not know that Nancy was in the garden – seething. If they had been there, at that precise moment, they would have heard her curse and call Abbey a *bitch*. *'I will get you 'bitch'! Mark my words … this will end, if I have anything to do with it.'*

She came back inside and again had changed her personality.

"Let me look at the ring again?" she asked. The *sweetness* dripped off her tongue, but no one noticed. "Abbey, it really is beautiful. Now you make sure you look after Jake. He's important to all of us in this room."

"I will," Abbey said. "I will always look after him."

Nancy smiled and thought to herself, *'Yes. Of course you will 'bitch', but you don't know me. I have not yet finished with Jake and if you stay with him then you will join in the game.'*

Nancy felt pleased with herself. She knew that Jake really loved Abbey and that gave her another avenue to explore. She could hurt both of them, and not even give it a second thought.

'Jake, I may have lost you forever, but you will suffer beyond anything you have ever known!' Nancy smiled. *'My revenge will be sweeter than ever.'*

Chapter 9

The drive to Wilkes-Barre on that Monday morning was a quiet affair. Both Jake and Abbey were reluctant to break the ice. Abbey knew that Jake was hurting and thought best not to say too much. They arrived at the small Methodist church and he walked straight to his father's grave, as if he knew where it was by instinct. The headstone had been updated as requested and it actually made Jake break into a small smile.

It read:

Gary Brian Lockhart 1928-1970
Loving Husband and Father
Underneath had been written:
Martha Carolyn Lockhart 1928-1985
Loving Wife and Mother
Together again

Abbey burst into tears as soon as she read the epitaph. Jake held her.

"It's okay my love. This is only fitting. She missed him every day of her life. I know she is happy now."

He dug a hole in the ground with the small shovel he had borrowed from the gardener. Then he took the urn with his mother's ashes along with her wedding ring, put the top back on, and placed it in the ground. Then he covered the urn with the earth and placed the flowers in the pot at the bottom of the headstone. Jake stood there looking down. Abbey walked a small distance away to let him be alone. He said his tearful farewell and rejoined Abbey. He hugged her tightly and whispered,

"My mother always wanted grandchildren. One day, we will come back with our children and let her see them."

She gave him a tearful kiss. "Yes, that would be nice."

They drove into Scranton to get lunch. Both of them picked at their food and talked about the crazy week they had just had.

"Are you okay?" Abbey asked Jake. "This must have been very hard for you to do."

"I will be," Jake replied. "I guess I just need time to get used to not seeing her, but I will visit now and again." Abbey comforted him and stroked his face.

Heading back to Rockaway, Jake reminded Abbey that she had not yet shown her parents the engagement ring. They headed to her house. It was early evening when they arrived.

Sam had arrived home ten minutes before Abbey and Jake turned up. He greeted them at the door.

"Come in, come in," he said. "How did it go? *Jake,* it must have been very hard. I went thought that once. It's not easy. I'm making coffee. Would you like some? Your mother will be home shortly," he informed Abbey. She showed her father her ring. "*Wow!* Now who's being spoiled?" He looked at Jake and laughed.

Jake liked Sam. He was so down to earth, he felt comfortable around him, always made him welcome. As for *Maggie* – she scared him a little. He was not sure which way to take her. Sometimes she was pleasant. At other times though – like when he called from Connecticut and she did not tell Abbey – she worried him, but he thought best not to upset the apple cart.

He thought to himself, *'One day I have to try and sit down with her and see if we can work out some sort of truce, or at least a compromise. I have done nothing to you Maggie, so I don't understand your problem.'*

His thoughts were interrupted as Maggie came through the front door. Much to Jake's surprise, the first words she uttered were directed at Abbey.

"Show me your ring."

Abbey held her hand up to the gaze of her mother's eyes. "Oh my goodness!" Maggie said. "It's fabulous. She's a lucky girl Jake."

She actually hugged him and shouted out to Sam, "Why don't we have that champagne now?" He had anticipated and was carrying it through as she spoke. Sam and Maggie toasted them.

"To the bride and groom to be."

Jake thought then that maybe he was wrong about Abbey's mother.

There was a message on the phone for Abbey informing her that school would be back on schedule the following day. Jake thanked her parents for the champagne, and Abbey walked him to his car.

"I'm still somewhat unsure about your mother," he told her.

"Don't worry *Jake*," Abbey replied, "she'll come around." She kissed him. "I love you."

"Those are the nicest words I've heard all day," Jake grinned. "Thank you." He held her a moment longer and kissed her goodbye.

He poked his head out the driver's side window.

"I'll call you tomorrow. I have to go to the lawyers in the morning, and then it's back to work." He waved at Abbey as he drove away.

That Tuesday morning, Jake was in his mother's lawyer's office at the stroke of nine. Nora and Leo were there as well. They had been summoned as had Jake. The lawyer came in to greet them.

"Good morning. I'm Gerald Simmonds. Please come in and take a seat." He was a short man, but very sturdy. "I have arranged for coffee, though Martha's Will is fairly straightforward." His secretary brought in the tray and poured each of them a drink. Mr. Simmonds opened up a folder in front of him. "As you may or may not know Mr. Lockhart, I have met Nora and Leo before at your mother's house. They witnessed the Will she had me prepare, so I will begin." He was like an old-fashioned schoolmaster.

"My house and all its contents and my life insurance, I leave to my dear son Jake. Mr. Lockhart, the insurance policy is for two-hundred thousand dollars."

Jake was astounded. He knew his mother had life insurance, but he did not realize it was for such a huge amount.

"Your mother also had a contingency plan for death duties. These will be covered by one of her bank accounts. *To my dear friends, Nora and Leo, I leave the sum of $20,000 and lastly to my church $1,000.*"

"As I said Mr. Lockhart, a fairly easy Will. I have sent the Death Certificate to the insurance company, and they will issue me a cheque shortly. I will then transfer this to your account, if you would be kind enough to give me the details. May I say in finishing, your mother was a shrewd investor. As instructed on her death, all her shares were to be sold and placed in her savings account to cover any costs. This I have done and I will deal with any persons with a claim. If, by the time I have finished, there are any monies left, it will be credited to your account. *Mr. Lockhart,* do you have any questions?"

He was in a mild fog. "No. I don't think so," Jake said. "Thank you for your time Mr. Simmonds."

Jake took Nora and Leo for a late breakfast, and thanked them for being a good friend to his mother, and for all their help with the funeral.

Nora inquired if Jake was going to live at the lake. He told them that he needed time to sort things out, but most probably would. He loved the house and had to make up his mind what to do with the apartment. He thanked them again and went to work.

When Nora arrived at school, she saw Abbey in the staff room. She explained where she had been, and apologized for not mentioning it before, but she had forgotten that they would be at Martha's lawyers. Abbey asked how Jake took the reading of the Will. Nora replied that he looked sad and had a lot to think about. She did not say anymore, she thought it best for Jake to talk to Abbey.

Nora looked at Abbey's ring. "It's absolutely gorgeous. When did you go shopping?"

Abbey smiled and told her about their Saturday excursion to New York.

"We had a wonderful time."

"You're a very lucky girl," Nora replied. "You've got a good man there. Look after him."

"I will," Abbey beamed. "I will."

Jake called Elizabeth to see if Nancy was still okay. She told him that she was out at the moment, but that she had been very quiet since yesterday.

"I think she is still recovering, but I will keep an eye on her."

He thanked her then he called Leo. When he answered, Jake asked if he had any idea what to do with his mother's clothes, where they could go, whether there was a charity they could be donated too. Leo thought a good idea would be to donate them to the church. His mother was always helping the less fortunate and working on the *garage sales.* Jake thanked him, and hung up.

He was not busy at work so Jake left early, and informed them that he would take the next day off as well. He went for a long walk by Indian Lake, he loved it here. Some of the boats already had their covers on. Jake thought these must belong to the holiday crowd, who have now packed up for the summer. Denville gets a huge influx of out-of-towners who own cottages in the area. *'It will soon be fall,'* he said to himself. As he walked along, he thought of Abbey and the *difference* since she came into his life. The more he thought about it, the more he liked the idea, *that next June they would be husband and wife*, then they could spend a lot more time together. This brought a huge smile.

At around 4:00 p.m., Jake drove out to his mothers to start packing her belongings. The phone rang. Before he had time to speak, the voice at the other end said, "Hi Martha. It's Betty."

Jake was a little confused. He stuttered his answer, "I'm sorry, this is Jake, Martha's son."

"Oh, hi…" she replied. "Can I speak to Martha?"

Again Jake apologized, "No. I'm afraid that won't be possible." Again he started to stutter. "My – um – my mother passed away."

"Oh my God! When did this happen? How did this happen?"

Jake explained the best he could.

The voice said, "I am really sorry. Please accept my deepest sympathy. I just can't believe it. We only had tea together three weeks ago, after church."

"It was very sudden." Jake tried to explain. He could hear the distress at the other end of the phone.

"I'm sorry," said the voice and hung up.

He started to pack boxes, but had to sit down. *'My God,'* he thought. *'How many more people don't know?'* The thought was daunting. He held his head in his hands, he realized they were wet he had tears in his eyes. As he was wiping them, the phone rang again. *'Oh no,'* he thought, but when he answered, it was Abbey.

"Are you okay Jake?"

He told her about the phone call, how it upset him. He was not a weak man, but this was hard for him. Abbey suggested he leave what he was doing until a later date. He agreed and arranged to meet her in town for dinner.

Abbey tried to cheer him up, but he could not eat most of his food. He told her about the lawyers and how his mother had provided for him. He asked Abbey if she would, when possible, go through his mother's jewellery. There were a couple of pieces that she wanted Elizabeth and Nancy to have the rest was hers if she wanted them. Jake really wanted her to do this for him.

She asked Jake if he would like help to pack up Martha's things.

"Don't do it alone," she pleaded. "I see how sad it makes you."

Jake smiled. "Thank you Abbey. You're beginning to read me like a book." She kissed him.

"Would you like to go to a movie? It might help you take your mind off what has to be done."

He agreed, they watched a new film called, *'Agnes Of God'.* They both enjoyed the movie and then drove over to Jake's apartment. Abbey wanted to be close to him before she went home. They made love, it was tender, she so liked to be here like this with him. The most important person in her life was Jake, and she had to let him know.

As always, he walked her to her car and kissed her goodnight. He actually cracked a joke, "Come this winter," he said, "I'll kiss you goodnight inside."

He smiled at her, she laughed and kissed him again and then drove away. Jake walked back inside. He did not notice Nancy – standing alone in the shadows – watching him.

She had arrived at Jake's around six-thirty, rang the doorbell, *no one home*. So she waited and waited and waited, around nine she saw him arrive with Abbey.

She hid behind the tree. They went inside. Instead of approaching them, she stayed in hiding. When Abbey left at eleven, she was still watching, cursing under her breath. As Abbey pulled away, Nancy stayed in the shadows. She did not approach Jake and watched him go back inside.

She started talking to herself as she walked to her car. *'I will make sure that bitch suffers. I will make his life hell, but I will be patient. They will both suffer ... if it's the last thing I do.'*

Jake could not sleep. He kept thinking of his mother and her tragic end. *'Why her? Why my mum? She was too nice a person for this. If there is a God, he must be hiding somewhere.'*

When he did finally sleep, his dream was awful. He could see his mother reaching out for him. He awoke with a start, sweating profusely. He made coffee to settle himself down and decided to wait until the weekend to go back to his mother's house. He still did not call it his home, not yet, that would take time.

After showering and getting dressed, he took his car to Daniel for a service. His friend was pleased to see him.

"Jacob!" he called out.

Only Daniel could call him that, no one else, he had always hated Jacob as a name, but did not mind his buddy using it, as he only did in fun.

"Hi," Jake answered. "My car needs an oil change and winterizing. Can you fit it in today?"

"For you … of course. Do you need a loaner? We have a couple to choose from."

"Sure, I could use a loaner," he said. "How is Elizabeth?"

"She's ecstatic."

Daniel told him about the baby moving around, this was all they talked about now.

Jake asked about Nancy. He wondered whether it was awkward to have her staying with them.

"Not really," Daniel said. "She is going home this weekend. Her parents insisted that she spend time with them, but she is not going back to university. It seems that when she is well enough, her father wants her to help run his company. He has always had high hopes for her and really did not mind that she does not want to go back to Connecticut. Her mother has been told to take it easy by her doctor, because she has high blood pressure."

Daniel explained to Jake that he thought she seemed different now, and *Nancy talks more than she used to*, which in his opinion was a good sign.

Jake agreed with his friend and told him that he would be in touch with her to see if he could help.

"After all," he said, "we have been friends a long time."

As Jake drove through Rockaway, for some idiotic reason Nancy was on his mind, but it did help take away the sad thoughts of his mother. He was thinking that his luck had changed. It seemed like Nancy would be fine and everything would turn out okay, so he decided to drop by and see both Elizabeth and Nancy. They were all smiles when he arrived, coffee was served, and Jake told Elizabeth that Daniel had informed him about the baby.

"I'm really looking forward to being a mother," she said.

Jake told her she looked radiant, and turned his attention to Nancy.

"So I hear you are going to run your father's company," he said jokingly.

Nancy laughed. "I don't think that will happen for a while, but you never know, my dad it seems wants to start taking life a bit easier. We will sort it out when I'm ready."

"How is Abbey?" she asked, pretending to be interested. "You two look great together, I really am glad that it has worked out for you." *She lied.*

Jake informed her that he was really happy.

"Good. I look forward to the wedding next year."

Jake did not see the smirk on her face, but Elizabeth noticed.

He kissed both of them on the cheek and left. He felt so much better now that Nancy had accepted that he was going to marry Abbey.

He picked her up at five-thirty from home. Abbey's grandmother Susan had invited them for dinner. She wanted to get to know her granddaughter's future husband better. She liked him. The evening went well and they had a nice roast beef dinner with all the trimmings and a vintage bottle of red wine to round it off. The more Susan talked to Jake, the more she thought that Abbey had picked the right man.

As they were leaving she hugged her granddaughter and actually did the same to Jake and welcomed him to the family.

Abbey commented on the way home that he had made a good impression with her grandmother.

Jake smiled. "She's a nice lady. I never knew my grandparents, so I'm going to adopt her as mine."

They both laughed. Abbey so liked to see Jake laugh. He had a wonderful smile and it turned her on. Just to see him smile was so important to her.

For the first time they actually made love in the car. Abbey could not wait to get back to Jakes. It was awkward, but they both enjoyed each other and found it quite exiting to pull into a *rest area* and have sex.

"Wow," Jake said afterwards. "What turned you on so quick?"

"Just you." Abbey smirked.

After dropping Abbey home, Jake drove to his apartment. Nancy was once again hiding behind the tree.

'Where's the bitch tonight?' she said to herself. She watched as he walked into the complex. Then she drove away still cursing Abbey's name.

'Jake Lockhart, you will feel pain. I guarantee it. I lost our baby because of you and one day you will know what suffering is ... and so will that cow ... Abbey.'

That weekend Jake and Abbey were at the house trying to sort though his mother's clothes when Daniel Elizabeth and Nancy turned up to help.

Daniel said to Jake, "We will get this all packed and ready. Then you can take us to the pub for lunch." He agreed and thanked everyone for helping.

Nancy smiled and added, "That's what friends are for Jake. Never forget we are your friends, though it does depend on what you buy us for lunch." They all laughed.

They sat inside to have their lunch. It was quite chilly for the beginning of October. Jake noticed that Nancy was back drinking alcohol. They were all starving and ate lots. They had a huge selection of bar food, wings, fries, zucchini, mozzarella sticks, lots of dipping sauces, and a fair amount of beer. Even Elizabeth drank a beer. Daniel knew she would suffer later when the baby got its revenge.

They all went their separate ways about three o'clock. Daniel and Elizabeth went home. Nancy said her goodbyes and was off to her parents. Jake asked Abbey if there was anything she wanted to do.

"Just back to your apartment for a snooze would be nice," she replied, which they did.

That evening they just walked to the theatre and saw a movie. Afterwards they stopped and had an ice cream and went back to Jake's and enjoyed each other, they then slept again.

On the Sunday morning they went to Indian Lake for breakfast. It was becoming a regular spot for them, Jake commented.

"When we are married, we will come here for breakfast at least once a week."

Abbey smiled and agreed, "That would be ideal."

They had Daniel and Elizabeth coming for dinner, so Jake asked Abbey if she could cook. He had never asked her this before.

"Yes, of course," she replied. "But I'm not Elizabeth."

"Who is?" he kidded. "She is the Chef de la Crème." Both of them burst out laughing.

Down in St. John, Jennie and Richard were in a bit of a pickle. She'd had an offer for her business, a really good offer. Richard thought it was too good to turn down.

"Sell it," he said, "and let's travel the world."

This idea appealed to Jennie.

"Just imagine," he said, "we can go where we want, when we want. Let's go to Europe and see everything. It would be nice, but the decision is yours. It's your baby. I'm just giving you my two cents worth."

Jennie sat there thinking.

"In some ways I agree," she replied. "It's not as if we need the money that I make. It's just … I think I will sell, but it will be sad to see Serendipity go, I've had it so long. It's part of my life."

She thought to herself, *'I'm lucky in having Richard for my husband. He has supported me though our marriage with never a question. So many people are getting divorced now it's scary. I don't understand why couples don't try harder to make it work. Yes, it's good to be one of the lucky ones.'*

"I will call the guy tomorrow and accept his offer. He has two gift shops in St. Thomas that are very successful. As long as he's willing to keep the staff, there should not be a problem. Some of them have been with me from the beginning."

Richard walked over and kissed her on the forehead.

"Listen," he said, "I would love to travel the world, but you being happy is more important. So if you have second thoughts, I will understand and accept whatever you decide."

Just then, Jennie came up with an idea. "Richard, just hear me out. What if I sell it and we do travel - do you think that as Abbey is getting married next June, we could offer them the cottage for their honeymoon while we are in Europe? Because I don't want to go before June because of the weather, I had enough cold in New Jersey."

"We will go to their wedding and then take off and enjoy ourselves wherever you decide to take me."

Richard cheered her up. "Why don't you call Abbey and put the suggestion to her? I personally think it's a great idea, and as she knows this area so well it would be nice for Jake, because Jennie as we talked about and agreed, one day Cinnamon Cottage will eventually go to Abbey."

"Okay Jennie, this is my plan," Richard looked at her and smiled. "First we go to London, then Paris, Monaco, Rome and Venice. How does that sound to you?"

"It will be delightful," Jennie replied. "I now know I made the right choice in choosing you as my husband." They both laughed.

Jennie called her sister Maggie. They talked for a while about Abbey, Jake, and the engagement ring. She could sense that her sister was not one-hundred percent behind the idea.

"What is it Maggie?" she asked. "Why the apprehension?"

"Oh, I guess it's just because they have not known each other that long, and we don't really know that much about him."

"Maggie, listen … I'm your sister and I love you. Abbey is not a fool, she has always known where she wanted to go in life, and I for one, think she is a very good judge of character. You should be overjoyed that she will be married, and one day make you and Sam grandparents. You're very lucky. Can I talk to her?"

"No Jennie. She is at Jake's for dinner. Why don't you call her tomorrow? She normally gets home by five."

"Okay Maggie," Jennie replied, "I will, and do me a favour. Cheer up."

After she had finished talking to her sister, Maggie poured herself a drink. She knew Jennie was right, and she also knew she was being stupid. *'If Sam found out how she was thinking, he would not be happy. He likes Jake a lot and thinks Abbey is the lucky one. So why can't I feel that way too?'* Maggie poured herself another.

Abbey and Daniel were stacking the dishwasher after dinner. Elizabeth managed to get Jake alone. She spoke in a very quiet voice.

"I think you should know Jake that I do not trust Nancy. She comes across all happy and nice, but I think it's just a front. I've been watching her and something tells me she still has not forgiven you."

Jake pondered on this and replied, "Let's see what happens. I hope you are wrong, but who knows. The good thing is, I told Abbey everything that happened between Nancy and me and she understands it was just a drunken mistake. But I know the last week you have been close to her and I trust your thoughts. I will talk to her and see if she still has a problem with me – I promise."

Jake walked them all down to their cars. It was getting late and he felt tired. He said goodnight to his friends and he held Abbey close and kissed her.

"I love you. It's starting to rain, so off you go home. I will call you tomorrow."

"I love you too," she said and kissed him goodnight.

He watched her drive away. Nancy was there, but Jake did not see her.

Everything was back to normal now that Jake had laid his mother's ashes on his father's grave and his mother's belongings had gone to the church. Jake felt a lot happier at work and managed to get back in his stride very quickly. There was money to be made, and he was ready to earn as much as possible.

Though his mother had left him the house and all that money, Jake thought the wisest thing to do was invest all he could for their future together. The only nagging doubt now was what to do with the apartment.

He had clients waiting for advice on where to put their money, what stocks and shares to buy. This was a tonic for Jake. He had no time to think, though thoughts of Abbey were always in the back of his mind.

Chapter 10

That evening Aunt Jennie called her at home and discussed with Abbey their thoughts on the honeymoon. She immediately jumped at the idea, but explained to her aunt that she would have to talk it over with Jake. They had not yet planned anything. With what had gone on in the past two weeks they'd had no time even to discuss the wedding. Abbey thanked her aunt and promised to get back to her as soon as possible. Aunt Jennie also mentioned to her that she had sold Serendipity to a larger company, and that she and Richard were going to travel. She would also like Abbey to come for a break at Christmas, as she knew school was out for at least a week. Abbey again promised her aunt an answer as soon as she could.

Abbey thanked Aunt Jennie.

"And please give my love to Uncle Richard."

Even though she was now grown up, she still called them aunt and uncle. To Abbey, this was just showing respect, and she loved them dearly. She had always thought of her aunt as her best friend.

Abbey was so happy she tried to call Jake immediately, but he was with a late client, so she would have to wait. Her father came home and they sat and talked. Abbey told her dad the whole idea from Aunt Jennie.

"I think it's a wonderful idea and I'm sure Jake will be thrilled. It's one of the nicest spots on earth," he replied. "Now I need to eat. I'm starving. Is your mother around? Let's see what she has prepared for dinner."

Jake did not finish until eight-thirty, but he loved the adrenalin rush from helping his clients invest, and pushing his commissions even higher. He called Abbey as soon as he could and apologized that he could not see her that evening. He would have to pack as soon as he got home. He had a two-day business seminar in New York starting in the morning.

Abbey did not mention her chat with Aunt Jennie. She thought it could wait until the weekend.

"I'll miss you," she told him. "What time are you leaving?"

He told her he was catching the seven o'clock train from Denville.

"I love you," he said. "And I will miss you too, but I will be back for the weekend, then I promise to make it up to you."

"Don't talk dirty on the phone," she said playfully. "You bad man, I love you more each day."

Jake quipped, "Maybe we will go for a spin in the car."

"That was really nice," Abbey laughed. "Like I said, you are a bad influence on me, but the idea sounds appealing."

Jake promised to call her from the Big Apple, but he was going to have two busy days. When he got off the phone with Abbey, he called Nancy at home. He wanted to know if she would like to come over when he got back from New York, so that they could chat. Nancy thought that would be super and looked forward to talking to him one on one. She explained to Jake that every time they were together other people were around. He would call her either Friday evening or Saturday morning.

Jake sorted out two of his best suits, shirts and ties, with decent shoes, a lot of very big company executives would be at this seminar, he wanted to make an impression.

Nancy had not informed Jake that she had started working with her father, that could wait until she met with him, but she was wondering what was on his mind.

She still loved him, but at the same time, she hated him. As for Abbey, that was more than hatred. As far as Nancy was concerned, she had stolen her man and she would pay dearly for this crime. She would suffer. Her mind was full of hatred. Even though she knew Jake loved Abbey, she would hurt them both – no matter what.

On her first day with her father, they made a visit to Brady Industries. Sam was pleased to see her.

"I have not really seen you for a long time, except for a few minutes after Jake's mother's funeral. You look very well."

He did not know about her hospitalization in Connecticut. Only her parents and the other four were aware of her addiction to drugs, but she was pleased to see him. It had been years since she had paid a visit with her father, maybe ten years she told Sam, seems like a lifetime.

They met with Simon after leaving Sam. He also had not seen Nancy for years.

'She looks hot,' he thought. *'Really hot.'*

They had coffee and discussed an order for her father's company. Simon could not take his eyes off her. Nancy was no fool, she knew he was giving her the eye, and she wanted to take full advantage. When they left his office, she had forgotten her purse on purpose.

"I'll just run back and get she informed her father. I will meet you in the car."

She went back to Simon's office. His secretary showed her in.

"I'm sorry." She looked at him with her big blue eyes. "I left my purse – here it is." She picked it off the floor. Simon was hooked. He cleared his throat and asked if she would have dinner with him. He felt a bit awkward, as she was the daughter of a friend, and apologized for hitting on her so soon after meeting again.

"I would love for you to take me out and wine and dine me," she answered.

"How about this evening?" he asked. "Or is that too soon?"

"Thank you," she replied. "That will be fine."

"I'll pick you up at seven."

She smiled and left.

At seven precisely, he pulled up at her door. Nancy was dressed in a two-piece suit that really showed off her figure.

"Wow. You look beautiful."

"Thank you," she replied. "You don't look bad yourself."

Simon was grinning. "You're very kind."

He looked at her. She was beautiful. She had grown into a very desirable woman.

He drove to his favourite Italian restaurant, the Regigalia in Cedar Knolls. Nancy also knew this was Jake's favourite hideaway. They talked a lot over their meal. Simon ordered a nice Chianti to complement the meal, he asked Nancy what she had been up to over the years.

She explained that she had been away at university, but had decided to join her father's company instead. Simon just took it all in and believed every word. She told him that she had a small hospital stay because she was exhausted and needed rest, and that Jake and her other friends had come up to visit. She did not want to be caught in a lie, but she never mentioned the real reason.

Simon told her that he knew she had been in hospital but did not know the circumstance. He did not mention that it was Abbey that had told him. It's not always good to mention another woman's name when out on a first date, especially with someone you think you could like a lot given time. He loved talking with her, she was a good listener, and as the evening went on, they continued to laugh even more.

When he dropped Nancy home, he asked if he could see her again, she kissed him and replied, "I can't wait. Call me." She ran indoors.

Simon rubbed his lips. *'That was one of the nicest kisses I think I've ever had.'*

As he drove home, he started singing, which he had not done in a very long time.

Nancy was jubilant. She had really enjoyed his company, which in some ways shocked her. She had only been thinking of her hatred for Jake and Abbey and it had consumed her. She decided it was time for her to enjoy herself. While she thought what to do with those two, maybe Simon could be her pleasant distraction. *'He is very handsome,'* she thought. *'Very handsome.'* She wanted to see where this would lead.

When Jake arrived home late Friday afternoon, he called Nancy to see if they could get together. She informed him that she had a date that evening, and agreed to meet him for breakfast on Saturday morning at Indian Lake.

He called Abbey so that they could get together. She drove straight over to his apartment. They went to a small Chinese restaurant for take out and took it back to eat.

They talked, and Abbey bought up the conversation with her Aunt Jennie, about the offer to use her cottage for the honeymoon. She wanted to know what Jake thought.

"I think it's a great idea," he replied. "I have never been that far south."

They made love and he held her. He felt so good when she was close to him. It was like he had locked the rest of the world away.

"I love you so much, Abbey Walker." He kissed her gently. They both slept, cuddled together.

Nancy had a wonderful evening with Simon. They had a beautiful dinner, and then went to the local pub, which had live music and dancing. She was very impressed with the way he could move on the floor. After a few drinks, he got really bold and asked Nancy if she would like to come back to his house, to his surprise, she agreed.

On the drive to his home, Nancy could not leave him alone. She kissed him and touched him. Simon loved every minute. Nancy had undressed him inside the front door. She had a need for sex. It had been far too long. He took her on the hall table and she thoroughly enjoyed him, and when they got to the bedroom she made love to him. Simon could not remember ever being so aroused.

When he awoke in the morning, after sleeping really sound, Nancy was gone, but she had left him a note. It read: *Simon. Had a breakfast meeting which I can't get out of, call me later if you want a repeat performance.* She signed it 'N'. *By the way, you were great.*

Jake was up when Abbey stirred. "Where are you going?" she asked.

"I'm sorry," Jake replied. "I should have told you last night, but I have a breakfast meeting with Nancy. It's important. I hope you don't mind, but I need to talk to her. There are a few things we have to clear up." He kissed her.

She did mind, but she now trusted Jake completely, so did not say a word. He left and promised to be back as quick as possible.

Over breakfast, Jake asked how she was feeling. Nancy explained that she was feeling great, had a new man in her life, and she wanted Jake to know that what went on between them, was now water under the bridge. She was glad that they both could move on. Jake thought this was great. He felt a lot easier with her, which brought a huge smile to his face. They talked about work. He was so pleased Nancy was working. He was sure this would also help.

"Nancy," he said, "I've always wanted us to be friends. You are and always will be special to me, and I'm so glad that we are back to normal."

"So who's the lucky guy?"

"Oh, I don't think you would know him," she replied. "His name is Simon Brady."

Jake was startled. "Actually, we have met. Daniel had a barbecue party and he was there. By all accounts, he's a nice person."

"Yes he is." Nancy looked at Jake. "Yes, he is."

When Jake drove away from Indian Lake, he was pleased with himself. *'So she has taken up with Simon. That's wonderful,'* he thought. *'Maybe things have changed.'* Though he could never forget the way she had treated him and the nasty phone calls she made.

Nancy was on her way home. Her mind was racing. She was like a cat that had got the cream. *'He believed me,'* she said to herself. *'He actually believed me. Yes Jake, I have my man for now, but you and Abbey will still pay for what you put me through. Yes ... you will pay dearly. I want you to suffer and I want that 'bitch' to know what I went through. When I let the cat out of the bag, she will hate you as well. When I tell her about our baby, and because of you I lost it.'* Nancy really did feel pleased with herself.

Jake picked up Abbey and drove over to Daniel's. He had told Abbey of his conversation with Nancy, and that everything was good between them now. She was happy for him, but he had promised Elizabeth he would let her know what was said.

Both Elizabeth and Daniel were pleased to see them. Abbey commented on how big her bump had got.

Elizabeth sighed. "Yes, it feels I'm giving birth to an elephant. I think it's a girl," she said, "but we shall see. Daniel would like a boy – most men do."

"Yes," Abbey agreed, "but we girls are less trouble." They both laughed.

Jake explained his meeting with Nancy and what they had talked about. He had forgotten to mention to Abbey that the new man in her life was Simon Brady. Everyone went silent.

"You mean she's dating Simon?"

"Yes," he said, "she is, and seems very happy. Why? Do you not like the idea?"

"No," Abbey hesitated, "it's just that, he's such a sweet guy. I hope she doesn't hurt him."

Daniel commented that he thought they would be well suited. Elizabeth thought it was time to change the subject.

"We have not told you both, but Daniel has put an offer in to buy his own garage down by Estling Lake. The owner is retiring. We have scraped together all we have, and I'm sure the bank will lend us the rest."

"It's a good business," Daniel informed them. "He has a lot of steady customers, and I am tired of working for someone else."

"Listen buddy," Jake said, "forget the bank. I can lend you the rest. Let's get you started. I want to see both of you get ahead. Remember,

I told you at your wedding, if you ever needed help I would always be there."

They all had coffee to celebrate Jake's offer.

On the way back to his apartment, Abbey commented, "That was a nice gesture Jake. You are a kind man."

"They're my friends Abbey. I mean they're our friends now. I just feel they need a bit of help and I am in a position to give help."

She kissed him and smiled. "You big softy."

When they arrived at Jake's, Abbey asked if she could call her aunt, he agreed.

She spoke with her aunt for about ten minutes. Jennie was pleased that Jake had accepted her offer and could not wait to meet him.

"I can't wait to be at your wedding," she told Abbey. "We already have your gift, and no you can't know what we got you." Abbey laughed. Her aunt reminded her about Christmas. Abbey told her she would have an answer after she had spoken with Jake.

"I'll call you back soon, I promise."

She walked over to him and kissed him tenderly.

"Jake, I forgot to tell you my aunt has invited us for Christmas. Do you think you could get away from work, and come with me? They are really looking forward to meeting you."

He looked at her. "Abbey darling, I would love to go, but only if Elizabeth has had the baby. I can't miss that for anything. It's a promise I have already made."

Abbey understood what this meant to him, so she thought it best to maybe forget going to St. John. She wanted to be with Jake more than anyone this Christmas, so she would phone her aunt tomorrow and explain.

That evening they went early to the movie theatre. It was packed for the sequel to 'Wild Geese', which Jake had thoroughly enjoyed, but this movie was a let down. They even left before the end, and went to the local pub for supper.

Muldoon's always had live music, and the Irish group that were playing were excellent. They ate their meal of fish and chips, had a drink, and danced to every other tune that was played. Jake was not a great dancer, but Abbey did not mind, at least he tried.

At around nine-thirty, Nancy and Simon walked in. They all said hello and Jake ordered a round of drinks. They sat and talked, everyone was friendly. Simon danced with Nancy and Jake realized what a good mover he was on the dance floor. Then he asked Abbey to dance, which she of course accepted. Jake and Nancy were talking, and Jake commented, "He's a nice guy Nancy. You have good taste."

"Yes," she replied, "I do, and I really like him."

"Let's hope it works out," Jake said.

"Yes, I hope it does too, but only time will tell."

Nancy was very friendly to both of them, which of course, pleased Jake. Every time he had spoken to her lately, their friendly relationship seemed to be getting back to where it once was.

Simon offered Jake and Abbey a lift home, as during the conversation they had mentioned walking to the pub. This was a nice gesture and Jake thanked him, as it was getting very chilly at night.

After Simon had dropped them off, he turned to Nancy. "You've become very quiet. Is it something I said?"

"*No. No,*" she replied, "not at all. I am having a wonderful time. Now take me back to your house and ravish me." But in the back of her mind were Jake and Abbey. She was thinking and revenge had reared its ugly head again. She had to plan very carefully if she was to succeed.

The sex with Simon was very intense. They made love on the kitchen table and then they had a bath together, and ended up making love on the rug in front of the television. This was passionate sex, and when they had finished, both of them were dripping wet.

Nancy was asleep as soon as her head hit the pillow. Simon sat and stared at her. He thought she was beautiful and stroked her hair. She looked so peaceful lying there. He knew he was in love with her.

Without doubt, he was in love, and in a funny way, this scared him. He lay down beside her and went to sleep.

Abbey and Jake sat talking for hours after they arrived back. He told her that he intended to sell the apartment and move to his mother's house. He felt funny calling it his house. It would still take time for him to come to terms with this.

They talked about Elizabeth and Daniel's impending addition to their family, which was due in mid December. No one knew if it was a boy or girl, they did not want to know, and all Jake cared about was that they would be okay.

He thought of them as family and would always make sure if they wanted help he would be there. He needed them in his life, nearly as much as Abbey, because without her he would have gone insane. She was now his rock.

Jake held her and whispered, "Let's go to bed."

She kissed him and before they hit the bedroom their clothes were everywhere. Their lovemaking was not rushed and they climaxed together. He kissed her gently on the nose, and told Abbey how much he loved her.

Her response was to rub his face and kiss him.

"I love you Jake Lockhart. More than I could ever have imagined." They fell asleep in each others arms.

Abbey's dream was of their honeymoon on St. John, and of the wonderful time they were having. They made love on the beach, just by the picket fence. They swam in the pool naked, which she had never done before. They visited every beach on the island and their lovemaking became more intense. She awoke in a panic – Jake was calling her name.

"Abbey, Abbey, wake up!"

"What is it?" she pleaded. "What's wrong?" She was very unsettled.

"It's you darling," he said. "You were having a nightmare. Your arms were going everywhere and you were kicking me. I was worried. It took me so long to wake you."

She held him. "I'm sorry Jake, but I don't think I was having a nightmare. Whatever I was having was wonderful. That's all I can remember."

He kissed her gently. "Then I'm glad I was not there. I would have ended up with a black eye. You looked like you were in a boxing match." They both laughed, he cuddled her and they slept.

Over the next few weeks everything was quiet in Rockaway. Abbey was making plans for the wedding. Elizabeth and Daniel were now getting anxious, as it was getting close to the birth. Jake was really busy at work making money hand over fist. Nancy and Simon were now an item. They were seeing each other every day. He had asked her to move in with him, but she said she needed more time. Maggie was not happy about their relationship. She still thought that Simon would be better off with Abbey.

Down on St. John, Jennie and Richard had completed the sale of her business, and were in the process of buying a boat so that they would not need to use the ferry to go back and forth to St. Thomas. They had put in an offer for a nice cabin cruiser, which was also perfect for traveling around the islands.

It would be their first boat after all this time living on the island. Jennie loved the idea that it could sleep four, and was fully loaded with kitchen and bathroom, and a nice sitting area below deck, just in case of rain which they did not get very often.

Richard liked the twin inboard engines, and on the test run he thought she handled very well. He could go deep sea fishing with Jennie, who had always wanted to learn how to catch their dinner.

Their life was changing. They spent a lot more time together, which pleased both of them. They loved each other very much and now it was time to live life to the fullest. As Jennie pointed out to Richard, *'Time seems to fly.'*

"And in my case," she laughed, "gravity has taken its toll."

Richard commented, "I disagree, you look lovelier now than when I married you." She smiled and told him, 'S*he liked it when he lied a little.*'

Since retirement, Richard had become much more relaxed. Jennie liked this side of him. His job had been stressful, but now he was tanned and fit. She thought to herself, *'I am lucky. We have had a good life together and I want it to continue for a long time.'*

Chapter 11

The snow came early this year in New Jersey and it was getting really cold. The dark nights did not suit Abbey. She did not like the winter that much and longed to live in a warmer climate. The only thing that made it bearable, was knowing Jake was close.

She took her grandmother Susan to New York, so she could do her Christmas shopping. This also gave Abbey the opportunity to look for a nice present for Jake.

She wanted something special, very special. She visited one of the top jewellers and picked out a nice gold watch, very masculine she thought but very elegant. Her grandmother approved.

"It's lovely dear," she commented. "He's very lucky."

Susan asked, "Now what can I buy him, because soon he will be a member of the family?"

Abbey suggested a leather wallet.

"He needs a new one badly. Jake's is falling apart at the seams. It's funny Gran. He is so fussy about his clothes and shoes, but his wallet is horrible."

They chose a black leather one, and Susan thought it would be nice to have his initials engraved at the bottom corner.

They went from store to store. Abbey found a beautiful outfit for Elizabeth's baby that was due any day. It was a really nice knitted yellow two-piece. She could not buy blue or pink, just in case she got it wrong.

They arrived back in Denville at around six. Sam was waiting to take them home and loaded all their parcels into the trunk. He laughed. He could not believe two people could have bought so much. Susan informed Sam, *'that she had only half of her Christmas shopping.'* She loved spoiling her family for the festivities that lay ahead.

Christmas was the time of year she loved most. Unlike Abbey, she did not mind the winters. Susan loved to walk in the snow, on the trails at the back of her bungalow. She had done this for many years with her husband. Abbey had never known her grandfather. He had been killed at the very end of the Second World War. He was on his way home when a German submarine sunk their ship. His participation in the war was over and he had come through without a scratch, only for this to happen.

Susan now had two teenage girls to bring up on her own. She so longed for those days before that *damn war* took her husbands life, but she did bring them up alone and was proud of both of them. They had made good lives for themselves, and had given her two beautiful grandchildren. Sadly though, Heather had died which had left a nasty void in her life, she hated the thought of death, seen too much of it she would say to herself.

Jake had been extremely busy at work. His client base was building very quickly and he could barely keep up with it. He was working twelve hours a day, and had hardly seen Abbey except on weekends. This was not what he wanted, but had little choice as he had a need to be successful.

This need drove him on. He did not want to be working until he was sixty-five. By then, he thought, *'the best years will have passed us by, I want the best for both of us, so we can raise a family and have time to share in that joy.'*

Abbey was a little concerned, as he seemed to her to be consumed by his job. She wanted to spend more time with him now, not worry about later when they are old and grey. She had spoken with him on this matter, but had not really gotten anywhere. He felt that this was his time, and he needed to use it as best he could.

Abbey had also voiced her concerns to Elizabeth and Daniel. They understood her anxiety, but they also knew Jake. When he put his mind to something, nothing could steer him away. It's like he always had something to prove, not to his friends or family, but to himself.

They assured Abbey that she was the most important person in his life. Every time they had seen Jake, all he talked about was Abbey this, and Abbey that.

"He wants to be able to provide a good life for both of you Abbey," Daniel explained to her. "Maybe getting over his mother's death is what's pushing him? Let me talk with him and see why he has become so engrossed in his work."

Elizabeth felt for her. She had been through a somewhat similar situation with Daniel, but they had worked it out and now he did spend more time with her, especially with the imminent birth of their baby. She assured Abbey that if anyone could get through to Jake, it was her husband. They had coffee and Abbey told Elizabeth about her upcoming trip to New York with her grandmother, but in the back of her mind was filled with thoughts of Jake. She tried to understand, but felt shut out.

She prayed that Daniel could make him see that she was concerned, and that they had to discuss why he had become so obsessed with his work. She wanted nothing to stand in the way of their happiness. He was more important to her than maybe Jake was willing to realize.

Abbey felt lost and confused. On weekends, he was so tender and caring. It was like he had become two different people. During the week he would hardly speak, or if she called he would give her a minute and then have to get back to work.

The thought had also crossed her mind that maybe he had found someone else. This feeling, she did not like.

After Abbey had dropped off her Christmas shopping at home, she drove over to Jake's. She had made her mind up to try and confront him in a friendly way.

Jake was really pleased to see Abbey. He held her close and kissed her very gently.

"I missed you," he said lovingly.

She now felt guilty, but decided to go ahead anyway.

"Jake. We need to talk. Let's sit down."

"What's on your mind?"

"Us," she replied. "I'm very concerned. We only see each other a few hours a week now, and on weekends only. All week you seem to busy and even when I call you on the phone, I only get a couple of minutes of your time." Abbey was trembling, and tears welled in her eyes.

Jake looked at her with concern. "What are you implying Abbey?"

"I'm not implying anything," she said. "I'm asking, why you don't seem to have time to be with me? I feel left out Jake. I just feel that work has taken you over. I have not seen you since last Sunday ... that's nearly a week ... and you rarely call me. Jake, we have not even had an engagement party. I just find it strange." The tears were now streaming down, she ran to the bathroom.

He sat there stunned. He did not really understand what was wrong. He loved Abbey more than anything in the world. *'Had he ignored her too much?'* Different thoughts were now running through his mind. Suddenly, the light went on.

"Oh my God!" he said out loud. "What an idiot I have been."

Abbey came back from the bathroom, her eyes were still wet. He jumped up and held her.

"I'm sorry darling," he said. "I'm truly sorry. I am a complete fool. I didn't realize. I would never hurt you intentionally. I have been a jerk. Please forgive me?" Jake himself now had tears in his eyes.

She held him.

"Oh Jake ... I love you. I felt you were letting go. It really frightened me."

"I love you Abbey," he said, "and could not imagine my life without you. I make this promise to you now – you will come first always – not my work."

Jake now knew that Abbey meant everything to him. He would have to make changes to his life or risk losing her. The thought of that was unbearable.

He kissed her on the nose, which made her smile.

"Abbey, you have my undivided attention. I need a kick up the backside for not realizing what I was doing to us."

That night in bed was like their first time all over again. They kissed. They made love. Jake and Abbey could not get enough of each other.

They were just dozing off when the phone rang. Jake jumped out of bed. It was Daniel's voice on the line and he sounded frantic.

"*Jake.* It's Elizabeth. She's in the hospital. The baby is coming!"

Jake assured him that he would be right there. He and Abbey dressed without even taking a shower, they were in the delivery ward fifteen minutes later.

Daniel paced anxiously, up and down. He was so glad to see them.

"She, she's in labour. The baby's due any time," he blurted out.

Daniel was always the calm, dependable type, but now was a complete nervous wreck. Abbey hugged him.

"She'll be fine," she whispered. "I'm sure it won't be long."

They all heard the baby cry together. The nurse came out and asked Daniel to come in to see his baby daughter.

Daniel kissed his wife and held his little girl.

"She's beautiful," he said. "She looks just like you."

He handed the baby back to Elizabeth and beckoned Jake and Abbey in. He picked up the tiny bundle. Jake was amazed at how delicate she was. He had never held a new born baby before.

"She's adorable," he said and laid the baby in Abbey's arms. Her face lit up.

"Oh Elizabeth, you are very lucky. She's unbelievable! So cute, and it looks like she is smiling already." She carefully handed the little girl back to Daniel.

Jake was the first to ask, "Have you decided what name to give her?"

Elizabeth answered him. "We had decided if we had a girl, we would call her Rebecca after my late grandmother."

"That's a lovely name," Abbey said.

Then Daniel chirped in, "And we won't mind if she's called Becky for short."

Jake and Abbey congratulated both of them and decided to let Elizabeth get some rest.

"We will come back later," they assured their friends.

As they were leaving, Jake turned to Abbey and said, "Where can we get something nice for Becky on a Sunday?"

"We don't need to," she replied. "I already bought an outfit. Before we come back, I'll slip home and pick it up."

Jake thanked her. "Again I have been neglectful. Thank God there is one of us who thinks." They laughed.

Abbey felt so much happier now that Jake had realized how she had been feeling over the past few weeks. She could now set aside her fears and move on with their relationship. They were asleep within five minutes.

The ringing of the phone woke both of them up. Jake crawled out of bed. He felt like a zombie.

Who could that be? He looked at his watch. It was ten thirty. He picked up the receiver, it was Nancy. Daniel had called her with the news. She sounded really exited.

"Jake, what time are you visiting?" He was trying to clear his head so he could answer.

"Sometime this afternoon," he managed to reply.

"Okay ... I will see you there." She hung up.

Jake got back into bed and cuddled into Abbey who had already gone back to sleep.

He woke again an hour later. This time it was his doorbell. He stumbled to the door, it was Monica. She wanted to know if he and Abbey would like to come for dinner that evening. Jake told her about the baby and agreed that they would join Monica and her parents for dinner.

He laughed, "But only if I am awake."

She smiled at him and said, "Always the comedian. See you at seven."

Abbey was also awake. "Who was at the door?" she yawned.

"It was Monica," he replied. "We have been invited to eat with them later."

"That's good," Abbey responded. "At least we won't have to worry where to go and eat."

They showered and went to Indian Lake for a little something to stave off the hunger pains until later.

When they arrived at the hospital, Nancy and Simon were already there.

"You look wonderful," Jake said to Elizabeth. "Motherhood must really suit you."

She smiled at Jake. She always had liked his sense of humour. "Thank you kind sir," she replied.

Abbey handed Elizabeth their present for the new born baby. Daniel was ecstatic, and did not want to let go of little Becky, but he reluctantly handed the child over to Jake for a while.

They stayed for about an hour, then left Elizabeth and Daniel alone. Other family was arriving to see the newest family member. Nancy asked Jake and Abbey if they would like to join her and Simon that evening for dinner. Jake declined and apologized, explaining that they already had an invitation.

"Some other time, would be great," he suggested, and they left it at that.

They went back to Jake's and relaxed before joining Monica and her family for the evening. Jake actually dozed on the sofa – which he rarely did.

Abbey tried to watch a program on TV, but could not get into it. While Jake dozed, she managed to get a *'yes'* out of him for their visit to St. John for Christmas. She called her aunt with the good news.

It was already December the fifteenth and Abbey hoped they could still book flights without too much of a problem. Jake told her he would sort it out first thing in the morning.

Abbey and Jake had a nice evening at the Gitano's. Jonathan and Mary always made them feel welcome. They had a good home cooked dinner with a wonderful apple pie that Monica had made. She had remembered to get whipped cream just for Jake. By ten o'clock, Jake was exhausted. He apologized and told them that he had to get some sleep. Jake thanked them for their hospitality and walked Abbey to her car.

"I'm sorry I cut the evening short darling," he said, "but with all the hours at work this week and then the hospital … I'm totally worn out."

He kissed Abbey goodnight, and assured her he would call the travel agent as soon as he got to work.

As he watched her drive away, he did not see Nancy in her favourite hiding place.

Jake went straight upstairs and went to bed. Nancy had been behind the tree for over two hours. She was freezing, but didn't care. When she had seen Elizabeth and Daniel with the baby – she almost lost it. How she kept her cool she could not remember. After having dinner with Simon, she made an excuse about having a headache and headed home. He kissed her goodnight, and she drove straight to Jake's apartment complex to lie in wait.

Nancy did not know how she was going to get her revenge on Jake and Abbey, but knew she would somehow ruin their relationship. Seeing the baby this afternoon had resurrected the memory of losing her child. They had to pay - especially Jake. She would make him suffer as much as she possibly could.

Nancy was having a great time with Simon. She thought she might be falling in love with him. He was attentive and caring, and she enjoyed him in bed, but at times her vendetta would overtake rationality.

She sometimes wished she could forgive Jake, and there were times when she thought it was possible. But then she would see him or Abbey and the venom would again, flow through her veins.

Nancy had even made an appointment with a psychiatrist, but cancelled at the last minute. The thought of Jake and Abbey together would overtake her emotions, and she would go back to her plotting. So far, she had no clue how to do the deed, but *'patience'*, she told herself, *'would prevail in the end'*.

When Abbey informed her mother of her plans for the holidays, Maggie was furious.

"What do you mean you are going to see my sister for Christmas? What about the rest of the family? We always have that time together, always!" she snarled.

Abbey looked at her mother and calmly replied, "I'm not a child anymore Mum, we have been invited and we are going." For the first time in her life Abbey was standing up to her mother, which in a way gave her some satisfaction. She knew deep down that her mother did not like Jake.

"Mum, why do you get like this? Let me lead my own life ... please. And tell me, why you don't like Jake? I think it's so unfair. I am going to marry him. I love him, so get used to the idea."

Her mother started ranting about him not being good enough for her, and told Abbey that if she went to St. John for Christmas, it might be a good idea to find somewhere else to live.

Abbey did not flinch.

"If that's what you want, then I will be only too happy to oblige. I love you Mum, but I will not put up with being treated like a five-year-old."

"This is my house!" her mother stormed back at her. "I won't have you using it like a hotel, staying at that Jake's when you feel like it and then coming home when it suits you. You are acting like a *whore!*"

Abbey ran upstairs. Those last words from her mother really hurt. She cried, *'How could her mother turn like this?'* She was still crying when there was a tap on her door. It was her father.

"Abbey, I need to talk to you." He came in and sat on the end of the bed.

"I've just been talking to your mother. I'm sorry little one. She does not mean what she said. I have to get her some help. I thought she was over this, but I was wrong. Forgive her Abbey, please. We need for her to see a doctor or something, and I'm going to need your help." Sam held his daughter like he did when she was a little girl.

He spoke very softly to her.

"Abbey, I think mum is ill. She has been drinking very heavily lately. I don't think she knows that I found out from the store that she has been buying five bottles a week, sometimes more. We have to get her to a decent clinic to dry out. I'm worried she will do something stupid. She loves you Abbey, you can take my word for that. It's just … sometimes she just doesn't seem to handle things too well."

Abbey kissed her father on the cheek. "I will help if I can, but what she called me is unforgivable."

"I know baby … I know," Sam replied.

As soon as Jake got to work, he called the travel agent as promised and booked two flights to St. Thomas. He still felt very groggy even though he had slept for nine hours.

He struggled through his work, called Daniel to make sure everything with Elizabeth and the baby were okay, and was informed that they would be home on Tuesday. While he was on the phone, Daniel asked if his offer to buy the garage was still good. Jake assured him it was and asked him to let him know how much was needed so he could have the funds ready. He had been so busy that he had not even invested his inheritance. Once he knew what Daniel and Elizabeth needed for their purchase, he would sort it out. There would be no interest charged. He had not told anyone, but that was to be a surprise for his friends. His mother had left the money to him and if he could do some good with it – then so be it.

During his next break he called the Real Estate agent and made an appointment for that evening to view the apartment. *'The quicker it's on the market, the better,'* he thought. Then he would move to the house when he got back from St. John.

He called Abbey at lunch time and gave her the good news that they had flights leaving next Monday the 23rd. She thanked him for letting her know so quickly, and would call her aunt that evening. She did not tell Jake about her mother. She thought it best not to let him have the details over the phone. He explained about the apartment and asked if she like to go out for dinner. He would be able to pick her up about seven-thirty after his meeting.

When Jake arrived at Abbey's house, Sam answered the door.

"Come in," he said. "I have just made a pot of coffee and we need to talk to you."

Over coffee, Sam explained about Abbey's mother and that afternoon he had secured a bed for her in a private clinic. He did not want anyone else but family to know.

Susan, Abbey's grandmother, was there with her until Sam could visit. He hoped Jake realized the problem was not any fault of his. "It's just that Maggie has twisted things out of proportion."

Jake took Abbey for something to eat. He noticed she was unusually quiet.

"What's wrong honey?" he asked. "Is it your mum? I'm sure she'll be okay."

"No," Abbey replied. "It's what she said to me." She told Jake that her mother had called her a *whore.*

He was flabbergasted. "She called you that?"

Jake took a moment. "It must be her state of mind Abbey. She can't know what she's saying. I know she doesn't like me a hell of a lot, but she loves you. Give it time, when she's better, you can get back to normal."

He took her home, though Abbey would have liked to stay at his place, she did not argue.

Daniel took Elizabeth and Becky home on the Tuesday morning. Nancy had decided to help out and had everything ready so Elizabeth could take it easy for a few days.

She would stay so that Daniel could get on with the purchase of his own garage. They had not told Nancy that Jake had put up the rest of the money. Elizabeth still did not trust her one-hundred percent, so they kept it out of the conversation. In spite of her faults, Nancy was wonderful with the baby. She bathed her and nursed her to sleep. It did give Elizabeth time to recuperate. She did need the rest, as the birth of her daughter had worn her out. Although she slept as much as possible, she was wide awake to feed Becky when she was hungry.

Nancy told her that Simon had asked her to move in with him, and that she was giving it a lot of thought.

"It's a big step and I want to be sure I'm ready."

Being there with the baby caused Nancy to reflect and think about how things may have been. She loved holding Becky in her arms. Just looking down at her gave her an inner glow. She wondered how her life would have changed if she had given birth instead of the miscarriage. Then the dark thoughts would return, and they would overpower her. Nancy felt trapped somewhere between a rock and a hard place and just wanted closure somehow. She wished many times that she could forgive and get on with her life.

But for Nancy, there was no easy answer. Her hatred built up inside her, and at times she had no control, though she would admit to herself that she felt like Jekyll and Hyde. Elizabeth thanked Nancy for being so considerate and tried to talk to her about her loss, but did not get very far. Nancy was too elusive with her answers. This only confirmed to Elizabeth that deep down inside, she had not forgiven Jake. She wondered why Nancy would lie about getting on with her life. She knew Jake thought that it was all resolved. She would talk to Daniel, and voice her concerns. If anyone could get through to Jake, it was her husband. She did not need this pressure at the moment, something had to be said.

Chapter 12

Down in St. John, Jennie and Richard had now taken possession of their new boat. Much to Richard's amazement, his wife had named it *'In My World'*.

"Strange name for a boat," he commented.

Jennie just smiled and replied, "I get fed up with boats that are called after people's names. I wanted something different and that is what we have."

"Okay," he said. "It's your choice."

Then he remembered that Jennie did use that expression in her conversations and quietly repeated a few, "In my world, there would be no wars. In my world, there would be no hunger. In my world, children would not suffer."

He chuckled, "Now I get it."

"Thank you," she replied. "Took you long enough." They both laughed.

"Come on," he said, "I will take you out to dinner to celebrate."

Over their meal they made plans for Christmas.

"I'm looking forward to meeting Jake," Richard commented to his wife. "Now what's this about Maggie? You have spoken to Sam and he's put her in a clinic."

"Serves her right," Jennies replied. "It's all over Abbey and Jake getting married. It's just plain stupidity. She wants to try and control the poor girl's life. To some degree, Sam agrees. She has also been drinking very heavily, all day every day. I know she's my sister – but enough is enough. I'm not being heartless Richard and my sympathy goes out to anyone with a problem that is not self-induced."

"My sister just feels sorry for herself and wants others to feel for her too. She has to try and get over it. I only hope this does not make Abbey suffer."

She paused to take a sip of wine before continuing.

"I don't have time to visit her at the moment, but I will go to New Jersey in the New Year and try and talk some sense into her. I'll give mum a ring and see if she is getting anywhere."

Richard asked Jennie if it would be a good idea to talk to Joanne next door.

He explained, "They are really close."

Jennie thought that was something she had not considered. She phoned her neighbour and invited to come over for a drink and a round table. Joanne agreed.

They all had a large glass of wine. Jennie explained the problems with Maggie to Joanne and hoped she had some suggestions about what to do. She told her that Abbey was coming to her for Christmas and she needed to get every thing ready.

Joanne said she would call Sam and see if she could go there.

"I have not seen snow in years," she replied. "It will be fun and I can sort Maggie out, I'm sure of it."

After speaking with Joanne, Sam was relieved. He knew how close his wife was with her friend, and appreciated her concern. He would get the guest room ready for her and if she wanted, Andrew was also very welcome to visit if he did not want to be alone for Christmas. Joanne had thought that a good idea and would let Sam know as soon as possible.

She called Andrew who was a little hesitant, but in the end he agreed to accompany her.

"It's just the cold," he said. "I don't like it."

"Be a man," Joanne said quite unsympathetically.

He laughed. "Things you do for love."

Abbey felt relieved that her mum's friend was coming as it took the pressure off her and Jake going to St. John. She paid a visit to her grandmother and explained that she and Jake were traveling to see Aunt Jennie for Christmas, and were leaving next Monday.

Her grandmother thought it was a good plan though she would miss her. She suggested that it would be an idea to come to dinner on Friday or Saturday so that they could exchange gifts before they flew out, she would also invite her father.

Abbey took the time to talk to her about her mother.

"I don't understand what had happened to her, and why she flipped on me."

Susan explained, "Deep down, I don't believe she has ever gotten over Heather's death, and now with you getting married she feels she is losing you as well. She's not, but she is not thinking straight."

When Abbey told her grandmother what she had been called, it upset her. "I'm sorry Abbey. Maybe this is worse than we first thought. Let's hope the psychiatrist can get through to her, and with proper care we can get her back to normal."'

"I hope so," Abbey replied. "She did frighten me, and what she said about Jake was really hurtful. She was screaming at me and basically told me to leave."

Her grandmother assured her that she was certain her mother did not mean the nasty things she said.

"Let's give it time Abbey. Let's get her well again."

Abbey had a long discussion with Jake about Christmas. They needed to organize themselves for the delivery of presents to Daniel and family, and that they had been invited for dinner at her grandmothers either Friday or Saturday – whichever was best. He agreed, and asked Abbey to make the arrangements if she had the time, and he would do as he was told. She laughed.

"You are a comedian Jake Lockhart."

Maggie was now being seen by Dr. Moore, a psychiatrist, every day. He also had a long talk with Sam and wanted a detailed history of his patient so that it would help him better understand the problem.

"It's not easy," he explained. "She does not want to discuss very much with me at the moment, and your input may be the trigger I need to get her to open up and talk. I have prescribed antidepressants to see if they will calm her."

Sam basically told him their life story, leaving out very little. When he had finished talking, the Doctor seemed pleased.

"You have helped me a great deal," he told Sam. "I now have something to work on."

Abbey and Jake visited Elizabeth and Becky.

"Daniel is busy sorting out his new garage, but should be home shortly." Elizabeth informed them.

"We've come bearing gifts for everyone," Jake said excitedly.

He had bought a giant elephant for Becky, he apologized that it was far too large to wrap, but it would look great in the nursery.

Elizabeth gave him a hug and whispered, "You big softy." They also had presents for both of them, but would wait for Daniel.

At last, he arrived home and they all went berserk opening whatever they could lay their hands on. They had not laughed so much in a long time. Daniel and Elizabeth bought a joint present for Abbey and Jake. It was a beautiful bone china dinner service. They thanked them. Then it was Jake's turn. He had a special present for Daniel. When he opened it, he could not believe his eyes. It was a pair of coveralls with the name of the garage on the front. It also had his name on the left breast pocket and beneath that was the word, *Proprietor.* Elizabeth burst out laughing. They had a glass of champagne to celebrate. This was truly a night to remember.

While Daniel and Abbey were in the kitchen making coffee, Elizabeth voiced her concern to Jake about Nancy, and she made it quite clear that there was still a problem between them. She could not tell him the story that Nancy told to her in secrecy in Connecticut because she had made a promise and would keep it.

Daniel and Elizabeth wished them a happy Christmas and a safe journey to St. John. Abbey added, "We will have dinner in the garden and think of the three of you."

On Friday, Jake called Nancy at her office. He was lucky to catch her in she told him. He asked whether she could join him for lunch and she agreed to meet him at the locale for noon.

He had already spoken to Abbey about Elizabeth's concerns and had decided to get this sorted out once and for all.

"Maybe Elizabeth is being over protective toward you," Abbey said to him. "Every time we have run into her, she has been very pleasant."

"Yes she has," Jake agreed. "But I know Nancy very well. She has a dark side, and I need to probe that, just to make sure that everything is okay."

Over lunch, Jake tried to get a response from Nancy about his concerns. He did not mention that he had spoken with Elizabeth. She was very calm, and addressed Jake's questions.

"Yes, sometimes I feel angry over what happened between us, but every day it gets better. I have a nice man in my life now," she explained. "I would not jeopardize my relationship with Simon. Believe me Jake it is going away slowly. I don't think about what happened as much as I used to. Time is a great healer, and I just need a bit more." She held his hand. "I promise."

Jake thanked her for being blunt. He appreciated that he was to blame, but he just wanted everyone to be happy. He agreed with her that Simon was a super guy. She then told him that she was going to move in with him in the New Year.

"I'm there most of the time anyway. I just want to find out if this can work."

Jake had to get back to work. He kissed her lightly on the cheek.

"I am happy for you Nancy. I guess only time will tell. It seems I was wrong about everything and I'm sorry, but I must dash. I hope to see you and Simon soon."

After Jake left, she sat there in thought. She knew he was right and that she should move on. The only time she was happy was when she was with Simon. But the joy disappeared every time she saw Jake. Back came those destructive feelings – feelings that took her over completely.

As soon as Jake got back to the office, he called Elizabeth and told her about his meeting with Nancy, and updated her on what they had discussed. She listened intently then replied, "Maybe I'm getting it wrong Jake, but I still get this nagging feeling when she is around."

Jake assured Elizabeth that it was best forgotten and not to worry. He and Abbey had talked at great length about Nancy, and she had agreed with him that it was best to look on the bright side for a change.

"Abbey is a good judge of people," he said and hung up the phone.

Elizabeth was still thinking about her chat with Jake. She still thought that somehow Nancy had blind-sided him. *'That woman is very clever,'* she told herself. *'I don't think this is the end to the saga.'* Elizabeth decided to try and distance herself from her friend. She knew now that her feelings toward Nancy were dwindling very rapidly. She thought to herself, *'At one time, she was my best friend, now I don't even know if I like her.'*

Abbey and Jake had a great time at her grandmothers. They ate dinner and exchanged gifts. Abbey received a stunning necklace. She was thrilled.

"Thank you Gran." She gave her a hug.

"This is for you Jake."

Abbey's grandmother handed him his gift. He opened it and smiled.

"Thank you Susan. It's just what I needed."

Abbey made him take out his old wallet and put all his stuff in the new one. Susan asked what that was at the bottom of his worn out one.

"Duct tape," he said. They couldn't stop laughing. "It stopped my business cards from falling out."

When Susan opened their gift, she immediately had tears in her eyes. Abbey had made her a collage and Jake had it framed. It was filled with both old and new photos of all the family. It had taken her a long time. She had scrounged pictures from everyone. Susan remembered a lot of them being taken. She hugged both of them.

"This is wonderful," she said. "I really like that one of you and Jake. You make a fine couple."

Sam did not make the dinner. With Joanne and Andrew arriving he was too busy. He got them settled in, and then he and Joanne went to visit Maggie.

When Joanne first set her eyes on her friend, she was shocked. Her eyes were sunken and she looked really tired. Joanne could not believe how grey her hair had gone since the last time she had seen Maggie.

She sat beside her and held her hand.

"I'm here for you," she said. Maggie tried to smile. "Do you want to talk?" Joanne asked. Maggie nodded her head. She turned to Sam, and as prearranged, he left the room.

Joanne was relieved when Maggie started talking to her. For the first time in years she opened up. She explained to Joanne that it was her own fault, not anyone elses. She needed to come to terms with a lot of silly issues. Maggie explained that she had been blaming everyone else and she knew that was wrong. Joanne asked her if she was happy with Sam. Maggie replied instantly.

"Yes. He is my life."

Then she told Joanne that she had been drinking far too much, and that the relationship between Abbey and Jake had moved along so fast that it frightened her.

"I felt I was losing my baby again, but I now realize she is a grown woman and she must live her life her way. I was very cruel to my daughter. And some of the names I called her … I'm ashamed of myself Joanne. I'm afraid she will never speak to me again."

She started to cry. Joanne was grateful that at least her friend knew she was to blame.

"Listen Maggie, Abbey loves you, and is very concerned. Sure she was hurt at the way you spoke to her, but she realizes you were not yourself."

Joanne was very stern. "Now listen to me Maggie. You are not sick. You just stressed yourself out. You need to calm down and accept that not everything will be as you want it. That's life I'm afraid." She went on, "If you can come to terms with your daughter's relationship with Jake, we will have you out of here in no time." She hugged her friend.

Joanne called Sam back in and went for a coffee to give them some time alone. Maggie held him and thanked him for being so understanding.

"I just want you back," he said, "back to normal. I miss you Maggie. I miss you a lot. I turn over in bed and you are not there. Get well darling. We all need you."

"Ask Abbey if she will visit?" she pleaded. "I need to talk to her Sam. I really need to hold her. I just hope she will forgive me. I want to be home for Christmas with my family."

Sam knew then that Joanne had been successful with her talk with his wife.

He felt some relief that Maggie was no longer feeling sorry for herself. He kissed her goodbye, and rejoined Joanne.

On the drive back home, Joanne assured Sam that Maggie would soon be home. She told him of their conversation, and how she opened up to her.

"As she knows it's just in her mind, I think she will soon be well. The only thing I ask Sam is that we get Abbey to visit before she leaves on Monday. Maggie needs to see her. It's important to her recovery."

Abbey did not stay at Jakes that Friday. She explained to him that as they had guests and she should be there. Jake understood and agreed. They made love and after they dressed he walked her to her car. It was bitterly cold. He joked with her that he would not go out on the town as she was leaving so early. He kissed her good night and ran in doors. He so wanted her to stay, but knew it was wrong to ask. He just hoped that the situation with Maggie would improve, because Abbey was suffering. He could tell … the sparkle was missing in her eyes.

Abbey was overjoyed at seeing both of them again. They all had coffee and Joanne and Sam talked about the visit to the clinic. Joanne asked Abbey if she would join her in the kitchen. They needed to talk. Sam had already agreed to let Maggie's friend talk to his daughter.

Joanne went farther with her talk to Abbey. She explained in detail about what her mother had said, and how sorry she was. Abbey listened and when Joanne had finished, Abbey explained that her mother had upset her so much that for the first time in her life she felt like an outcast, she was frightened.

Joanne understood and pleaded with her to come with her tomorrow to see her mother.

Abbey was silent for quite sometime before she answered, "Okay Joanne. If it will help, of course I will go with you. I just hope that we can do some good."

"I'm confident we can," Joanne replied.

They went back in the lounge to join the others. Sam whispered to Joanne, "Everything okay?" She just winked at him and commented on the lack of wine. They all had a good laugh, but Joanne got her way.

Abbey called Jake and told him that she would have to meet him later than arranged because she was going to see her mother on Saturday afternoon. He wished her luck and was pleased that she was taking the first step toward mending bridges.

"By the way," he said, "I have sorted some of my clothes, but I will need your input for what else to take."

"I love you," were his last words.

The four of them sat for awhile talking about everything but Maggie. They stayed away from that subject so not to upset Abbey.

Abbey did not sleep that well. She kept thinking of how her mother had changed over the past few months. She understood her concerns over how quick she got engaged to Jake, but could not understand why she disliked him.

Jake was a kind, gentle person and Abbey had no idea she would fall in love so quickly with him, but she was glad that she had. Life without Jake now would be devastating.

Her father Sam had always been supportive and even he had no idea why her mother had reacted in such a manner.

On the Saturday morning, Abbey awoke from a fretful sleep. She was frightened of how the day would go, but she had to try and make peace with her mother.

Abbey called her Aunt Jennie in St. John as arranged to give details of her arrival time. Her aunt was pleased to hear from her and explained that they would meet them on St. Thomas at the dock by the ferry, but would not divulge why. They had always made their own way to St. John.

Aunt Jennie told her, "We have a surprise for you, please wait and see."

Abbey, along with Joanne and her father, arrived at the clinic at noon. Sam went in to see Maggie first while they waited outside.

Joanne noticed that Abbey was shaking and held her hand. She whispered to her, "Be strong and I know things will be okay."

When her father emerged from the room, he looked at Abbey and said, "Your mother would like to see you."

As she entered her mother's room, she burst into tears. She had never seen her look so pale. Maggie beckoned her over and held her tightly.

"I'm sorry baby," she cried. "I'm so sorry. Please forgive me. I have been so stupid. I did not mean any of those horrible things I said to you."

Abbey laid her head on her mother's shoulder.

"Of course I forgive you. I love you."

They were now both crying. Her mother wiped the tears from Abbey's eyes.

"Thank you," she replied. "I needed to hear that from you more than anything."

Abbey sat up and looked into her mother's eyes. She could tell that she meant every word.

"I love you Abbey and I always will. When I'm better, I promise to be a better mother ... I promise."

She completely shocked Abbey with her next statement.

"I need to ask a huge favour of you. Please, it's very important."

"Ask away," Abbey said. "If I can do it, I will."

Her mother looked at her and said, "I need to talk to Jake. I will understand if he doesn't want to talk to me, and I would not blame him. I have been really horrible to him."

Abbey held her mother tightly. They both had tears again.

"I need to apologize to him. I realize now baby, how much you love him, and I know he loves you. Do you remember that night he was in Connecticut? When you came home from having dinner with Simon, the first thing you did was ask if anyone had phoned. I lied to you. Jake did phone and he sounded very concerned. I knew you had words and it helped in my scheme, but I see now I was totally wrong about him. I hope one day he can find it in his heart to forgive me for being such a bitch."

Abbey kissed her mother and promised to talk to Jake later that day. She left the room so that Joanne could take her turn. She sat outside with her father and told him everything that she had discussed with her mother. Sam was relieved and thanked his daughter.

"She needs you Abbey," he said. "I think she needs you more than ever now."

Sam was feeling the strain. It took him back all those years ago when Heather died. It was if it was happening again. He needed to be strong for Maggie and for the second time in his life – he felt it was his fault.

Abbey could tell there was something wrong. She could see the tears in his eyes. She held onto him and promised to help all she could.

"Do you want me to cancel going to St. John for Christmas and stay home?"

He assured her that was not necessary. "Go and have a wonderful time."

After Abbey dropped Joanne and her father home, she drove straight to Jake's. She ran to his apartment, forgetting she had a key she rang his doorbell. When Jake opened the door, she flung her arms around his neck. She was trembling. He kissed her and asked how it went.

They sat on the sofa and Abbey gave Jake a full break down on the conversation with her mother.

"So it went really well. I'm pleased for you," he replied. "And if you want, I will go with you to see her. She needs support from everyone, and I will do it for you because I love you."

She kissed him gently. "Thank you darling. We can go tomorrow before lunch and then you can treat me to ribs at Charlie Browns. I need ribs desperately."

Their gentle kissing then turned to real passion and within a few minutes they were making love on the rug in front of the fire. The radio was playing soft rock in the background and when they had finished, they lay back. Suddenly, Jake burst out laughing. The song playing on the radio at that exact moment was *'Dr. Hook'* singing *'When your body's had enough of me and I'm laying right out on the floor. When you think I've loved you all I can, I'm gonna love you a little bit more.'* Abbey cuddled into him and told him she was so looking forward to St. John. She could not wait to get there.

Jake kissed her on the nose, and reminded her that she had to help him finish packing tomorrow.

"I'm sorry," he said, "but I'm not very good with suitcases."

Abbey smiled at him and said, "You know Jake, I am so glad I fell in love with you."

He looked at her and told her, "Abbey, I fell in love with you the moment I laid eyes on you." Jake kissed her nose again and said, "Come on, I need to be fed. I'm starving. How about Chinese?"

"Lovely," she replied.

On the Sunday morning, the first thing Jake did was give his neighbour a key, and then he informed Monica that the Real Estate agent might pop in if she has any showings.

"She has a key," he told her, "but if you could keep an eye on the apartment, I promise to bring you back a huge present."

"You don't have to," she replied, "but it would be nice."

Abbey wished her a merry Christmas and gave Monica her present.

Then they drove to the clinic to see Abbey's mother. Jake was very hesitant. He did not let on, that in a strange way, he was a little scared. He did not want to say the wrong thing, as he knew he was not favoured by Maggie.

When they arrived, Joanne was already in the room with Abbey's mother. She had also arrived early. When she emerged, she told them that Maggie was feeling a lot better and was looking forward to seeing them. Jake was still feeling apprehensive, but muttered to himself, *'Nothing ventured, nothing gained.'* He and Abbey walked in.

Maggie greeted them both, kissed Abbey and shook Jake's hand.

"Thank you for coming," she said to him. "I know it could not have been easy for you."

Jake just smiled. While Abbey and her mother talked about their trip to St. John and how Aunt Jennie was looking forward to meeting Jake, she whispered something to Abbey. He did not hear what was said, but she smiled at him and a moment later she left the room.

Maggie asked Jake to sit by her. He hesitated, but complied with her wish.

"I've been a fool Jake," she started. "A damn fool … and I wish to apologize to you in person. You deserve to be treated much better. Jake, I am ashamed at my behaviour toward you and I hope one day you will be able to forgive me."

Jake was quiet for a long time, but then when he did speak, Maggie really listened to him. He found it awkward, but he tried to explain as best he could.

"I love Abbey more than I ever thought possible, and her happiness means everything to me. I could never understand why you did not want our relationship to work. I still don't. All I would like you to do Maggie, is enlighten me. As for my forgiveness … that seems very shallow, because I will marry Abbey with or without your blessing."

She looked at Jake. "I don't blame you for being bitter," she said.

"I'm not bitter," he replied. "I'm confused. I thought your daughter being happy would have been one of the most important issues in any mother's life. Instead, you made her unhappy you were really cruel to her. That Maggie is something only Abbey can forgive."

"Jake, I was blinded by my own stupidity. I did not want your relationship to work, because I wanted Abbey to have everything that was possible – which I have to admit did not include you. I had it in my head that she would be far better off with Simon Brady. Jake, I was totally wrong. I see now that the most important person in her life is you." She paused before continuing.

"Now that I have come to my senses, I can see now why she picked you and I'm glad she did. You are obviously the right guy for my daughter, and I promise never to cause any more grief. I hope one day we can become friends."

"Only time will tell Maggie," Jake replied. "Only time will tell. Abbey loves you dearly, and I hope I never see her as upset as she was that day you laid into her. Get well Maggie and let's take everything one day at a time."

Jake left the room and bumped into Sam. He was anxious to know how it had gone. Jake explained that it was definitely better, and that he and Maggie understood each other a lot more than they did before.

Abbey went back in to say goodbye to her mother. She hoped she would have a nice Christmas, and would call her from St. John. She kissed her mother and as she turned to leave Maggie held her arm.

"Abbey," she said, "Jake is a lot more of a man than I gave him credit for. In his own way, he told me off for the way I have been acting. I certainly admire that. Now, you have a nice holiday and I will see you when you get back."

They said their goodbyes to everyone and Jake drove Abbey straight to Charlie Browns, as promised.

"Now you can get your fix of ribs."

She kissed him and they walked into the restaurant arm in arm.

Over lunch, Abbey tried to find out what had been said between Jake and her mother. He explained nicely that her mother had asked for his forgiveness, and that she admitted trying her best to sabotage their relationship, so that she could end up with Simon.

Abbey smiled at him. "Jake, he could not take your place in a million years."

He then went on and told her that at last her mother had seen the light, and realized that they were meant for each other. Abbey leaned across the table and kissed him.

"Yes, we are," she whispered. "Yes, we are."

Chapter 13

They flew out of Newark at 8:30 a.m. for St. Thomas and changed flights in Miami, eventually arriving at their destination at 4:20 p.m. They took a taxi from the airport in Charlotte Amalie to the ferry dock. Jennie and Richard were waiting patiently.

Abbey hugged her aunt and introduced them to Jake. They all shook hands and then they were shown Aunt Jennie's new toy. Abbey was shocked.

"So this is your surprise. Wow! It's lovely and the name is fantastic."

Knowing her aunt so well, Abbey knew exactly why it was called, *'In My World'*.

"That's definitely a nice boat," Jake commented.

"Thank you," Richard replied. Then he asked Jake if he knew anything about boats.

"No sir," said Jake, "but it sure looks like a beauty."

Then Richard told Jake, "If you like, while you are here, I can teach you."

Jake was amazed on the ride to the Island of St. John. *'It's really nice in this part of the world,'* he thought to himself. He felt a little uncomfortable with people he did not know.

Abbey snuggled into him and rubbed his cheek.

"It is paradise here Jake. It really is."

He kissed her on the nose and said, "I believe you darling. It is something else."

Aunt Jennie watched them very closely, and nudged her husband and whispered, "Look, do you see how happy they are?"

Richard responded quietly, "Yes, it shows."

When they pulled into the harbour at Cruz Bay, Jake could not believe his eyes.

"Holy mackerel!" he exclaimed and looked at Abbey. "I have never seen a prettier place. I really haven't."

Then he drove them to the cottage. As they lived on a public beach, they were not allowed a jetty of their own, so the boat had to be moored in the harbour. Jake knew as soon as they pulled in the driveway that he would like staying here.

Aunt Jennie had made up their room. Abbey was a little surprised that they were allowed to share a room, but her aunt explained, "I'm not a prude and I know that you came here for a holiday and to spend time with each other, I have no intention of stopping, or standing in the way of two people that love each other."

Jake and Abbey had a wonderful time over the next few days. Richard and Jennie took them everywhere. He taught Jake how to handle the boat. He learned very quickly, which impressed Richard. On Christmas day, they had roast turkey on the patio, with glorious sunshine. They could not keep Jake out of the pool. He swam and swam, and could not get enough of the water.

He and Abbey also swam in the bay. Jake was surprised at the warmth of the water. They made sand castles and acted just like a couple of kids. All the time Aunt Jennie watched over them, she was impressed with Jake and was so happy that her niece had found the right man.

She would talk to her husband while in bed, and he agreed that he liked Jake a lot.

"He's a fine young man," he commented to his wife. "In some ways, I think Abbey is the lucky one to have found someone so caring."

"Yes," Jennie added, "he seems to have a very sensitive side to him, but I'm so glad my sister has come to her senses. That must be a great relief to Abbey. She seems a lot happier now than the last time I spoke to her back in Rockaway."

Abbey and Jake would lie on the sand and relax. He had never really had a holiday. When the summer break would come, he always spent it by the lake at home with his friends. This was so different, so tranquil. No wonder Abbey called it paradise

when she had told Jake all about herself back in the early days of their relationship. St. John was always her favourite place to be. He could now see for himself what she meant.

He was complimentary on just how Jennie and Richard had made him so welcome.

"I feel like one of the family already," he said, "and your aunt is so different to your mother, and I don't mean that in a nasty way. It's just that she seems so easy going."

"She has had a different life to my mother," Abbey said. "Not so much pressure in certain ways."

She was still a little apprehensive talking about her mother.

While they were on holiday, they had made love every night – even once one evening late on the beach. They were in the corner right by the picket fence. Jake took off her bathing suit. He loved to look at her naked body. He caressed her breasts and ran his tongue all over her, she responded by playing with him, and then they made love. The sound of the ocean and the thought that they could be seen seemed to spur them on, though deep down Jake was worried that someone might walk by. Richard and Jennie had gone shopping in St. Thomas and not long after they had enjoyed each other, Abbey spotted their boat pulling into Cruz Bay.

"I think we timed that just right," she said to Jake.

"Yes," he agreed. "Another few minutes and we would have been caught with our pants down." They laughed.

The following day, Jake insisted that they go for dinner to a nice restaurant. It would be his treat to thank both Jennie and Richard for their hospitality. They had a wonderful evening consisting of lobster and quite a few bottles of wine.

Jake found the pair of them fascinating. They shared their stories of life on the Island. Richard retold tales from his memories of his time as Police Chief and some of the criminal characters that he had come across over the years. And finally, Jennie's business acumen with her successful acquisition of the shop and how well it had done.

There was a lot of talk about the wedding and where it would be. Abbey informed her aunt that she had booked their local church for June, but every other detail she wanted to sort out with mum and dad. That would have to wait till she got back to Rockaway to see how her mother's health had improved. Abbey had spoken to her parents on the phone and all seemed well. Her mother was now home and according to her father, she was much better. Jennie was pleased at the news and would call her sister the following day. The same day Jake and Abbey were leaving.

Abbey sat with her aunt on the patio having coffee. The men were still asleep. "Too much wine," her aunt told her. They chuckled. Abbey told her aunt about her contract with her school. It had ended the previous Friday, but there was good news on the horizon. One of the older teachers was retiring in April and Nora, who was very tight with the Principal, had informed Abbey that she was the front runner for his position.

She would be informed if and when she had secured a permanent position. She was keeping her fingers crossed because she really liked working at the school. The staff was all terrific and being so close to home was a bonus.

Her aunt asked how Jake had handled the situation with Abbey's mother. She could not give a definitive answer, as he had not opened up that much after their talk. He had told Abbey that since her mother had tried to break them apart, he still did not trust her too much.

The men appeared much the worse for wear. Jake needed coffee badly. The last time he felt as bad as this was back in Connecticut, which were memories he would sooner forget. Richard was also feeling it, but he managed to smile through it and blamed Jennie nicely for trying to get him drunk and take advantage of him. They all burst out laughing.

Abbey kissed Jake good morning and decided she would do the packing, and give him time to gather his thoughts. Jennie asked him if he had any idea when he was moving to the house. Jake replied, "As soon as I get back to town, I will start packing all my belongings. I expect the apartment to go soon, as there had been quite a bit of interest."

On the boat ride to St. Thomas, Abbey was very quiet. When Jake inquired if there was a problem, she informed him she never liked leaving St. John because she always felt good on the island. He immediately knew why, and reminded her that they would be back for their honeymoon. Just hearing those few kind words was enough to cheer her up.

When they arrived in St. Thomas, they said their goodbyes on the dock. Both Jennie and Abbey hugged each other with tears in their eyes.

Richard said to Jake, "They have always been close, more like mother and daughter." He shook hands with Jake, and informed him that it was a real pleasure having met him.

Jake replied, "Likewise."

Jennie let go of Abbey and asked Jake to make sure he took care of her. He promised her he would. She also asked him to try and be kind to her sister, because that was very important to Abbey. He smiled and kissed her on the cheek.

"I will," he replied. "I will."

They then took the taxi to the airport for their flight home.

When they arrived in Newark, the bitter cold hit them immediately. Daniel was waiting to take them home. He was really pleased that they had a good break from the winter, because it had been very cold. Jake also noticed that there was a lot of snow on the ground.

"Yes," Daniel informed him, "it snowed for almost two days."

They dropped Abbey home first.

Jake held her and whispered, "Thank you for the lovely time in paradise."

He told her he would call her later. He did not want to say goodbye, but there were a lot of loose ends he had to tie up with the apartment and work. Abbey understood and kissed him. Sam appeared with Simon to help Abbey with her luggage.

"Nice to see you again Jake."

"Thank you sir. We had a lovely time."

Simon shook hands with Jake. "I hear you had Christmas dinner by the pool."

"Yes," Jake replied a bit shaken that he would be at Abbey's house, but he did not say anything.

Daniel dropped Jake at his apartment and drove straight home to see his wife and daughter.

Jake had a lot of messages on his answer machine. The most important was the Real Estate agent's happy voice with two offers on his apartment, and would he call as soon as possible.

He thought it a bit late, so he would call her in the morning. Jake felt uneasy. In the back of his mind, he was plagued with thought as to why Simon would be at Abbey's. He tried to block it out, but for some unknown reason, it kept bothering at him.

Later that evening, he called Abbey. She came to the phone still laughing.

"Sorry Jake, but we were listening to some stories and jokes from Simon. mum's a lot better and she can now stay home. She actually asked after you when I got back."

Jake arranged to have dinner the following evening and she would drive over to his apartment around seven. He hung up the phone, and again that uneasy feeling about Simon was there.

All his other messages were from work, so they too could be sorted tomorrow. He was tired after the long journey and decided to have an early night. He did not eat supper, but settled for a cup of coffee and a cookie. As he lay in his bed, he missed Abbey, and thought to himself, *'I will have to get used to being alone until we are married.'* The next thing that hit him was the alarm going off, for all his niggling doubts he still slept like a baby.

He made his morning cuppa and set about answering his calls. The Real Estate agent informed him they were both genuine offers and that neither party had a property to sell, so should she go ahead and close the deal. Jake agreed, and asked her to keep him informed. He showered and went into the office.

Abbey had spent the previous evening with her family, Joanne, Andrew and Simon. He had helped Sam bring her home from the clinic and had stayed for supper. Maggie was feeling much better and needed company. She was so glad to see Abbey that you would not have guessed any bad feeling had ever existed. She and Abbey laughed at Simon's humorous stories from his past and it seemed to Abbey that her mother was back to normal, for which she was in her own way, very grateful.

Joanne and Andrew were heading back to St. John in the morning and Simon had graciously offered to drive them to New York where they had booked a flight to St. Thomas. Joanne had taken a liking to Simon. She found him to be charming, amusing and helpful. In a way, she understood why Maggie had so wanted Abbey and him to hook up, but it was not to be. Then again, being an author, she said to herself. *'You never know what's around the corner.'*

Abbey had gone to bed dreaming of St. John. She loved it so much. It was a different world there. She hoped one day to live on the island, and be near her favourite aunt.

Simon had gone home to Nancy. He apologized for being late, but she did not mind at all. When he explained that Abbey and Jake arrived home while he was there —she loved it, because she knew Jake would not have liked the idea. Nancy had put another piece to her puzzle, and whispered to herself, *'Thank you Simon.'*

The following evening Abbey drove to Jake's apartment. She was looking forward to having dinner with him. He asked her what she would like to eat, her reply was simple – *you.* She undid his zipper and started caressing him. Jake gently undressed her. He kissed and licked her entire body, taking his time and nearly bringing her to a climax. He leaned her against the wall, lifted her legs and in one thrust – entered her. They rode back and forth until they came together. After they were finished, they stood there locked together for ages not wanting to untangle.

Jake gently kissed her and whispered, "That was absolutely the most enjoyable sex I have ever experienced."

They took a shower together. He washed her back caressed her breasts and they started all over again. Abbey straddled him and the lovemaking began, and again they both took it slowly to try and make it last forever.

When they were both exhausted, they walked to the Chinese restaurant. It was really cold, but they did not seem to mind. Jake almost ate everything on the menu, he was so hungry. Abbey smiled at him and made a comment.

"So what made you so hungry?"

"You did," he said, winking.

Abbey decided to stay the night and for the first time they went to bed extremely tired. They cuddled and as soon as their heads hit the pillow they were asleep.

The following morning Abbey helped Jake with some packing. He had obtained a huge amount of boxes from the company that was going to move him. He had a lot of junk to throw out, but had decided to keep his furniture and dispose of his mother's, as his was more modern.

Nora and Leo had arranged for Jake's mother's furniture to be picked up by a local charity that helped the less fortunate. Everything went, apart from a few special items that Jake wanted to keep, the grandfather clock and pictures, his mother had in her lifetime obtained some nice original oil paintings - no one that well known, but very collectible.

Abbey decided to go home and spend some time with her mother as she was now on her own. Joanne and Andrew were leaving this morning, so she wanted to say goodbye and thank them for their help.

When she arrived home, Simon's car was in her driveway. Andrew was helping with the luggage.

"Good morning Abbey," Simon said when he saw her. "And how are you this fine cold day?"

"I'm feeling great," she replied. "You are kind to run them into New York."

"I don't mind," answered Simon. "I have to go into the Big Apple anyway on business, so this kills two birds with one stone."

Abbey said her goodbyes and went and sat with her mother in the lounge.

"You are looking so much better," she told her.

"Thank you dear," Maggie said. "I have not felt better in years. Is everything okay with Jake?"

Abbey assured her it was.

"I'm really glad," her mother said. "I tried to apologize to him over my conduct, but he seemed a bit put off with me. I can't say I blame him. He was the at the forefront of my stupid meddling. It really is nice to see you Abbey, and I promise never to come between you and Jake again."

She kissed her mother. "It's done mum. It's finished. Let's not bring the subject up again. I just want you back." Her mother hugged her.

The sold sign had gone up at the apartment complex. Jake was pleased it sold so quickly. He had three weeks to move out before the new owners took possession. He drove over to his mother's house. He still called it that, even though he spent most of his life there.

He was amazed at how big it was with the furniture removed. He did not have enough to fill the house, but his thoughts went to Abbey. They could go out together and choose whatever else they needed to make it their home. He liked that idea immensely. It would be as much fun as when he moved into his apartment. Elizabeth had helped him then, but now he had his Abbey.

Nancy was working very hard, and her father rewarded her by handing more clients over to her.

"She has the knack," he told his wife. "She knows just how to get orders. It's amazing! Another year and she should be able to take over all the business and we can start to enjoy more freedom."

His wife liked that idea.

Because she worked for her father, Nancy found that she had a lot of free time on her hands. When Simon mentioned to her that Sam and Maggie had talked about going to St. John in January, he thought it would be a good idea. He wanted to buy a condo or cottage, so that he and Nancy could spend some time away from the horrible winters.

Nancy said it was a great idea, and hoped that Abbey would go with her mother. Simon said he did not know if that would happen, but he would suggest it to Sam.

"I mean," he explained, "she is not working for a while until she gets a proper teaching position at the school and what I gather is that won't happen until April when the other teacher retires."

When Simon returned from New York, Nancy asked Simon who had accepted his invitations to the New Years Eve party.

"Well…" he said, "there are you and me, Daniel and Elizabeth, Sam and Maggie if she is well enough, and about twenty other people from work."

Nancy suggested they ask Jake and Abbey. He thought that was a good idea as he had overlooked asking them. He immediately called Abbey at home. She thanked him and accepted without asking Jake – *'She would love to go'.*

Nancy was pleased. She was about to set the wheels in motion. *'Soon,'* she said to herself. *'Very soon, I will get my revenge. I can't wait to see their faces when I pull it off.'*

Jake and Abbey had words when she phoned him with the news of the party. He thought he should have been asked first. Abbey told him not to be so stubborn, but again that nagging feeling came back to haunt

Jake. *'Why is it,'* he said to himself, *'only Simon can make me feel this way over Abbey?'*

As he put down the phone, he though it was ironic that the background music playing was *'Dr. Hook'* singing, *'When you're in love with a beautiful woman you watch their eyes. When you're in love with a beautiful woman, you look for lies.'*

Jake had to somehow come to terms with his insecurity over his relationship with Abbey. He loved her beyond words, yet somehow he still doubted her. He knew he was being foolish, but could not explain to himself why.

Though Jake was reluctant to go to Simon's bash, he picked up Abbey and her parents. On the drive, he thought to himself, *'Maybe Maggie would not stay long,'* which suited him completely. He did not say anything to Abbey because she was still angry with him over his reaction to the invitation.

There were a lot of cars in the driveway, but it was big enough to accommodate them all. Jake parked for a quick getaway if needed. Nancy greeted them at the door and ushered them in quickly out of the cold. She kissed Jake on the cheek and said how nice it was to see him again. She was also very pleasant to Abbey. The party was in full swing, people were dancing, and the food was out of this world. Nancy mentioned that Simon had the caterers do all the preparation for this evening.

Simon came over and greeted them. He gave Abbey and Maggie a kiss on the cheek and shook hands with Jake and Sam.

"Welcome to my home," he said. This was Jake's the first time, but Abbey had been here on a number of occasions when she was a teenager.

Simon asked Abbey to dance and she readily accepted. She liked dancing with Simon because they both had a passion for it. Nancy took Jake's arm and showed him the house. When they returned, Abbey was still dancing and Nancy could tell by the look on Jake's face that it was not sitting well. She loved the thought and watched him out of the corner of her eye.

When Abbey returned to Jake's side, she was out of breath.

"That was wonderful," she told him.

Jake remained civil and commented what great dancers they were, but inside he was eaten away with jealousy. He was not a dancer. Sometimes, he wished he had learned.

Abbey really enjoyed the party – so did Nancy. She watched everything like a hawk, but stayed in the background. Even when Simon asked her to dance, she made an excuse that she had a slight headache and told him he would be better off dancing with Abbey and much to Jake's annoyance he did. When Maggie decided that she was tired, Jake said he would run her home. Sam insisted they get a taxi, but Jake would not hear of it. To his utter dismay, Abbey decided to stay and enjoy herself. The only one this pleased – was Nancy.

"It's okay Jake," she said to him, "we will look after her."

Abbey asked Jake if he would come back and pick her up, but he declined, saying he was tired.

"Please yourself," she said. Then she turned, walked away from him and immediately danced with Simon.

Jake felt tortured, but realized that it was his own fault for being such a jerk. Abbey did not want him to go, but since he was, she at least wanted him to come back for her so they could bring in the New Year – their first together. When Jake left, Abbey went to the washroom. She was upset and had to dry her eyes.

Nancy was overjoyed. It was wonderful to see them fight. She loved it and would make sure it would continue, and get worse.

As he was dropping Sam and Maggie, she turned to him. What she said surprised him.

"Jake, go back for Abbey and be by her side for midnight. It's important. She wants to be with you. Please … I'm asking you. She loves you Jake. Swallow some of that stubborn pride of yours. If you love her like I'm led to believe … go back."

Maggie got out of the car. Jake sat there taking in her advice.

Jake came to his senses and drove back to Simon's. He had listened to Maggie and what she said made a lot of sense. He was just being awkward. As soon as he arrived, he headed straight to Abbey who was seated on one of the sofas. He immediately apologized to her for being a stubborn idiot. She flung her arms around his neck and thanked him for realizing how hurt she was when he left. She asked him to dance with her.

"I'll try," he said, "but if I step on your toes … just slap me."

It was the first time they had laughed that evening.

Nancy was not happy when she saw Jake had returned. Her ego was deflated.

'Damn it!' she said to herself. *'This is not what I had in mind. I will have to try and throw a wrench in the works another way.'*

Midnight came and the party erupted in song. Jake kissed Abbey and promised he would not act like this again. Everybody did the rounds wishing all a Happy New Year. Simon could not find Nancy. She had gone upstairs. When he did find her, she was crying. He held her and tried to find out if she had a problem. She lied and told him she did not feel well, and asked if he would explain to the guests why she was not there.

Jake drove Abbey home. She wanted to see her mother and make sure everything was okay. He told her that it was her mother that had convinced him he was being childish. She kissed him goodnight and said she was so glad he came back, and that she would call him in the morning.

He drove home feeling stupid, and could tell by the way Abbey looked at him she was not impressed with his behaviour. Even though he had gone back for her, there was an undertone in the way she spoke to him.

Chapter 14

On New Years Day, Abbey and her parents were in deep discussion over her sister's phone call inviting them to St. John for a break. Jennie thought the warm weather would help her sister recuperate, and Sam had agreed he would arrange with Simon for a couple of weeks vacation later in January.

Jennie also wanted Abbey to come back to stay, as at the moment she was not working. Maggie and Sam thought this was a great idea to be together again as a family. Abbey agreed she would travel with them. When her mother asked if she wanted to talk to Jake about it first, Abbey's reply was, *'No, I do not need his permission.'* Maggie did not ask any more questions, in case it looked like she was interfering.

Jake spent the day packing. He wanted to move all the small stuff himself. He had arranged the moving company for Monday morning that way he could get back to work Tuesday.

Abbey had not called him as promised. He started to worry a little that maybe he had really upset her last evening, so he called. Maggie answered the phone and wished him a Happy New Year. Then she put him on with Abbey. He immediately apologized again for his behaviour the previous evening and she told him *'it was water under the bridge, and not to worry about it.'* She also informed him that she would be going to St. John with her parents, so she could give her mother support. Jake did not like the idea, but said nothing to upset her again. Instead, he lied and told her what a good daughter she was.

Abbey informed him that she would stay home that day, as she was not feeling that well and that she would call him tomorrow. When she had awoken that morning, she felt sick and had thrown up. She thought she might be coming down with something and not long after talking with Jake, she went back to bed.

Jake visited Elizabeth and Daniel later in the day – just for some company. He was a bit down. Elizabeth could tell, but decided to not go there. She knew he could sometimes be moody.

He ate supper with them and went back to his apartment. Again, he did not see Nancy watching, but seeing him come home alone gave her a high. She went home to Simon, knowing that now was the time to hatch her plan and she knew that this time it would work.

The next two weeks, Abbey and Jake did not see a lot of each other as he was busy at work and arranging the house. She did go and help, but the sickness she felt every morning was getting her down. She had had enough and decided to go the doctor who did all the tests and took blood, just in case she had a virus.

On Sunday the 12th, they spent the day together as Abbey was leaving Tuesday for St. John. There had been no sex between them for two weeks. This had worried Jake, but Abbey said she did not feel like making love. They had supper together in the house for the first time. Jake had made a roast, because it was so cold, though Abbey did not each very much. Later that evening, Jake drove her home and kissed her goodbye. She promised to call him from St. John later that week, as the next day she would be packing and helping her mother. She also had another appointment with her doctor, which she did not mention to Jake.

Nancy and Simon were also having words. He had arranged to travel down to St. John with Sam and family. Nancy had agreed to go with him, but she informed him that she could not go as her father had arranged a trip to Boston to see a new client and insisted that she go with him. Simon was unhappy, but he believed her story completely and was sorry that they could not be together. He was going to propose to her on the island.

On the Monday evening, Jake was coming out of the pharmacy when he spotted Abbey and Simon across the road. He was just about to call out when he noticed Simon had his hands on her shoulder. As he continued to watch, they hugged each other, and then he saw Simon kiss her. He turned and walked away. He was devastated. 'What the hell was going on?'

He did not call Abbey that evening for an explanation. Instead, he just brooded like a twelve-year old. Although she had phoned and left him a message to give her a call, he was too annoyed to call her back.

Tuesday morning, Simon drove into Sam's driveway. They were waiting for him, all packed and ready to go. Abbey had not told her parents what the doctor had said. She wanted to wait until she had spoken to Aunt Jennie first. She wanted advice on the best way to let them know she was pregnant. The only person who knew was Simon, and that was by accident. He just happened to share the same clinic, though he had a different doctor, and had gone to get a repeat prescription for his inhaler as now and again he had the odd asthmatic attack. Abbey had bumped into him coming out of the clinic. She needed to tell someone and his friendly face was there at the right time and place. This was what Jake had witnessed – Simon congratulating her.

Abbey was concerned that Jake had not contacted her. She had left another message, but with no response.

Jake had paced the floor all night not knowing which way to turn. He had not called Abbey because he felt betrayed. He knew Simon had always liked her, but it was intolerable to see him kiss and hug her like that.

He called Simon at home that evening, but no reply. He took a chance and called Nancy at her parents. She told Jake she needed to talk with him and arranged to meet him for coffee and she would explain. After she hung up the phone, she was thrilled. *'Now,'* she said to herself, *'play it properly and you have succeeded.'*

When Nancy walked in, Jake could tell she was upset.

"What is it?" he asked. She was hesitant. "I don't know how to tell you this Jake, but Simon dumped me. He told me there was someone else in his life and asked me to move out."

Of course, the whole thing was a complete fabrication, but Jake believed every word.

"Where is he now?" Jake asked.

"He's gone to St. John with Abbey and her family."

Jake was stunned. He could not control the shaking that came over him.

"What are you saying Nancy ... that Abbey is seeing him behind my back?"

"I guess so," she replied and started to cry.

Jake could not console her. At that moment, he could not do anything.

"When did he ask you to move out?"

She told him, "New Years Day."

She did not mention to Jake that Simon had told her Abbey was pregnant. She did not know if Jake even knew. She played her game well very well. Jake said he had to go – and left.

Nancy could not believe her luck. Everything had fallen into place without having to do too much. Tonight she would celebrate with a good meal and a few drinks. She started to laugh and said to herself, *'Jake ... it's payback time.'*

Jake drove around in a daze for hours. He believed Nancy. Why would she lie about something like that? He could tell she was upset at being treated so badly by Simon. He had to decide what to do. He did not sleep that night and the following morning he decided to call Brady Industries. He knew the secretary, Linda. They had been in the same classes at school, and he knew she was not one to keep secrets.

"Hi Linda. It's Jake Faulkner."

"How are you Jake? We haven't spoken in years."

"Yes," he said. "It's nice to hear your voice again." Though really, he did not care. "Can I speak to Simon?" he asked.

"No. Sorry Jake. He's on vacation with his girlfriend."

"Oh!" Jake exclaimed. "Really? Has he gone anywhere nice?"

"Yes," she replied. "I shouldn't tell you this. He likes to keep his private life away from the office, but because it's you … I don't see why not. He's gone to St. John in the Virgin Islands."

Jake slammed down the receiver.

He went into the office and quit on the spot. The Manager tried to talk with him, but Jake would not listen. He was enraged and his anger was getting the better of him. He put all his files on the desk and walked out. He had not eaten now in two days. All he did was drink coffee. He started to shake again. He tried his best to pull himself together, but it did not work. He went home and sat there in the dark with his head in his hands.

He fell asleep on the sofa and did not wake until late the next morning. He decided to call St. John. He disguised his voice when Jennie answered and he asked to speak with Simon. She did not put her hand over the phone, so Jake was able to hear each word clearly.

"Richard is Simon around?" He heard Sam answer. "No. He's out with Abbey." Those words were the final nail in his coffin. Jake gently put the phone down before Jennie could tell him herself.

Jake's life was suddenly in utter turmoil. He had quit his job. He had lost the woman he loved, and was in a state of total exhaustion. He packed his suitcase, called all the utility companies and went next door to give Leo a key to the house. Nora was at school. Jake explained that he was going away for a while and asked if he would mind keeping an eye on the house. Leo tried to find out what was wrong, but could get nowhere.

Then Jake drove to Daniel's garage and told him what had happened, but even he could not console Jake.

"Are you sure?" he said to him. "Maybe the wires just got crossed."

Jake assured him he had checked thoroughly, even phoning St. John for conformation. Daniel was stunned.

"Jake, come and stay with us for a while."

Jake declined.

"I have to get away buddy," he said, "but if you don't hear from me for a while, don't panic. I won't do anything stupid."

While he was busy talking to Daniel, his phone rang at home. It was Abbey trying to contact him, but to no avail.

She had been frantic worrying why he had not been in touch. The phone just kept ringing, and even the answering machine was off.

"Where are you Jake? Where are you?"

She was even more worried now. She sat there.

Simon had gone to look at some properties for sale and her father decided to go with him. She had gone the day before, but it had tired her out.

"Penny for your thoughts?" Aunt Jennie said. She had come in from the pool and saw Abbey sitting there with a strange look on her face.

"I can't get hold of Jake," she replied. "I don't know where he can be. He has not answered his phone in days."

"Have you tried him at work?" Jennie suggested.

So Abbey called the office, and asked to speak to Jake. The Manager informed her that Jake no longer worked there. Abbey was stunned.

"What is it?" her aunt asked Abbey. "Why are you crying?"

She explained that Jake had quit his job and she did not know what was going on.

"I'm sure there's a simple explanation," her aunt assured her. "Don't worry about it. When you do speak with him, he will tell you the whole story."

Then Abbey blurted it out. "I'm pregnant Aunt Jennie. I had it confirmed the day before I came here."

"Oh my God!"

Jennie was shocked, but she was happy for her. She hugged her niece.

"What was Jake's reaction?"

"He does not know. I couldn't get hold of him to give him the news."

"Have you told your mother?"

"Not yet. I wanted to speak with you first. With her not being well and all, I wanted to wait."

"I understand," Jennie said. "Maybe it would be best to wait until she is back to normal. Talk to your dad. He is very understanding."

Abbey said she would.

Her mother was seated on the patio in the sunshine. Abbey joined her.

"How are you feeling today mum?"

"I feel very good," she replied. "It's very relaxing here and I am so glad you came with us. It's nice being a family again."

"Yes mum, it is."

She did not let her mother see she was upset.

Later that day she managed to get some time alone with her father. She told him the whole story. He was not upset, but he was concerned about Jake.

"What is he doing Abbey? Did he mention he had a different job?"

"No," she replied. "I just don't know what's going on with him."

"Don't worry," he assured his daughter. "I'm sure you will get it sorted when we get back. That's if he does not call you first, which I'm sure he will, when he has something to say."

Simon was staying at the nearby hotel, and had been invited to dinner by Jennie and Richard. Not a word was spoken about Abbey and her pregnancy, though Jennie did inform her husband in bed that night. Richard was quite shocked.

"Well I'll be," he said. "Who would have thought that Abbey and Jake did not take precautions?"

The following morning Abbey tried again to reach Jake, but still no word on where he was or what he was doing. She felt sick, not because of the baby, she just felt something was really wrong.

Nancy called on Jake, but he was not at home. Leo saw her through his kitchen window and walked over.

"Waste of time knocking," he said. "Jake isn't there. He has gone away for a few days."

"Do you know where?" she asked.

"I haven't a clue," Leo informed her. "He would not tell me where he was going."

Nancy thanked him and drove off.

'Yes, yes, yes!' she said to herself. *'It worked. It has finally worked.'* Her smile was as big as a house.

Jake had been driving all night. He had crossed the border into Canada that morning. His first stop was Kingston. He took a hotel room, ate some food and slept. He stayed around the town for a couple of days then drove up to Ottawa where he booked into a hotel room overlooking the Parliament Buildings.

Meanwhile, on St. John, Abbey was beside herself with worry. She had called Jake's home and the phone was dead, the number was no longer in service. She decided to call Nora at home. She told Abbey exactly what Leo had related to her that Jake had left town for a while and they did not know how to contact him. Abbey broke down when her mother asked what was wrong. She told her everything. Maggie held her daughter like she had not done in years and they cried together. Jennie got Richard to get in touch with the police in New Jersey to see if they could find out anything. They assured him they would investigate as a favour to a former police officer.

They were very quick with their response. Jake had left town and they did not know where he had gone, but they would continue to try and find where he was.

Abbey wanted to go home, but her aunt did not think that was the answer.

"Let Jake sort out his demons," she said, "and then maybe everything will be fine."

Simon phoned Nancy to see if she had heard anything. She lied and told him she did not know anything.

Jake visited all the clubs. He got drunk a few times, ended up sleeping with a few girls though for the life of him he could not remember their names. He went to the American Embassy and applied for a work visa. He did not need the money, but he did not want to go back to Rockaway. He wanted to start a new life somewhere different. He knew he had to come to terms with losing Abbey, but most nights he cried himself to sleep. He missed her more than he thought was possible. This tragedy hurt him even more than losing his mother. He hated to admit that, but it did. On his way to Canada he had stopped at the grave to tell his mum and dad what he was doing and how much hurt he felt over Abbey. He hoped they understood that he had no choice but to leave or go completely insane. He told them that he believed it was his fault Abbey had gone off with Simon. *'I acted like a child,'* he said, *'and now I have to pay.'*

He picked up his visa from the Embassy, it only took a few days and started going to every financial institute looking for work. It was a good economy at that time and he was sure he would find a position. His resume was excellent, and within a week he had been offered positions with three different companies. The one he decided to work for was fairly new, but he liked the idea of starting at the bottom again and perhaps working his way up. His knowledge of the stock market was as good as anyone and he was sure this was the way to go.

Jake rented an apartment overlooking the Rideau Canal. It was small, but furnished, which suited him. He was on the twelfth floor and it gave him a superb view of the Canal, which at the moment was just a very large skating area. He could not believe how many people were on the ice.

He now had an apartment, a job to start and he would adjust to life here as quickly as possible. He needed this to help take away his pain. He thought of Abbey every day. More than he wanted too, but he knew it would take a long time, if not a lifetime. In some ways, he did not want to forget. He knew he would always love her, no matter what she had done.

Abbey and her family arrived home, as soon as she unpacked Abbey drove straight to Daniel's house. Elizabeth was home, but did not want to see her.

"How dare you come here?" she said. "After all you have done."

Abbey was confused.

"What do you mean after all *I* have done?"

Something about her reaction confused Elizabeth and caused her to hesitate a moment.

"Come in," she said gruffly.

They sat in the lounge. The baby was sleeping in the other room. Abbey demanded to know what was going on. Elizabeth immediately reacted by becoming defensive.

"What do you mean what's going on?"

"Where's Jake?" Abbey demanded.

"I honestly don't know," Elizabeth said. "All I know is what Daniel told me. He has left town because of you carrying on with Simon."

Abbey was shocked. "Carrying on with Simon! What the *hell* are you talking about?"

Elizabeth reluctantly relayed to Abbey everything Jake had told Daniel, leaving out nothing. Abbey started to sob. The tears flooded down her cheeks.

"Are you denying it?" Elizabeth asked.

Abbey could not control her emotions, she could not stop crying. Elizabeth was patient and waited until Abbey could speak.

"Of course I'm denying it. I have not and would not ever cheat on Jake. I love him too much to do something so stupid."

A terrible feeling swept through Elizabeth. Maybe it was women's intuition, but whatever it was made her scream, "Nancy … that bitch!"

"What do you mean?" Abbey begged, still sobbing.

Elizabeth was furious. Her entire body trembled in anger. "Nancy was behind all this. I'm certain of it. That rotten, no good scheming witch … she conned Jake into believing everything," she said. "She conned us all."

She stopped to take a breath before explaining farther. "As I mentioned earlier, she told Jake that Simon had dumped her. I guarantee he knows nothing of what has gone on."

Elizabeth called Daniel and asked him to get in touch with Simon.

"And get him to come to the house Daniel," she said. "You are not going to believe what has happened, and I can bet, neither will Simon."

Daniel was baffled, but did as he was asked.

When Simon had arrived home there was no sign of Nancy. He was very puzzled, because all her clothing was gone. He tried calling, but there was no answer, and when the phone did ring it was Daniel, who asked him to come over to his house immediately.

Simon arrived at Daniel's. He was utterly confused, as he did not have a clue what was happening. Elizabeth ushered him into the lounge. Her mother had taken the baby so they could sort out the problems in peace.

Abbey was sitting on the sofa, still in tears. Simon did not like the look of this and asked Daniel to explain. He tried, but found it difficult to do because he did not know where to begin.

Elizabeth had finally composed herself and decided to try explaining the best she could. She gave Simon the whole story that had been related to Daniel by Jake, including the call to Brady Industries and his call to St. John. She told him about Jake hearing that Simon was out with Abbey.

She then asked Simon for an explanation, which he also found difficult to relate. He explained to all of them that he and Nancy had agreed to travel to the island for a short break and to look at properties for sale, as he was in the market for a holiday home.

The reason he was out with Abbey was she had agreed to help him look as Nancy had to stay behind to work. He now realized that was a total lie. He had not and never would go behind somebody's back and cheat. It was difficult, but he confessed to them that while on St. John he was planning to propose to Nancy, because he had fallen in love with her.

Abbey had not said a word. She just sat there in a daze. Elizabeth really felt for her, as she had given Abbey a piece of her mind until she realized out the truth. Daniel was still in shock over what Simon had told him. Nancy had successfully conned all of them. Jake had gone who knows where. Abbey was so stunned about the whole thing that she looked like she would scream at any moment. Even Simon had been betrayed. He could not believe one person could do this much damage, but Nancy had succeeded.

Then Abbey spoke, "Okay, we have all been taken for a ride, but what are we going to do about it? We have to find Jake. He must be in utter turmoil."

"There's also something else you need to know." Abbey went on. "I'm having Jake's baby, and he doesn't know. I could not get hold of him before I left."

The tears were back, but she fought through them. "I love Jake. I always have. Simon has been a good friend, but nothing ever happened between us. I hope you believe that because it's the truth."

Simon nodded his head, and then he said, "Abbey is right. We have to try and find Jake. That is the most important issue at the moment. I will deal with Nancy when I catch up to her."

Elizabeth hugged Abbey, and apologized.

"I'm so sorry for not trusting you," she said. "Please forgive me."

Though Abbey was hurt, she said she understood why they had believed the story.

"Nancy must have been planning to do this all along. I'm sorry Simon." She looked at him. "You did not deserve to be caught in the middle like this."

Then Daniel spoke. "Okay. We all have issues with Nancy. What goes around comes around. We will sort that out later. How do we find Jake? He could have gone anywhere, and I for one do not have a clue where to look. According to Leo, his neighbour, he took all his clothes and left him a key to look after his home, but did not give out any information as to where he was headed. All he could tell me was that he said he would be gone a while, and that's exactly what Jake told me. I tried to get answers from him, but he was too upset. The only thing he assured me was he would not do anything stupid, because as far as he was concerned this whole dilemma was his fault."

Abbey asked Daniel what he meant by *his fault?* He explained that Jake felt he had let her down. He had been acting like a child, so he deserved to lose her, even though he loved her more than life itself.

This time, both Abbey and Elizabeth were crying.

"This is a God awful day," Simon commented. "Poor Jake … what must he be going through? There must be something we can do?"

"I'm open to suggestions," Daniel replied, "but I do not have a clue where to start."

Abbey suggested that maybe she could ask her Uncle Richard if he had any ideas. He had been a policeman most of his life, and through his connections in New Jersey, he tried to find Jake, or at least find out where he had gone while they were in St. John, but had not had any luck. That was then, and this is totally different.

"I have to find him. I just have too," she said.

They all agreed to meet the next evening to see if any of them could come up with a solution. Simon left them and drove to Nancy's. She was not home, but her father invited him in. They had known each other a long time, and when Simon explained what Nancy had done, both he and his wife were devastated. He told Simon that she had left. They had found out yesterday from their lawyer that she had taken the inheritance that her grandmother had left in trust for her, and left town. They tried to console Simon, but he was too annoyed with what had happened.

"I'm a big boy," he told them. "I will get over this, but what she has done to Abbey and Jake is totally unforgivable."

Simon drove home to an empty house. He was feeling pain like he had never felt before. He had fallen completely in love with Nancy, but now he believed she may have used him from day one.

Chapter 15

When Abbey got home, her mother and father were quite concerned. She told them the whole story. It really upset Maggie who was still trying to come to terms with the way she had treated Jake.

"What can be done?" she asked Sam. "There must be something we can do."

When Abbey suggested Uncle Richard may be able to help, Maggie stood up and said she would call immediately.

"I need to do this for Jake's sake. I owe him."

After speaking with her brother-in-law, and giving him the details, he said he needed a couple of days to see what he could find and would call as soon as possible, but he could not make any promises.

She sat down with her daughter. Abbey looked tired. They fixed her some soup and put her to bed. She thanked her mum for trying to help. The last words Abbey heard before she fell asleep were, "Don't worry, we will find your man."

In the meantime, Richard had informed Jennie what had gone down in Rockaway, and why Abbey could not get in contact with Jake. He made phone calls until the early hours of the morning. He had called every Police Officer he knew. None could really help, except Robert O'Neil, an ex undercover cop in New York. He had been a Police Officer for twenty-five years until he took early retirement to become a manager for a security company. He hated the job, so he set himself up as a Private Investigator. He had become very successful, and now had a staff of twenty working for him.

He had not spoken to Richard in years, but after listening to his story, he agreed to help and assured his old friend that he would visit New Jersey within a few days. Richard gave him Sam's number and address, and Rob told him he would keep him informed of any developments, but also let him know this would be time consuming and expensive. Richard just told him to go ahead anyway – there would be no problem with payment.

Jake had settled in his apartment, and was also starting to make some strides at work. It was slow going, but he was managing his portfolio very well. The clients he had been assigned, liked him, so he was over the first hurdle. Many times during the day, his thoughts would wander to Abbey. In some strange way, he hoped she was happy. Even after everything that had happened, he would always love her, no matter what he did or where he went.

After work, he would walk down by the Canal. He was fascinated at the amount of people skating – people of all ages. Jake had never seen this type of activity used at this level. He had skated on the lake at home as a youngster, but there never had more than a dozen skaters at any one given time, even on the weekends. There may have been twenty to thirty, but here in Ottawa there were hundreds all the time.

He had also noticed how many diverse ethnic groups there were. He commented to himself, *'There must be people from all around the world living here in the Capital.'* He had met Russians, Bosnians, Italians, Irish, Germans and Australians. He had run into so many different nationalities in such a short time.

He had found a nice little Indian restaurant on Rideau Street. He discovered he had developed a taste for curry, so he visited it at least twice a week. He was surrounded by restaurants and pubs. Coming from a small town, it was quite a different atmosphere than he was accustomed to. He could have any type of food he desired, even though he did not have a big appetite, he knew he would not starve.

He paid a visit to the Rideau Centre and bought himself a pair of skates. He wanted to get his fitness level back, and this would be a great way to do this. After falling a thousand times, he started to get the hang of skating again. He was amazed at how many people had helped him up off the ice. At least he was surrounded by nice people.

Jake was really pleased that he had chosen to work at Cohen and Cohen. All the staff was pleasant and if they could give advice to help they would. The owners were also supportive in every way. The only drawback was his loneliness. He would spend endless hours in his apartment, staring at nothing. He felt all he had were memories. Besides missing Abbey, he also missed his friend's Daniel and Elizabeth, and holding the baby when he went for visits. But he would have to get used to it, because he had decided not to contact them. He had to make a new life for himself, if not here in Ottawa, then somewhere else. He felt a clean break may be the answer to his problems. His lawyer back in Rockaway was the only contact from his past life.

He had agreed to pay the house taxes and any other bills that came. Jake had made sure he had left enough from his mother's Will to cover anything for years. He thought about selling the house, but decided to keep it just in case one day he returned.

That Friday evening, a gang from the office invited him to join them for drinks and he reluctantly accepted. They were a fun group, some older, some younger, very friendly, especially after a few drinks. Jake listened to the conversations, and he actually laughed for the first time in weeks. Some of their antics were hilarious. That was the same evening he was introduced to Danielle.

She had come into the bar with a few of her friends and David, one of his coworkers, had introduced him as his American friend Jake. She was strikingly beautiful and Jake could not help but notice her big brown eyes. They reminded him of Abbey, which bought back a feeling that made him feel sick. He went to the washroom, but he was okay, he was not sick and decided not to be rude and went back to the gang.

Danielle asked if he was okay, and he assured her it was just something he ate.

The bar on Elgin St was now very busy. Danielle commented to David that she thought Jake was very cute and wanted to know what he knew about him. Was he married, engaged or going steady? David admitted he did not know anything about Jake except that he was new at the company. He had come to Canada a few weeks ago, but he liked him, though he was a very private person. She took it upon herself to try and find the answers.

Danielle came straight out with her questions to Jake.

"Are you married?"

"No," he replied.

"Engaged?"

"No again."

"Steady girlfriend?"

"Not anymore."

Jake was feeling a little flustered. He had never been interrogated before, but at least she did it in a nice way. Eventually he began to feel a bit more at ease with her. So much so that for some unknown reason, he told Danielle what had happened to him and about Abbey and all the problems that had arisen back home.

She looked at him and smiled.

"That is why you have a sad face, but I certainly understand why. Thank you for being so honest with me. It must be hard to adjust to life without the one you love."

She then shared her life story with Jake, who listened intensely.

"I was born in Montreal in 1962. My father was born in Quebec and my mother was an Italian immigrant, from Naples. I have one brother who is in the Armed Forces. We moved to Ottawa in 1979. My father works for the Federal Government, and my mother is a Bank Manager here in Ottawa, actually just down the street." She chuckled.

Jake found her to be open and funny. He asked where she worked and when she explained, he was not surprised.

"I'm a model," she answered. "I basically work all over the world, London, Paris, New York, wherever my agency sends me."

Jake was intrigued.

"Wow. What a lifestyle."

"Yes," she replied, "but it's very hard work. You just never seem to stop. I only got back from London two days ago and next week I'm off to Singapore. People think that because you travel all over the world, it must be fantastic, and it is, but it is also very tiring. Sometimes when I get back home, I sleep for days. My ex-boyfriend got fed up with me being away so much and the relationship ended on a sour note. So you see Jake, I have been through the wringer myself."

Danielle and Jake talked until the early hours, and when the bar announced it was closing time, they were surprised where the time had gone. Danielle gave Jake her phone number and asked him to call her as she would like to see him again. He told her he would call and that he would like to see her again also. Jake suggested that maybe next time they could go out for dinner, which Danielle thought was a great idea. She lived in the west end of Ottawa, so Jake hailed her a taxi. Then she kissed him goodnight and was gone.

Jake walked home with mixed feelings in his head. He had met a super girl and they had talked for hours. He liked her a lot, but Abbey had been in the back of his mind the entire time. He somehow had to get over this so he could move on with his life, though he knew it was too soon to have a relationship with any woman.

When he got in, he made coffee and turned on the radio. It seemed ironic to Jake that every time he did this it was *'Doctor Hook'*. He wondered if this was what they referred to as – *fate* – because the song this time was *'Sexy Eyes'* and it reminded him of Danielle and Abbey. They both had beautiful eyes. He turned it off, in a way it scared him.

It felt to Jake that he was living his life through the words of their songs, though it was one of his favourite bands, he had no answer to why it seemed to happen.

Jake finished his coffee and went for a walk. He liked this city at this time of the morning. All the bars had cleared out, and though it was extremely cold, there were still people walking about. Back home at this time, there would not be a sound.

He watched lovers walking arm in arm and laughing, and he wondered if he would ever be happy again like he had been in Rockaway with

Abbey. That was the happiest time of his life, and in some ways he did not want to forget.

A few days after Richard had contacted Rob O'Neil. The Private Detective called Sam, and made an appointment to see him. When he arrived, Simon was also there. He had dropped over to see how Abbey was doing. He was concerned for her health because of what had happened, but Abbey was strong. She was okay, and after speaking to her aunt who told her that Richard had found someone to find Jake, she felt a lot better.

Rob was a huge man, 6' 4" and built like a quarter back even though he was in his late fifties. He sat down with all of them and outlined his plan, which to Maggie seemed rather complicated, but Rob went on. He would first check in the States to see if he had used his Social Security Number or any of the banks. He had a friend in the FBI that would help him. He had also filed a *missing person* report to see if that would generate any leads.

He explained that this would take time and money. Simon interrupted him and said, "Rob, I will take care of any money you need. If you want some up front, I will give you a cheque now."

The Private Detective warned them that this would take time, and they must have patience. Simon wrote him a cheque. He assured them he would be in contact as soon as he had heard anything, and then he left.

Sam took Simon aside and told him he was not responsible for paying the detective. They had funds to easily cover this, but Simon insisted, because in a way he felt partly responsible. Nancy had caused all of this, and he should have seen it coming.

"Please let me do this Sam," he pleaded. "If only for my own piece of mind."

Over the next two weeks, Abbey became impatient at not hearing from the Private Detective, but her parents gave her reassurance.

"Remember what he said Abbey. It will take time. He knows what he is doing and Richard says he is the best – and he should know."

She called her aunt in St. John and was on the phone to her for ages. Jennie suggested that she come down to stay, but Abbey wanted to be at home in case there was any news.

When Jennie got off the phone with Abbey, she spoke with her husband, and explained that she thought her niece was going out of her mind. Richard was not surprised.

"Abbey must be patient," he replied. "It's not easy to find someone who really doesn't want to be found, but if anyone can find him it's Rob. Jennie, he is most probably the best cop I have ever known. He will leave no stone unturned until he finds Jake, and I assure you he will find him."

"Oh I do hope so," Jennie said. "I do hope so, for Abbey's sake."

Abbey had been offered a full time position at the school, but she had no choice but to turn it down. She was now four months pregnant and did not think it fair to take up a job only to leave a few months later. She spoke to Nora about this problem because she had recommended Abbey for the position, but Nora was in total agreement with her young friend. Nora asked if there was any news on Jake. A teary-eyed Abbey said she had not heard anything yet.

She spent most of the time thinking and talking to herself. *'Where are you Jake? Please call me. Give me the chance to tell you it was a big mistake. I love you Jake. I always will.'*

Nancy had skipped town. She knew that if she had stayed, there would have been a lynch mob waiting for her once everything had been sorted out, but she was really pleased with herself. *'I pulled it off. It was worth the wait.'* Her only concern now, was her parents who had stood by her through thick and thin.

She called them and tried to explain her side of the story, but her father would have none of it.

"You have ruined lives with your vengeance campaign. I can't accept your explanation. It is not acceptable. What you did Nancy, was wrong. You even told us you were in love with Simon. How could you have hurt him that way? He was devastated when he found out. There are no excuses. Your mother and I have dealt with his company for years and I have always liked him, and then this, just so you could hurt Jake. It's totally unacceptable. I'm ashamed you're my daughter. Please, don't call me again."

Nancy was stunned. She could not believe her own family would turn against her, but they had. This she had not planned. She started to cry and realized the gravity of her actions. She did not want this, as she loved her mother and father. She could not bear the thought of never seeing them again. Boston was a nice place and her hotel was very comfortable, she sat and pondered what she should do.

That night, Nancy did not sleep. She walked the floor of her suite for hours. Getting her revenge on Jake was not worth the life she would have without her family. For the first time in her life, she was suffering like she had never known. Even when Jake had left her in Connecticut, she did not feel like this.

'What can I do?' she said to herself. *'What can I do? I did not think it would lead to my family disowning me. God what have I done?'*

She decided there and then that she would go back and face the music, even if everyone hated her, she would go back.

It had been six weeks since the detective had been in touch and when he finally called, Abbey was there. He explained to her that Jake was nowhere to be found in the States. His friend in the FBI assured him he was out of country somewhere. His next step was to try and see if he had traveled to Canada. He would start his search in Toronto and move westward, but he still assured Abbey that he would find him.

Abbey did not like the news, but had no choice to accept what he had told her. *'Oh Jake ... where have you gone?'*

She related her phone conversation to her parents. They were disappointed, but told Abbey to hang in there. At least he was not giving up.

Sam called Simon at home. He knew he would be there on the weekend. Simon agreed with him.

"We can't give up. We have to carry on until we find him for Abbey."

He told Sam that Nancy had left him a message on his answering machine. She sounded upset, but Simon was too angry to care. He knew her father had roasted her, and he was glad the shoe was on the other foot, but deep down he still cared for her. Love does not go away that easily, no matter what has happened.

Sam invited him for dinner that evening. He thought he would be good company for Abbey. Simon thanked him and would definitely be there. Then he called Nancy's father and told him about the phone message from her. George Ross asked Simon to have nothing to do with her.

"She has caused too much pain for everyone. Forget her," he suggested, "and get on with your life. Don't let her weasel her way back. She does not deserve pity or forgiveness."

Simon agreed with Nancy's father on the phone, but he could not shake the feeling of wanting her. He had fallen head over heels in love with her. Although he could not explain why, he would forgive her in an instant.

Jake met up again with Danielle. She was back from Singapore and he invited her out for dinner. She readily accepted, because she wanted to see him again. While she was abroad, she had thought about him quite a lot.

Over dinner, they talked about their nonexistent love lives. She was very interested in what more she could find out about Jake. He told her about his mother's death and how tragic it was, and that he found it hard to get over his loss. He told her how Abbey had helped him even though now she was gone. Danielle asked him if he was sure it was over, because something just did not sit right with his story. She understood that Jake believed it, but she wondered if he had gotten the whole truth.

She told him she had another photo shoot in Australia for some big beer commercial. She did not really want to go, but the money was too good to turn down.

"Besides, I can't be a model forever. All the younger girls are now getting noticed." This seemed to be the trend she informed him.

Jake liked her company. She was easy to talk to and very easy to listen to. She told him about her big love affair that had ended after three years, and how her boyfriend Adam had just decided one day enough was enough and walked out. She had not seen him since, but it took her a while to get over the breakup. Jake listened to her story, and could not take his eyes off of her. *'Maybe because she reminds me of Abbey so much,'* he thought.

On a whim, Jake invited Danielle back to his apartment after dinner for coffee. She was hesitant, but agreed as long as she could get a cab home. She could drive, but did not find it necessary as she was never in town long enough to appreciate owning a car.

Jake assured her he would call a cab whenever she was ready to leave and he would be the perfect gentleman. Danielle believed him, which is why she agreed to go with him. Over coffee, Jake explained that he only rented on a month to month basis. If he decided to live here permanently, he would purchase a property at that time, as he had one in New Jersey he could sell. This was to have been the house that he would share with Abbey.

Danielle then kissed him very tenderly. They held each other and kissed a long kiss that seemed never to end. Her lips were soft and tasted of strawberries. All of a sudden, Jake stopped.

"I'm sorry Danielle," he said. "That was really nice, but I'm not ready. I wish I was, but I'm not."

She understood completely and did not bat an eyelid, though she would have gone further if he had wanted.

Jake was feeling guilty. He did not want to hurt her. He did not want to hurt anyone – except Simon. *'Now that would give him pleasure. He took the one person in my life that I needed more than anything,'* he said to himself.

Jake walked Danielle down to her taxi. She again kissed him goodnight and whispered in his ear, "I hope you call me again. I will wait to hear from you." Jake promised he would.

That night Jake thought of how nice Danielle had been, even after the way he had brushed her off. She was kind and thoughtful and if he was to have a serious relationship again, he could not wish for a lovelier woman. Again his thoughts went back to Abbey and he wondered how she was and what she had been doing. The one thing he had not understood was why she never told him their romance was over and given him back his ring.

At the office, David asked him how he was getting on with Danielle. He explained to Jake that he had known her ex-boyfriend for years that is how he met her. They used to come to dinner with him and his wife, but after a couple of years, they realized that all he thought about was himself. He used to brag about how he had this famous model eating out of his hand. Davis was quite pleased when the relationship ended, because Danielle was a sweet girl.

Jake informed David that they had been out and he would be doing so again, but of course, he would have to wait till she got back from Australia.

His workload had gotten heavier and he was now getting some of his own clients which helped him to keep his mind off bad memories, but not all the time.

He had the surprise of his life when a few days later he had along distance call. He thought it might be his lawyer, but it was Danielle calling him from the other side of the world. She just wanted to let him know she was thinking of him, and hoped he was okay. He told her he was and that he had also thought of her and hoped they could meet up when she got back. She assured him she would like nothing better then the line went dead.

Jake awoke sweating. He had dreamed that he had spent the night making love with Abbey, but he realized after waking this was just a dream. But it was a dream he liked. It took him back to better days, when he used to wake and watch her sleep beside him. This was a time he had never been happier. He remembered the first time he met her at the roadside and the impression she had left on him. It was something he never wanted to forget.

He made his coffee and showered. At work, he kept trying to remember the dream, but eventually the day got busy and he had a lot of work on his desk.

He was called to the owner's office. His given name was Jacob and everyone here called him by that name. Jake hated being called Jacob because at school, certain people would do it just to be annoying. But he tolerated it here and put on a brave face, his boss wanted to inform Jake that they were very pleased with his progress, and that a pay rise was being offered. Jake thanked him and told the boss he like working for his company and was very happy he was given the opportunity.

'Overall,' Jake thought to himself, *'this was a good day, but it's a shame I can't go on the Canal.'* The warmer weather had caused it to be closed for the season. *'Maybe next year,'* he thought. *'Maybe, if I stay.'*

Danielle was back and they went out again. This time they had a pub dinner, a few drinks, and Jake actually danced to the live music. She was a good teacher and after about an hour Jake was actually getting quite good, which surprised him as he had never properly tried before. Danielle assured him, "Another couple of lessons and I will have you dancing as well as anyone."

This pleased him.

Danielle went back to Jake's after quite a heavy night of eating drinking and dancing. They were both worn out. She asked Jake if she could stay the night.

"I don't mind sleeping on the sofa."

"You take the bed," he insisted.

"Will you join me?"

They kissed and undressed each other. He carried her to the bedroom. She played with him as he caressed her whole body. Their lovemaking was average at best this first time, but they had both been satisfied. She cuddled into him and went to sleep.

Jake lay silent beside her. He was wide awake and feeling guilty. He did not want to hurt Danielle. She had done nothing wrong. He liked her, but she would never be Abbey. He knew this, but he thought that perhaps she could fill the void in his life, and he needed something.

Jake realized he had grown up a lot since leaving New Jersey and as far as he was concerned that could only be a good thing. He watched her sleep just as he had done on many occasions with Abbey. She was beautiful and her breasts moved up and down as she breathed. They were very firm and Jake found this extremely arousing. She opened her eyes and looked at him. They made love again. This time slowly and passionately. When Danielle climaxed, her whole body shuddered. She kissed him and told him how wonderful that felt. And for the first time, he also enjoyed the lovemaking. He felt like a man again. They lay back down and slept in each others arms.

When they awoke on that Saturday morning, the sun was shining and they had coffee on the balcony wrapped in a blanket. It was still quite chilly in the wind. They showered together and within minutes the two of them were completely aroused. Jake entered her for the third time in less than ten hours, and this time they climaxed together. They walked up Elgin Street and ate breakfast at a small diner on the corner. Jake had never eaten such a large meal. He was absolutely starving. Danielle ate like a rabbit even after a night of passion. As she explained to Jake, "My career will be over soon enough. I have to watch my figure."

Chapter 16

In Rockaway, Daniel and Elizabeth had invited Abbey and Simon to dinner. He picked her up and drove to their home. One of the reasons they had been invited was that Elizabeth had something to tell them which she was sure they did not know. It especially concerned Abbey, but she had to get this off her chest – it was eating away at her.

She found it difficult now that she was face-to-face with Abbey ready to explain. She asked her what Jake had told her about the time he went to Connecticut and all the problems with Nancy.

Abbey said, "Jake told me everything … eventually. I mean, it happened before I had really known him."

"What did he tell you?" Elizabeth asked.

Now Abbey felt a little uncomfortable.

"He explained that they had been out drinking one time and they ended up having sex." She looked at Simon. "I'm sorry you had to hear that."

"I already knew," he replied. "Nancy had also told me what happened."

"Thank God for that!" Abbey exclaimed.

Elizabeth took a deep breath. She had no choice now, but to drop her bombshell. "But what she did not tell you – was that she was pregnant."

Abbey's mouth dropped.

"What are you saying Elizabeth? That Jake got her pregnant."

"Yes," she answered, "he did, but he never knew. She swore me to secrecy. I only told Daniel yesterday."

Abbey's eyes filled with tears.

"Let me finish." Elizabeth pleaded. "She was furious at Jake for not letting the relationship flourish. A few weeks after finding out she was pregnant ... she lost the baby. I think that's what pushed her over the edge."

"So that's why she wanted revenge?" Simon asked.

"Yes," replied Elizabeth, "and she got it."

"So Jake was the target all the time," Abbey said. "She just wanted to get back at Jake for what she felt he had done to her."

"In a way ..." Abbey went on, "I feel a bit sorry for her. At the time, she loved him and in her mind, he let her down. Even though he told me it was the biggest mistake he had ever made."

Daniel had not said a word, he just listened intently. He knew he could not change anything that had happened, but he thought of his friend Jake. He did not deserve this, and poor Abbey, what she must be going through. Then he joined in the conversation.

"Has there been any further news from the Private Detective?"

"No," Abbey sighed. "They have switched their search to Canada. They think he might have gone there."

Daniel agreed. "Yes. I believe he would. He spoke to me years ago about maybe one day working there. But I do not have a clue where in Canada."

Simon said he was confident they would find him. The only problem was when.

"We are now in April and it took them almost two months to search in this country, and searching here must be easier."

Abbey squeezed his hand.

"As long as they find him, that's all that matters. I just hope he is okay and that after it is all explained to him that he will come back. That is my only fear. I miss him more each day. I pray that he has not found someone else. After what went down, who knows what's going through his head."

Elizabeth made coffee after dinner. No one was that hungry and she had a lot left over. Normally when she cooked, they ate everything, but this time she understood. Simon informed them all that Nancy had tried to contact him. She had left him a message, and she sounded upset.

"All she said was, '*I am sorry*'. I do not know where she is, but I hope she calls back so we can get this mess sorted out."

Abbey knew how Simon felt about her. He never stopped talking about her in St. John. It was Nancy this, and Nancy that, she knew he loved her. '*This must be really hard for him as well,*' she thought, but never mentioned it. Abbey did not know if she could ever forgive her.

Richard had taken it upon himself to call his friend Rob O'Neil. He asked how it was going. Rob told him he had one of his operatives in Canada, and that they knew he was there somewhere, because a work visa had been issued to him from the American Embassy. They were trying to see if he had left an address for his guy to follow up on. Richard thanked him and informed him he would let the family know.

Jennie called the family and gave them the news that Jake was in Canada. Maggie took the call.

"Thank God they are getting somewhere," she said to her sister. "Abbey is really suffering, and I don't want her having trouble with the baby. She is tired all the time, and she never could handle stress that well – just like her mother."

Jennie laughed. "You came through it all Maggie."

"Abbey is stronger than we give her credit for," she replied.

When Abbey arrived home and her mother gave her the news she wept with joy and hugged her mother.

"I do hope they find him soon," Maggie said. "Then you can both settle down and raise my grandchild."

Abbey smiled at her mum

"I am so glad you are back to normal," she replied. "This is the mum I love."

Not long after Simon had driven home the phone rang. He picked it up.

"Hello," Nancy said. He started to feel a little shaky, so he sat down.

"Hi," he replied. "Where are you?"

"I'm home. I have asked my family to forgive me for my stupid actions. I don't know if they will, and I can't blame them. Can I see you Simon? I need to talk to you."

"I don't know," he replied. "Nancy, I just don't know if that would be a good idea."

"Please Simon. I'm begging you. I just need to explain and then I will get out of your life forever if that is what you want."

Reluctantly, he agreed. He wanted so much to hold her, but he also wanted to strangle her at the same time.

Jake had decided to have a heart to heart with Danielle, even though he had really enjoyed their night of passion together. He liked her, he liked her a lot, but he did not feel it could go further and he did not want to hurt her unnecessary, should that time come. She was back in town, so he called her for a dinner date. She readily agreed to meet him at his little Indian restaurant on Rideau Street.

When she walked into the place, a lot of heads turned and Jake knew why. She was strikingly beautiful, and had the figure of a goddess. She kissed him on the cheek and before he could open his mouth, she told Jake she needed to talk. He listened to what she had to say, and was quite relieved when she had finished.

"Jake, the night we spent together was wonderful. I mean really wonderful. I had a need and you filled that need. I really like you Jake. You are a very caring and considerate man. The sex with you was fantastic, but it was just that – sex. I don't want to give you the wrong impression. I do not sleep around. That night with you will always be a fond memory, but I'm moving to London England. I have been accepted at the very best modeling agency. I have signed a two-year contract, and I will be leaving next week. The thing is I like you and maybe even one day I could fall in love with you.

Though at this time in my life I do not need to have any distractions, and if we carry on you would become just that. I hope you understand. If you don't want to buy me dinner, I will leave."

Jake smiled at her.

"Danielle, have dinner with me, and let's part as friends."

"I completely understand what you are saying and I agree. Your career is more important. I have to be honest and tell you the reason I wanted to meet you tonight was basically, to tell you the same thing. At this time of my life, even though I need to move on, it's too soon to get serious."

They finished their dinner and had talked about everything except romance. Jake called her a taxi and told Danielle that if she ever needed a friend to talk to call him. She kissed him goodbye and thanked him for a lovely time, then she was gone. He knew he would never see her, or hear from her again, that was one thing he was certain of.

Jake walked home thinking he should call Elizabeth and Daniel. He missed his friends terribly. Instead, he composed a letter to them both, explaining what he was doing. He did not say where he was in Canada, just that he was okay. He told them he missed them both, and would write again, but he did not put a return address or telephone number. His only other comment was to say that he hoped Abbey was okay and that she was happy. He signed it '*Jake, your friend forever*'.

On that Saturday he drove to Toronto for the weekend. He mailed his letter from there. He paid a visit to the CN Tower and other places of interest. Jake had not realized just how big this city was. It reminded him in certain parts of New York, huge apartment buildings and really busy main streets. Jake was glad he had not decided to live here. It was just too busy for a small town boy.

Sunday afternoon he drove back to Ottawa. He liked the clean streets and the people were friendly. He was glad to be back. It was a nice sunny day, so he took a walk by the Canal. It was starting to get dark, so he had a meal in the pub on Elgin and went back to his apartment. The only thing he did not like was the loneliness. He had made a few friends, but they were all married and it made him feel somewhat of an outcast.

A few days after Jake had been to Toronto, Daniel received his letter. He called Abbey and she immediately drove over. Elizabeth was exited.

"This is good news," she said to Abbey. "At least we know he's okay."

"But where is he?" Abbey asked.

"We don't know," Daniel replied. "All we know is that the postmark is Toronto. At least you can call that detective and let him know."

Abbey called her father and explained about the letter.

"That's fantastic!" Sam said. "I will call Mr. O'Neil right away. At last we have something to go on."

Abbey asked Daniel what was in the letter.

"Jake said he missed his friends and stuff like that." He smiled at Abbey and put her out of her misery. "He also hoped that you were okay and happy." Daniel added, "Obviously, he must still think of you."

"Oh, I do hope so," Abbey replied.

Although it was good news, she felt sad that he had not left a forwarding address, or telephone number that he could be contacted at.

Elizabeth comforted her.

"They will find him Abbey. I'm sure of it."

"And when they do …" she said, "will he come back?"

"He will when he finds out you are having a child, Abbey," Daniel replied. "I'm not an expert, but your well being is still a concern according to the letter."

Abbey went home, somewhat elated, somewhat sad.

'I miss you Jake,' she said to herself, *'but I also feel like slapping you. Why didn't you stay and confront me instead of running away?*

Was what you were told really that believable? How could you even think I would be unfaithful? We were to be married next month. You knew I was making the arrangements. I had even booked the church. Oh Jake – just call me – please. I am going out of my mind.'

When Rob O'Neil got the message from Sam, he contacted his man, John Edwards in Canada and gave him the news. Rob was not a fool.

"If he posted the letter in Toronto with no return address, or any other detail to show where he is, then it's a good bet, he is not living in that city. But I would think somewhere close."

He told Edwards to check Montreal.

"If he's not there – try Ottawa. I'm sure he would find work in the financial field, it's what he knows. Start checking with all of the larger companies first. I will have my friend at the FBI check the banks. He must have an account somewhere."

Rob knew now, that they were close to finding Jake. He also knew if he did not want to be found, it would take a long time. He was amazed that they had not been able to get many leads. It was normally a lot easier to find people, but this was now into its fourth month, and was costing Simon Brady a lot of money. *'That's life,'* he thought to himself.

In the meantime, Simon had agreed to meet Nancy on neutral territory. They met at the café on Indian Lake. She apologized to him for her behaviour, and for lying to him.

"What about Jake and Abbey?" he asked her bluntly. "Did you get some kind of enjoyment out of ruining their lives?"

Simon was not prepared for her answer and frankly, it shocked him.

"Yes I did. I am sorry I hurt you and my parents. As for Jake and his *whore* … I couldn't care less. He had to be made aware of what he did to me, and how much he hurt me. He walked away and left me. I was alone, and pregnant. If you expect me to be sorry, then you're sadly mistaken because – I'm not!"

Simon was blown away. He could not believe she could be so heartless and he told her straight out.

"I fell in love with you. We had something special and you just threw it away. You used me and my reputation for your own vengeance. We all ended up being your victims … and yet, you are not sorry."

Nancy's reply was very curt, "Yes, I did use you … I did not want to, but the opportunity arose and I took advantage of it. Simon, I also was falling in love with you. Don't you see? They do not matter. We can be together again."

"Nancy … we can never be together again. I may love you, but in time, I will forget you. What you did is unforgivable, and as far as I'm concerned, you can go straight to hell! You are evil. You need help. But right now … you need to get out of my sight! I hope I never see you again."

Simon walked out of the café and out of her sick, pathetic life. He was proud of what he had said to Nancy. Someone had to stand up to her. He knew there and then that was over for them, but deep down Simon was not thinking of himself. He wanted Abbey to be happy. He knew Maggie had always hoped it would be him walking her down the aisle, but he had only ever thought of Abbey as a friend – and now – his friend really needed his help.

He drove home and made a few phone calls to Daniel, to Abbey, and even called Richard in St. John, but still no further news. Simon wished there was something more he could do – 'But what?' he thought to himself. 'I just don't know where to start.' He decided to call Rob O'Neil in New York. Rob told him they were concentrating their efforts on Ottawa, because they had drawn a blank in Montreal.

Summer had arrived and his concern was finding Jake before Abbey gave birth. She was due in just over a month and he knew that the stress of this unfortunate incident was getting her down. He would visit tomorrow and tell her everything that Nancy had said. He felt it was only fair that she knew.

He picked up the phone and called Nancy's father. Simon gave him the whole story and was pleased when Mr. Ross told him that they did not want her in their home.

"She has gone Simon. She is my daughter, but I don't have any idea how she could be so spiteful. I just hope one day she wakes up and realizes the chaos she caused, but I don't hold out much hope."

Jennie called her sister and explained that with everything that had happened, they had changed their minds about going to Europe. What they wanted now, was an invitation to come and stay there, Maggie of course agreed. She knew Abbey needed all the support she could muster, and her aunt had always been very close to her. They would be there within the week, which would give Maggie time to get everything ready.

When her daughter came home from Elizabeth's, she told her of the conversation with her aunt. Abbey was really pleased. She was now finding it hard to drive. She informed her mother that *her bump* was getting in the way of the steering wheel. It was the first time her mother had seen her laugh in a very long time.

Abbey went to bed early as she was tired after visiting Elizabeth. She had her dinner and said goodnight to her parents. As she lay on the bed and her thoughts turned to Jake. She talked to herself a lot lately, but it gave her comfort.

'Well,' she said, *'you are going to be a father soon, even though you don't know it yet. I now know the whole story Jake, and I guess I don't blame you for leaving. I just wished you'd had the courage to stay. This would all be over, and we would be together for the birth of our child. I have no idea whether it's a boy or girl. The surprise will be something to look forward too. Come home Jake. Please come home.'* She fell asleep.

Late that evening, while Abbey was sleeping, Rob O'Neil called Sam.

"Good news. We know he is living in Ottawa. My buddy at the FBI has just confirmed that he has a bank account in the city at The Scotia Bank on Sparks Street. He is now trying to find out how he gets paid and by whom. We should be able to locate him through his job."

Sam thanked him and immediately called Simon to give him the good news. His first concern was Abbey, so Sam assured him he would wake her.

Simon called Rob O'Neil and asked the detective to do him a favour.

"Of course," Rob said, "you're the one paying for all of this."

"When you find him, don't let Jake know. We will take care of that."

Rob agreed and wished him a goodnight.

Sam and Maggie walked quietly into Abbey's room. She was sound asleep on top of her bed. She had not even undressed. Maggie gently stroked her daughters face to wake her. Abbey opened her eyes. It took a minute to realize who it was. When she finally cleared her head Abbey asked if there was something wrong.

"No," her father replied, "we have good news."

"What is it?"

He sat on the edge of the bed and held her hand.

"They know more or less where Jake is living, so it should only be a few more days and this nightmare will be over."

The three of them cuddled each other on the bed. This time Abbey's tears were tears of joy.

"Thank God. It seems like it's been a lifetime," she said.

Sam went downstairs to make some tea. Maggie sat holding her daughter.

"I am so glad," she told her. "With any luck, you should have him back soon, and we can be a proper family together."

Abbey kissed her mother on the cheek and hugged her.

"Thanks mum."

They sat on the bed drinking tea. Sam looked at Abbey, she was smiling. He was relieved that his daughter was about to get through this dilemma and hopefully move on with her life. The last six months had been very hard on him. He had always wanted their happiness to come first.

John Edwards had been informed that Jake worked for a company called Cohen and Cohen on Albert Street. He staked out the place for three days, with Jake's photo in his hand. His boss, Rob O'Neil, had informed him not to make contact. *'The family that had hired us will do that.'* But there had been no sign of Jake.

It was ironic that while the private eye staked out his workplace, Jake was in Montreal with important clients of his company and his boss. They were setting up special portfolios. This was one of the biggest clients that the company had dealt with and Jacob Cohen wanted Jake to accompany him on this project. They finished all the business on Friday morning and headed back to Ottawa. Jake was exhausted so went straight home. His boss dropped him off outside his apartment, congratulated him on a job well done and drove off.

He made himself a snack watched television for a while then went to bed early. For the first time in months, he slept all night.

On Saturday morning, he went up Elgin to the diner where he and Danielle had visited. *'Seems like a long time ago now,'* Jake thought. He sat down and ordered everything on the breakfast menu – he was starving. Jake did not notice the man across from him pull out a photograph and look at him. He was too busy eating.

'That's him,' John said to himself. He walked across the road to the telephone booth and called his boss at home reversing the charges.

"I found him."

"Don't get to close." Rob cautioned.

"I won't. I'm just going to follow him to see if I can find out where he lives."

As soon as he hung up, Rob O'Neil called Sam. The answering machine came on, so he left a quick message, "It's Rob. Call me."

Since he had not been able to get hold of Sam, Rob O'Neil called Simon and gave him the story from his man in Ottawa. He explained that he had not been able to reach Sam. Simon informed him that they were at his mother-in-law's and would not be back until tonight. Simon told him that he was going straight to Ottawa himself.

"I will be leaving within the hour," he said. "Thanks for everything."

Simon tossed a few things in an overnight bag for his trip north. He took his address book with him so that could call Abbey and her parents later.

Chapter 17

Simon left at around 10.30 a.m. He took Interstate 80 and then on to 81. He drove north as fast as he dared, stopping in Watertown for a meal before crossing into Canada at the Hill Island Bridge, the same route Jake had taken all those months earlier. He had made good time and had no trouble at the border. When asked why he was visiting. He told the Customs Officer – *'business'*.

He then headed east toward Montreal and turned up Highway 16 to Ottawa. He muttered to himself that *'he did not like the roads as much as those in New York State'*, but pushed on. He arrived at 7.30 p.m. It had been an arduous drive and he was tired. He booked into a hotel on Wellington Street and called the private eye at his hotel. He had been given the number by Rob O'Neil. John Edwards answered on the second ring and arranged to meet for a drink in the hotel bar.

Over drinks, John gave him Jake's address and directions. Simon thanked him for his hard work.

"You must be glad to be heading home."

"Yes," John replied. "This one was long and tedious, but we got there."

"I did not realize what you guys have to go through," commented Simon. "Thanks again. I will take it from here."

It was nearly nine, so he called Sam at home. There was still no answer just the machine. He left a message that he would call back later. He called again at ten. Maggie picked up the phone.

"Hello Simon. How are you?"

"I'm fine Maggie. Can I speak to Sam?"

He thought it might be better to tell him than Abbey. When Sam came to the phone, Simon explained everything. He told him that he was in Ottawa and would call on Jake in the morning, and hopefully bring him back home. Sam thanked him.

"You did not have to do all this."

"Yes ... I did Sam," he replied. "I need to sort this out with Jake. I will call you tomorrow. Give Abbey my regards," he said, and hung up.

On Sunday morning, at around 9 a.m., Simon arrived at Jake's apartment tower. He looked at the door ring numbers and saw his name, Jake Lockhart, Apt 1211. He hesitated and was just about to push the buzzer when a kind old lady opened the door. He took the elevator to the twelfth floor and stood outside Jake's apartment door for at least five minutes before he knocked.

Jake had just gotten up. He was still tired after the demanding week in Montreal. When he heard the knock at the door, he wondered who it could be. In a thousand lifetimes, he never would have guessed who stood waiting on the other side of the door.

"Simon Brady! What the hell do you want?" Jake shouted at him. "Haven't you done enough? You are the last person in the world I want to see."

He was just about to slam the door when Simon put his foot in the way.

Jake grabbed Simon by the shirt. He was contemplating whether or not to knock Simon on his ass when he interrupted him.

"I thought you loved Abbey?" Jake was near his breaking point.

"Of course I love Abbey!" he said through clenched teeth. "I've always loved her."

Jake let go.

Simon, who had not flinched, calmly continued, "Then let me in. I have a story to tell you that you are going to find hard to believe."

Jake turned his back and walked away from him. Simon entered the apartment and closed the door.

"This had better be good," Jake said. "You have five minutes, then you leave, or I'll throw you out of here."

Simon smiled.

"Sit down Jake. You are now going to hear the truth of what really happened, but first let me tell you Abbey was never unfaithful to you. You ran away like a dog with his tail between his legs, instead of staying home and finding out the truth." He paused, expecting Jake to say something. He didn't, so Simon continued.

"Let me start at the beginning Jake. I was going to St. John to look at the chance of purchasing a holiday home. I had already purchased two return tickets, one for me and one for Nancy. The morning before we were to leave, Nancy informed me she could not go as her father wanted her to close a business deal in Boston. That was her first lie."

Jake stared at Simon. He was somewhat bemused.

"What do you mean her first lie?" he asked. "Let me carry on Jake and it will all fall into place. I went to St. John with Sam, Maggie and Abbey. We were on the same flight and I took them to the airport we were seated together on the plane. Abbey sat with her mother, I sat with Sam. When we arrived in St. Thomas, Abbey's aunt and uncle picked us up and took us to St. John. I stayed in a nearby hotel. They were kind enough to invite me over the next day for breakfast. After breakfast, I went off to look at properties. Abbey accompanied me because Nancy had gone off to Boston. Abbey had been phoning you, but getting no answer. She started to worry. When we got back later that day, she phoned you several more times – still no answer."

"I was cross," Jake interrupted. "I need a coffee."

"Yes please," Simon said without being asked.

As they drank their coffee, Simon carried on with his story.

"While Abbey was on St. John, she called your office who told her you had quit. Then she tried your home again and learned the phone had been cut off. Believe me Jake, she was very upset. She had not heard a word from you. When we arrived back in Rockaway, she went to see Daniel and Elizabeth. They told her your story and what you believed had happened."

"I checked my story," Jake replied, "and it all seemed true. Nancy told me you had dumped her for Abbey. What was I to believe? I called your company and they said you were on holiday with your girlfriend. And when I called Jennie and asked to speak to you, I heard a voice in the background say that Simon was out with Abbey."

"Simon, are you trying to tell me that this was all hogwash?"

"Yes Jake. You see … Nancy had lied about everything and you believed her. Then again, so did I. We are all her victim's Jake. She played us all for fools."

Jake went quiet. Simon watched him as he paced up and down his lounge.

"Oh my God!" Jake said. "What have I done and what must Abbey think of me?"

"What she thinks of you, I don't know," Simon told him, "but she does love you. That, you can count on. I think you should come back with me and sort this mess out."

To Simon's surprise, Jake explained that he could not just pack up and leave.

"I have got to go to work tomorrow and explain the situation. They have been good to me, and we have just done a major deal. It's going to take me a few days to finish it up. I also have to get hold of my landlord here and settle the account. I can't come back for at least three days."

Simon understood and admired Jake for not leaving things in a mess. His opinion of him went up and he thought to himself, *'Abbey, you did make a good choice after all.'*

As Simon got up to leave, he shook hands with Jake and asked him to call Abbey.

"He promised he would," then added, "I guess it's a good thing I never hit you."

Simon laughed. It was the first time in ages for him too.

"I will head back today. I'm just glad this is all over. It's been hard on everyone, especially Abbey. And for your information, as far as we know, Nancy has left town for good."

After he was gone, Jake sat and thought what he could say when he called. He was scared and a little hesitant. *'I deserve to lose her after acting so stupid. I never even gave her the benefit of the doubt.'* He picked up the phone and dialled. Sam picked it up.

"Hello," Jake said quietly.

"At last," Sam said.

He yelled for Abbey. Before she came to the phone, he asked Jake if he was okay and if Simon explained what had happened.

Jake replied that he had.

But what he still did not know was that Abbey was pregnant. Simon had decided it was not his place to tell him.

Abbey came to the phone.

"Jake. Jake. Is that really you?" she shouted in excitement.

"Yes," Jake replied. "It's me. How are you Abbey?"

"I'm okay now," she said.

"Where are you?"

"In Ottawa."

"Are you coming home?"

"Yes, as soon as I tie up some loose ends."

"When will that be?"

"I would think about Wednesday, or Thursday."

"What did Simon tell you?"

Jake told her exactly what Simon had told him.

"Is that all?" she asked.

"That's the whole story," Jake replied.

"So he left the rest to me." Abbey said.

"The rest?" Jake asked.

"Yes," she replied. "Are you sitting down? Jake, we are having a baby in less than three weeks."

Jake was totally stunned.

"We're having a baby?"

"Yes," Abbey said it again. "We are having a baby."

"Sweet Jesus!" Jake's mind was racing. "When? How?"

Abbey explained. "That is why I was phoning you the night before I left. I came over to your place, but there was no answer. I wanted to give you the news."

"I'm sorry," Jake said sincerely. "I'm truly sorry. I should have stayed and at least tried to find out for myself. I thought you had dumped me. I love you Abbey. I always have. Please forgive me."

"Jake, I love you. There's nothing to forgive. Just come home safely. We *both* need you."

Then he asked her, "Boy or girl?"

"I don't know," she replied. "I wanted to find out when I gave birth."

"It doesn't matter," he said, "as long as the baby's healthy."

Jake was over the moon. He stayed on the phone for ages. They spoke as though he had never been away.

"I promise to get home as soon as possible. Do you still want to marry me?" he asked sheepishly.

"Yes Jake," she assured him. "I am still wearing your ring. Hurry home darling. We have a lot to discuss and I just want to see your face again."

Her mother came to her side and held her

"Oh Abbey, thank God. I just want you to be happy, and when Jake gets back we will do everything possible to help. That is a promise baby."

Abbey was so glad that she now had her real mother back, the mother she grew up with and was always there for her.

Jake wished he could just get in the car and drive, but he felt obligated to wrap up everything in Ottawa. He called his landlord. That was one problem out of the way. *'Thank goodness I was only renting month to month.'* He would go to see Jacob Cohen first thing in the morning.

Abbey was ecstatic. She put her hand on *her bump* and spoke to the baby. *'Your daddy will be back soon. Please hold on, I need him at your birth.'*

Maggie was so happy that this ordeal had come to an end. She thought Simon had done a wonderful job of explaining everything to Jake. She just hoped that he would warm up to her, as he would soon be her son-in-law.

When Simon did eventually get back to Rockaway, he went straight to Abbey's to make sure Jake had called as promised and to let her know that he looked, tired but healthy. She could not thank him enough for what he had done.

"Listen Abbey," he said, "I needed to do this for my own peace of mind."

Then she asked him about his meeting with Nancy, so he told her all about their conversation.

She felt for him because she knew he still loved her, even though it was over for them.

Abbey was so pleased to see her aunt and uncle when they arrived on the Monday morning. Her father was at work and her mother had gone shopping. Abbey stayed home as now she found it tiring to go too far. She ushered them in and told them her good news. Her Aunt Jennie smiled at her.

"You see it did work out. A little late, but everything is going to be fine."

Having her aunt with her gave her spirit a boost. She felt so alive around her. They sat down and Abbey gave her the whole story from start to finish.

When Abbey finished, Jennie was absolutely incensed.

"How could anyone be so mean? I mean this woman has a serious problem. She should be locked away somewhere."

Richard agreed.

"You hear of things like this, but you don't ever expect them to happen on your doorstep."

Chapter 18

Though Simon had told everyone that Nancy had left town – he was wrong – she had not. She was hiding out at a small motel less than twenty miles away. She had been contemplating everything that had been said between her and Simon, and decided that she had not yet finished with Jake and Abbey. Nancy's mother had gone behind her husband's back and contacted her daughter. Her mother told that Simon had been to Canada and spoken with Jake and that he would be back in town in a few days.

This did not please Nancy. She felt that everything she had done had been in vain. Her mother was pleased that this had come to an end. Nancy, who was still scheming, agreed with her. As far as she was concerned, she would try some different tactics, and she did not have much time left to work out a plan to hurt them.

She hired a car and staked out Abbey's home to see who came and went. Her opportunity arrived on the Wednesday morning. Abbey came out of the house with a woman who Nancy did not know and they went for a walk. She followed them. They did not go far, when the woman with Abbey crossed the road to get a newspaper from the roadside box. Nancy rammed her foot down on the gas pedal and mounted the sidewalk catching Abbey completely by surprise. She felt the bump and sped off. Aunt Jennie screamed and ran across to where Abbey lay. There was blood everywhere. A homeowner who had seen what had happened called an Ambulance and went to see if she could help.

Abbey lay motionless. However, just before the Paramedics and Police arrived, she opened her eyes. Jennie was very concerned. It was obvious she was in pain. She moved aside for the professionals who got her into the Ambulance as quickly as possible. As the ambulance pulled away, Jennie ran back to her sister's house as fast as she could.

Her husband saw her run up the driveway and opened the door.

"What's the matter? Where's Abbey?" he asked.

Jennie had to catch her breath before she could explain what happened.

"My God!"

He stood there in utter disbelief. Maggie came in from the backyard and saw them standing in the doorway. She could see it on their faces – something was wrong.

"What is it?"

When Jennie told her what happened, Maggie's knees buckled. Richard grabbed her. She had fainted. Jennie went to get a wet cloth, while Richard called Sam at work and explained to him what had happened. He said he would meet them at the hospital. Richard did not tell him his wife had passed out.

Maggie came around and they were just about to leave when Jake phoned. She could not calm herself enough to tell him, so Jennie took the phone from her sister and went through the details again. Jake's pulse raced and his ears were pounding.

"Is she, is she okay?"

All Jennie could tell him was that they had rushed her to the hospital, but that she was awake when she had been put into the Ambulance. Jake thanked her and said he would leave immediately and would go straight to the hospital when he arrived, which should be sometime this evening.

He sat for a moment and prayed, "Please God ... I lost her once. Don't let me lose her again ... not now." He wiped the tears and told himself, 'Be strong Jake. Abbey will need you to be strong.'

Jake had said goodbye to all his colleagues and had packed his car with his clothes. He headed home. It was only 10 a.m., and he knew he could be there within eight hours if he went well above the speed limit the entire way. Jake drove like an idiot. He was lucky not to be stopped by the police.

When they arrived at the hospital and asked at reception for Abbey Walker, they were told she was in Intensive Care. They went up in the elevator to the 3rd floor. There was a Police Officer seated outside her door. He explained to the family that they were able to get a description of the driver from a witness. The officer asked if they had any idea who it might be based on the description. It was a very vague outline, they could not help.

They walked into Abbey's room. There was a doctor beside her bed.

"How is she?" Maggie pleaded. "How is my baby?"

The doctor informed them that he had sedated her because she was showing signs of high anxiety.

"The good news," he said, "is the baby she's carrying, is fine. We have done extensive tests and there are no problems there. As for your daughter," he explained, "she has three fractured ribs. Her wrist was broken and we have put a cast on that. She has some very nasty bruises to her head and neck. We need to monitor them quite closely, but I'm very optimistic that she should make a full recovery."

They breathed a collective sigh of relief. Then he took Sam and Maggie aside and informed them that if any complications did arise, they would consider inducing the birth to be on the safe side. They thanked the Doctor and rejoined Jennie and Richard. Jennie was very concerned about the swelling on her neck, but like Maggie said, *'We have to trust that the Doctor knows what he is doing.'*

Sam called Simon at work and kept him up to date about the accident. He informed Sam that the police had already called on him, as they found the car in his driveway and that the person who had rented the car was Nancy Ross.

"I tried to call you at home Sam. I pray Abbey will be okay."

He told Sam that the police had issued a warrant for Nancy's arrest and the charge was attempted murder. Sam trembled when Richard asked him what was wrong – he could not answer. Eventually, he told them.

Simon called Daniel and Elizabeth to tell them what had happened. They were in disbelief that Nancy could do something so horrendous. They thanked Simon and dropped little Becky at her mothers and went straight to the Intensive Care unit. Sam informed them that Abbey had not stirred. It was now a waiting game. They each took turns sitting with Abbey. Maggie informed them that Jake was on his way home.

"Oh thank God," Elizabeth replied. "Thank God."

It was raining heavily now as Jake passed the spot where he first met Abbey. His heart felt like it wanted to come out of his chest, but pressed on. He was nearly home. He arrived at the hospital at about nine. Maggie was the first to see him.

"Hello Jake," she said, throwing her arms around him.

"Where's Abbey? I must see her."

She could sense his anxiety and immediately took him to Abbey's bedside. He could not believe what he saw. He barely recognized her. There were cuts and bruises all over her face and her arms. He asked Sam if there was any news on her condition.

Sam took his time and repeated what the Doctor had told them.

"He thinks she will make a full recovery." He noticed the tears in Jake's eyes and put his arm around Jake's shoulder. "I'm glad your home son," he said, giving Jake a hug of support.

When Daniel and Elizabeth returned from the cafeteria, they saw Jake standing with Sam. They both ran and hugged him.

"Oh Jake," Elizabeth cried. "We missed you. We really missed you."

"I missed both of you," he said in response, "but I'm back now. And I'm back to stay."

She could see how upset he was about Abbey. He went in alone and sat by her bed and held her hand. His face was wet with tears, but he did not wipe them. He just talked to Abbey, hoping she somehow could hear him.

"I'm home darling. Please get better. There is so much I need to tell you. I have been the biggest jerk in the world, but I have always loved you. I need you Abbey. I need to hold you and kiss you and I need you to forgive me for doubting you."

Just then, the Doctor came in to check her vital signs, Jake had to leave for a few minutes. He joined the others outside. Richard asked him if he would take a little walk with him, he needed to have a talk man to man.

He had finished talking to Jake about everything that had happened, but he informed Jake, he was not finished yet. Sam surprised him by saying that he thought under these circumstances, and had he been in Jake's shoes, he most probably would have done the same. Jake smiled and thanked him.

Richard ended by saying, "You're back now and you have the chance to make things right. Don't screw it up, or I will set Abbey's Aunt Jennie on you."

They looked at each other and started to laugh. When Jennie asked them what was going on. Richard just replied, "It's a private joke, between men."

By eleven everyone, had left except Jake. He sat by Abbey's bedside, still talking, hoping she could hear him. He felt his back was against the wall. Why would Nancy resort to doing such a crazy thing? Not only has she hurt Abbey, but she has now ruined her own life. The police had put out an *'All Points Bulletin'* for attempted murder. If they find her, she will go to prison.

He draped his legs over the chair and fell asleep. Jake was totally exhausted, but he held on to Abbey's hand as if his life depended on it.

With the help of her mother, Nancy had taken a flight from Newark Liberty International to Mexico City. Her mother dropped her at the airport just before lunchtime. She knew there was a good chance she would never see her daughter again, but she felt compelled to help her escape. Mrs. Ross watched as her daughter Nancy boarded the plane, all she could do was wave goodbye. She knew what she had done was wrong. If her husband found out, it could jeopardize their marriage, but this was her blood – her only child – she had to do it.

Mrs. Ross drove home saddened, but her only thoughts were of her daughter. She wondered where she would eventually end up going. She knew Nancy would have to hide somewhere in the world, but that lifestyle must be better than spending time in the penitentiary. She could not bear the thought of her little girl behind bars.

Nancy had timed this perfectly. By the time the New Jersey Police knew who to look for – she was gone. After arriving in Mexico, she bought a car from a used dealer for cash and that's where the trail ended. They did not know where she had gone. A person could hide forever in Mexico, if they have money, and Nancy had plenty.

When George Ross asked his wife where she had been, she told him part of the truth.

"Just for a drive, to think about our daughter and what she has done."

"What she has done?" he replied. "What she has done ... is despicable. I hope she pays for her crime. If that girl dies, it will turn into first-degree murder."

Nancy's mother said she had a headache and went to her bedroom. She prayed for Nancy to contact when she could. She would never turn her in – never. She also prayed that Abbey would be okay.

Abbey opened her eyes. Panic took over. *'Where am I?'* Then she remembered the ambulance. She tried to sit up, but it hurt. She looked around the room. To her amazement, she saw Jake asleep in the chair. She called out to him. Jake awoke with a start. He thought he heard his name being called. He rubbed his eyes.

"Jake," Abbey said again.

A feeling of great relief came over him as he realized it was Abbey calling him.

"Thank you God," he said as he bent down to kiss her. "Thank God. Abbey you're okay." His tears were of joy.

Abbey's expression turned from bliss to panic as she tried to put her hands on her stomach to feel the baby.

Jake reached across and assured her the baby was fine.

"They have done all the tests. The heartbeat is strong. You will both be okay." He could not believe his luck.

"Why did you leave me Jake? Why?" she begged him to answer.

But Jake could not answer her. He looked at his Abbey. He tried, but he could not find the words.

"I'm sorry." It was all he could manage to say.

"Are we okay Jake?" she asked him. "I mean you and me. Are we going to be okay?"

"Yes," he said. "We are going to be fine. I love you, and after thinking I had lost you ... my love for you has grown. I have become stronger as a person while I was away. Abbey, I had a lot of growing up to do. I need to be with you now and I will never let go."

She hugged him as best she could.

"That's all I wanted to hear," she replied. "We have a lot to sort out, but we can do it. We have to do it. I love you Jake," she said. "I always have and I always will. When you left, my world fell apart. I never thought anyone could feel so helpless, but I did. Hold me."

He did as she requested, and he felt secure. It reminded him of when his mother held him in her arms – he smiled.

She asked Jake what had happened. She remembered the car, but did not have time to avoid it. Jake explained everything to Abbey's horror.

"So it was Nancy. Why Jake? Why?"

"I don't know," he answered. It was all he could tell her. "I just don't know."

The Doctors came in to do their tests.

"Don't leave me Jake."

She was still a bit frightened. Jake explained that he needed to call her parents to give them the news.

"I won't be long," he assured her.

He quickly called Maggie and Daniel to let them know Abbey was awake and everything looked good. Then Jake returned to her side. The Doctor told him her vital signs were good and the swelling was going down.

"You are very lucky," he said to Abbey. "Very lucky indeed."

He had already explained that the baby was fine, but he would not even consider discharging her until after the birth. Jake thanked him and sat down beside her.

Before the family arrived, Jake and Abbey discussed what they should do. He suggested that he could get the house ready, so she could come home with him. That was one option. The other was to go back to her parents. Whatever she wanted was fine with him.

"I want to be with you Jake," she replied. "I want our baby to be with us as a family. We can sort out all the rest when we are ready."

"I was hoping you'd say that." Jake kissed her tenderly. "I missed you darling. My life was empty without you."

"In a way, it serves you right," Abbey said, "but I hope we have both learned something. You're back and that's all I ever wanted. It's what I dreamed about every night."

The family arrived and Jake left to go home. He wanted to sort the house, have a shower, and start cleaning up. He could not believe his eyes when he went through his front door. The house was immaculate – not a speck of dust anywhere. He turned to go over to Leo and Nora's. They were in the doorway.

"We saw you arrive," Leo said. "How's Abbey?"

"She's going to be fine," he replied. "Who did such a great job in the house?"

"We have a cleaner that comes by Jake," Nora said, "so we enlisted her help. When Abbey phoned to say you were coming home, we set about cleaning the house. I'm sure you would prefer to see it as you left it."

He thanked them both and was promptly invited to breakfast. As he had not eaten in nearly twenty-four hours, he did not refuse.

He felt clean after eating, shaving and showering. He changed into some clean clothes and went back to the hospital. Abbey's grandmother, Susan was sitting with her when Jake entered the room. He did not know what kind of reception he would receive from her, but that was laid to rest immediately. She hugged him and welcomed him home.

"I will leave you two *lovebirds* alone," she said. "You make sure you take care of my granddaughter Jake or you will have me to deal with." She smiled and kissed him on the cheek.

Jake held Abbey's hand and kissed her gently. He told her what Nora and Leo had done.

"They really are caring friends. I guess I didn't know how lucky I have been."

"Jake," Abbey asked, "can we discuss baby names? We have never had the chance to discuss this and I think we should while we are alone."

Jake grinned. "Sure Abbey. You start."

"If we have a boy, I would like to call him Bradley," she said.

Jake replied, "And if it turns out to be a girl, I like the name Emily."

"That's a lovely name Jake. Emily Susan Lockhart, or Bradley Gary Lockhart."

"They both sound good." Jake was touched that she had considered naming a son after his father. He kissed her again.

As they had agreed on names, Jake's focus shifted to the baby's room.

"We don't have any furniture, or a crib, or clothes. What colour should it be painted?"

Abbey laughed and explained that she had the crib and all the stuff that would be needed for the time being. She would like the room to be yellow and decorative. Jake assured her he would enlist Elizabeth's help and get it ready.

"Her brother is an Interior Decorator and I'm sure you would not mind her help."

Abbey agreed immediately, she trusted Elizabeth completely.

He did not want to leave her side, but she was tired and needed some rest. Jake went to visit his old boss and eat humble pie. He asked for his old job back and luckily for him, he did not hold grudges. It was a small town, so he had heard most of the story through the grapevine. He knew why Jake left suddenly, and understood the problems he must be facing to get his life back together. After a long talk, they agreed he could start back after the birth because, as Jake explained, "Abbey needs me by her side."

He knew he was asking a great deal, but he assured his ex-boss that as soon as she was settled, he would work as hard as ever. Only during the day though, because he would have a family to go home to, and that was more important to him than anything. They shook hands on their agreement, and Jake went back to the hospital.

He did not want to leave Abbey for long periods of time. Jake knew the baby would be born soon, and for the first time in months, he was where he should have been all along.

As the days went on, Abbey's recovery improved. Jake had spoken to Maggie and Sam about their daughter moving in with him. Maggie smiled when she said, "I never thought my little Abbey would ever live in *sin*, but as long as you look after her Jake, I will be one-hundred percent behind you. I give you my word."

Emily was born on August the 18th, at 7.30 in the morning. Jake was by her side, as promised. The rest of the family was in the waiting room of the Maternity Ward. Jake was beaming when he delivered the news, first to Sam and Maggie, that they had a beautiful granddaughter, and then he informed everyone else. Abbey's grandmother was delighted when Jake told them the baby's name was Emily Susan. For the first time in ages Jake felt he had a new family.

Abbey was allowed to leave the hospital four days later. The three of them went home together. Jake had never felt better. The baby's room was finished and Abbey loved it.

"Elizabeth, you have done a wonderful job!"

Even though she was not there, she thanked her.

Over the course of the next few days, they had a lot of visitors. When Simon called on them, Jake took him aside and thanked him for being there for Abbey and for everything he had done to get them back together. Simon shook hands with Jake and congratulated both of them.

"Well done and be happy."

Jake and Abbey had already discussed marriage and christening and Jake asked Simon if he would consider being Emily's Godfather.

"We feel she should always know who to trust."

He was delighted and thanked them for considering him. Then Simon held little Emily and promised always to protect her.

Simon turned and headed for the door. He stopped and turned just as he was about to leave.

"I think you should know," he began, "that Nancy is somewhere in Mexico hiding. It looks like we will not hear from her again." He shook his head, left the house and walked to his car.

They waved goodbye to Simon and stood in the doorway.

"I will be happy living here," Abbey said as she turned to Jake and kissed him. "I have you and Emily. I feel we have gone full circle, but I could not be happier."

"You know, Abbey," Jake replied. "I was dead wrong about Simon. He really is a very nice person."

"I'm so glad all this stupidity with Nancy is over. We have plans to make Jake Lockhart." Abbey put on her most innocent look. "When are you going to make an *honest woman* of me?"

"Soon," Jake promised her. "Soon."

But his thoughts had gone to Nancy, and he was glad they would never see her again.

Although Simon was happy for Abbey, Jake and little Emily – he himself was very unhappy. He felt like his life had altered since meeting Nancy. He did not know how long it would take to get that evil woman out of his dreams.

Nancy had not forgotten. She would never forget and even as they walked back indoors, thousands of miles away, she was scheming.

'You will see me again ... I promise.'

Coming Soon

Abbey's Dilemma

By Paul James Jeff

Chapter 1

Abbey ran from the house screaming. She stumbled at the edge of the lawn and fell face first into the snow. As Abbey rolled over, she could see Nancy now as clear as day, looming over her, the knife blade glinting in the moonlight. Abbey called for help again. Suddenly Jake appeared in the doorway, staggering, covered in blood. Abbey called to him. He seemed to be moving like a zombie.

"Help me Jake," she cried. "Help me."

He stumbled and fell. She could see no movement. She called out again – no response.

Nancy moved in even closer. The knife in her hand seemed huge. She lunged at Abbey, thrusting the knife into her shoulder. Abbey screamed in pain. As the blood spurted upwards, she shouted at Nancy to get away but Nancy was on her again. The knife thrust into Abbey's arm. She had never felt pain like this. Suddenly, Nancy stood still. She looked at Abbey.

"I want to make this last bitch. I want you to suffer slowly."

Nancy lifted the knife, laughing hysterically.

"Jake is gone Abbey. Jake is dead. Now, it's your turn."

As Nancy brought the knife down, her face was twisted. She looked totally demented. Abbey called out for Jake – there was no reply.

"I told you bitch, he's dead."

Nancy lifted her arm. Again the knife was dripping in Abbey's blood.

Nancy laughed, "Now you die."

Biography

Paul was born in England, and immigrated to Canada in 1990.

He is happily married with two grown children and one grandson.

Paul has traveled, all over Europe, the Caribbean, many parts of the United States, and Canada.

He has now completed his second novel Titled "Abbey's Dilemma" and is currently working on another called "Chasing The Wrong Dream."

Paul has also written songs and poetry.

He is a member of *The Ottawa Independant Writers.*

pauljamesjeff@sympatico.ca

www.pauljamesjeff.com